Mountain Blaze

by

Debby Grahl

The Carolina Series

Mountain Blaze

Contact Information: info@thewildrosepress.com

Cover Art by *Kim Mendoza*

The Wild Rose Press, Inc.
PO Box 708
Adams Basin, NY 14410-0708
Visit us at www.thewildrosepress.com

Publishing History
First Champagne Rose Edition, 2020
Trade Paperback ISBN 978-1-5092-3248-2
Digital ISBN 978-1-5092-3249-9

The Carolina Series
Published in the United States of America

Dillon smiled and Diana thought it the sexiest smile she'd ever seen. There was a slight cleft in his chin, and fine lines formed at the corners of his eyes. Diana inwardly groaned. The butterflies were back.

"I'd hold onto you. I wouldn't let you fall," he softly said.

With his slow southern accent, the words sounded like warm honey rolling off his tongue. The depth of his eyes and the sound of his voice mesmerized her.

The horses stood side by side. Her and Dillon's legs touched. He leaned toward her, and the light aroma of wood smoke, hay, and his spicy cologne filled her nostrils. Diana knew what he was about to do but had no willpower to stop him. He cupped her cheek and their lips met.

Gentle at first, his lips glided over hers. He increased the pressure until she opened her mouth and his tongue slipped in. Diana moaned and wrapped her arms around his neck. His arms around her waist, he deepened the kiss. Before she realized what he was doing, without breaking their kiss Dillon lifted her from Flora and placed her across his lap.

Cradled in his arms, Diana clung to him, delicious sensations filling her. Her body came alive in a way that surprised her. The only thing that mattered was this man and this moment.

Flame moved, bringing her back to reality. Diana's eyes fluttered open, and she stared into Dillon's, deep with passion and need.

Dedication

To my cousins, Darla and Mike Kleiner,
who showed me the beauty of North Carolina

Chapter One

Chapel Hill, North Carolina

"Does my butt look big in these jeans?" Diana Thompson asked her friend Jennifer, as she peered over her shoulder at the dressing room mirror.

Jennifer Perell, seated among piles of clothes, rolled her eyes. "Seriously, you're asking me that question?"

Diana gave Jenn a slight smile. "Quite the cliché, right?"

"Since you're small enough that your butt looks good in anything, I'd say so. Now put those with the others, and let's go have lunch. We've been at this for hours, and I'm starving."

Dismayed, Diana took in the array of tops, jeans, jackets, and dresses filling the tiny room. "Jenn, I'm sorry. We can go." She reached for her own clothes. "I don't know why we're here anyway."

"We're here because something is bothering you, and instead of telling me what it is, you dragged me through every store in Chapel Hill. So spill it, and stop making us both crazy."

Diana made room on the bench and slumped down next to Jennifer. She placed her head in her hands. "I don't know what to do."

"Diana, I've known you for three years and in all that time I've never seen you this frazzled. I'm going to take a guess and say your behavior has something to do with the wedding."

Sniffing back tears, Diana nodded.

"Considering you're about to cry, I assume it's not good."

Diana gazed at her engagement ring and let out a long breath. "Jenn, I don't think I love Trent enough to marry him."

"Oh, boy, this is definitely not good. Let's get out of here. This calls for drinks and junk food."

Diana wiped the moisture from her cheeks and smiled into Jenn's warm friendly face and clear green eyes. "You always have the perfect solution."

"Hey, as the saying goes, that's what friends are for."

Diana slipped on her coat and followed Jenn from the department store. She'd met Jenn at a Tar Heels football game during their junior year at NC. Jenn, seated in the bleachers above her, irate over a penalty call, had jumped up and spilled her soda down the back of Diana's jacket. Horrified, Jennifer had insisted on accompanying Diana to the restroom where they attempted to clean up the mess.

Now, as they sat in a booth at a local Mexican restaurant, Diana knew she was the one person she could confide all her doubts to.

"Check this out," Jennifer said, pointing at the menu. "All-you-can-eat tacos. Great comfort food."

Diana laughed. "You can't get better than that."

The waitress placed chips, salsa, and their margaritas on the table.

After giving her their order, Jenn asked, "Okay, so tell me why you don't think you love Trent enough to marry him."

Diana took a long sip of her drink while deciding the best way to explain her feelings. "I'm afraid that though I love him, I'm not crazy in love with him." She brushed her long, dark auburn hair back from her shoulder and leaned forward. "Am I making any sense?" Before Jenn could reply, Diana continued. "My feelings for Trent are more the way you'd feel toward a dear friend, not someone you're going to pledge your future to."

"Since I've never been madly in love, I can't tell you how you're supposed to feel," Jennifer replied. "But I have been madly in lust, so what about sex? Does he ring your bell?"

Diana rubbed her temples. "Sex is pleasant enough. But if you're asking me if I see stars, the answer is no."

"Pleasant? Who wants pleasant? You want mind-blowing, screaming triple-orgasm sex, not pleasant. No wonder you're having doubts. Who wants to marry a man who's boring in bed?"

"There's more to a relationship than sex."

"Absolutely, but who would you rather have, a man who could make you see stars, or one who makes you count sheep?"

"Oh, for heaven's sake, he's not that bad." Diana busied herself wiping spilled salsa from the table, then in a low voice said, "Although, I only have one man to compare him to."

"The hot Italian you met in Florence before college? I take it he didn't ring your bell either."

"Maybe it's not them. Maybe there's something

wrong with me."

"Diana, there's nothing wrong with you. Trust me, after all my mistakes with men, I'm no expert on relationships, but I feel you really need to take time and think about this marriage. Did you tell Trent how you feel?"

Diana folded and unfolded her napkin before setting it to the side. "Of course not. What would I say? Oh, by the way, even though we're supposed to get married in four months, I'm not sure I'm in love with you."

"That probably wouldn't go over well. Okay, what about postponing the wedding until you sort your feelings out?"

Diana shook her head. "Again, what do I say? And what about his parents? I've become close to Judith and I adore his father. They're both totally into this wedding. Not to mention my own parents. My mom wasn't happy when I told her I was going to NC and not a college up east. When they came for graduation and met Trent's parents, you would have thought they'd known one another for years." Diana frowned. "You should see our moms making the guest list. Not only is my entire family coming to the wedding, my mother has invited half of Philadelphia. I feel as if I'm on a runaway train heading for a cliff."

"Okay, let me think about this," Jennifer said as their first platter of tacos was placed in front of them. They ate in companionable silence until Jennifer declared, "I might have an idea. What if you got away for a few days? Time apart might be what you need to figure out your feelings."

Diana cocked her head. "Where would I go?"

"Home to the mountains with me. Remember I told you my grandparents have a small horse ranch located a little west of Ashville with cabins they rent out. I'm going for Thanksgiving, and if you don't have plans, come with me."

"I'm surprised you were able to get Thanksgiving off."

"I put in for the days quite a while ago." Jennifer sipped her drink and sighed. "Soon it may not matter anyway."

"What do you mean? What's wrong?"

"It's my parents. They think now that I have my MBA, I could do better than working at the hotel."

"But you love the Huntington."

"I know, but my parents think I should find a position with some big corporation."

Diana grinned. "Like the Huntington Hotel Corporation?"

Jenn grinned back. "In my dreams. I love the hotel industry. While I was growing up, my family didn't do much traveling. For one thing, we couldn't afford it, plus we all had to help out with the ranch and the guests. Working for Huntington International, I have the chance to see the world."

"Well, if that's what you want, go for it. It's your life."

Jenn shrugged. "I know. We'll see. Anyway, back to coming with me. What do you think?"

Diana knitted her brows. "Actually, Trent and his family are going skiing in Aspen over Thanksgiving, and I don't ski. I was asked, but it's silly for me to go out there and sit around while they're gone all day. Since I've finished my last tutoring job, I could go home, but I don't want to make the drive. So, I planned on staying here."

Jennifer punched her fist in the air. "Yes, then it's all set. You're coming with me. I'm off work beginning Wednesday, so we'll leave early and get there around noon."

"Wait a minute. You haven't even found out if it's okay with your grandparents."

"I'll call and let them know, but they won't care. In fact, I'm not even sure who will be there. Since my family is scattered all over the U.S., some years there's a house full and other times only a few of us. Most wait for Christmas. My parents didn't see my sister Shannon last Thanksgiving, so they'll be out in California with her. Also, November is a good time to visit the ranch. My grandparents won't have anyone checking into the Lazy M until March." Jennifer frowned. "But I have to warn you the ranch is up in the mountains and kind of rustic. Upscale Philly it is not."

Diana gave a dismissive wave. "I'm sure it will be fine." She narrowed her eyes. "I'm not a snob."

"No, you're not, but I'd leave the designer shoes at home."

"Very funny." Diana smiled to herself. Her and Jennifer's backgrounds were about as far apart as you can get. Diana's father was partner in a prominent Philadelphia financial firm, and her mother, after growing up in Philadelphia society, was VP of Bella cosmetics. Diana attended private schools and spent her summers touring Europe.

"Do you know how to ride a horse?" Jennifer asked.

Diana shook her head.

"Well, girlfriend, we can take care of that."

****

Dillon McCoy tugged down the brim of his Stetson and leaned against the corral as the red Jeep made its way up the steep gravel drive. He hadn't seen Jenn in quite a while and was looking forward to it. Five years younger, she used to make a real pest out of herself by following after him. He grinned remembering the gangly tomboy.

The Jeep stopped, and Jenn flung open the door.

"Dillon," she called running toward him, throwing herself into his arms. "I didn't know you were here. When did you get in?"

"Hey, Pest, how you doing?" He picked her up and twirled her around. "Put on some weight, haven't you?" he teased as he set her back on her feet.

"Horse's ass, I have not." She playfully punched him in the arm. "Now let me introduce you to my friend."

The smile froze on Dillon's face as the beautiful woman came toward him. Big brown eyes were set in an oval face. Her nose was small and straight and her lips slightly full. Dark auburn hair draped down her back in soft waves. Dillon was admiring her trim legs encased in black jeans when Jenn spoke.

"If you're done ogling her, I'd like you to meet Diana Thompson. Diana, this is my rodeo cowboy cousin, Dillon. I have to warn you he probably has a string of broken hearts from here to Montana."

Dillon gave Jenn a sharp glance before removing his glove and taking Diana's outstretched hand. "Don't pay any attention to her. She exaggerates. Most women don't look at me twice." When their hands touched,

Dillon found himself not wanting to let go. What the hell was wrong with him? He'd met a number of pretty women, but they'd never made him feel like a wild stallion who'd cornered a filly.

Diana slipped her hand from his. "It's nice to meet you." She motioned to the scenery surrounding them. "The snow-covered mountains are beautiful, and the pine trees smell incredible."

"Glad you like it." Dillon found her soft voice with its slight east coast accent pleasant on the ears. "I hope you enjoy your stay." The large diamond ring on Diana's left hand flashed in the sunlight. He might be looking at the filly, but the filly wouldn't be looking back. He studied her more closely, taking in the fur-trimmed leather jacket she wore. Lucky for him she was married, because if he wasn't mistaken, her jacket probably cost more than he made in six months. "Will your husband be joining you?" he asked.

"Oh, I'm not married." Pink suffused her smooth cheeks. "Not yet anyway."

She quickly glanced away but couldn't hide the troubled expression in her eyes.

Dillon glanced at Jenn and arched one brow, silently asking, "*What's up?*"

"Not now," she mouthed. Aloud she said, "Well, we're anxious to unpack, and I want to show Diana around."

Dillon nodded. "Gran and Gramps put the two of you in the main house. I'm staying in the cabin."

"The cabin was built by my great grandparents when they arrived here from Kentucky," Jenn explained to Diana. "After my grandparents married, they built the larger house further up the hill. We use the cabin for overflow when we're all visiting."

"Gran probably has lunch ready, so you should go on up," Dillon said.

"Great. Will you be joining us?"

He shook his head. "I thought I'd ride out to check the fences and see if any need repairs. Gramps doesn't do it as much as he used to. I packed a sandwich, but I'll see you all at supper."

"I have a favor to ask you. Diana doesn't know how to ride, and I thought you wouldn't mind teaching her."

"No, Jenn," Diana exclaimed. "Dillon is busy. I'm sure you can teach me."

Dillon laughed. "You wouldn't say that if you'd ever seen her ride."

Jenn nodded. "He's right. I've never mastered the concept that you're supposed to move with the horse, not bounce up and down like a jumping bean." She shook her head. "No, if you want to learn, Dillon's your man."

Dillon glanced at Diana's designer jeans and her stylish ankle boots with their two-inch stacked heels and frowned. "I hope you have other boots and old jeans."

Jenn rolled her eyes. "I told her to pack casual clothes."

"That's what I'm wearing," Diana replied with dismay.

Jenn lifted her hands and let them fall. "I'm taking her shopping in Pine Bluff. I'll make a country girl out of her yet."

Dillon smiled. "Then I'll see you two later."

Chapter Two

Diana carefully made her way across the slick uneven ground back to Jennifer's Jeep. Handsome wasn't the word to describe Dillon McCoy. Drop dead gorgeous was more like it. Talk about baby blues. His eyes alone, under those thick dark lashes, could kick any woman's heart rate into overdrive. Add his killer smile with the cleft in his chin, a mustache the same honey brown as his hair, a smooth southern drawl, and a tall muscular build in jeans that fit way too well, and you had one hunk of a man.

She'd heard of people being instantly attracted to someone, but hadn't experienced it herself. She opened the door and slid into the passenger seat feeling as if a thousand butterflies had taken flight in her stomach. Who would have ever thought a man in a cowboy hat could be such a turn-on? She let out a long breath. What was the matter with her? She was engaged and shouldn't be thinking these thoughts.

"By the expression on your face, I'd say you've fallen under the spell of Dillon McCoy," Jennifer said as they headed up the road toward the main house.

Horrified that Dillon might have also picked up on her interest in him, Diana cleared her throat. "It's nothing more than appreciation of a good-looking man."

Jennifer smiled. "Don't worry about it. You're not alone. Women take one look at him and are ready to drop their drawers."

The image that conjured in Diana's mind made her palms damp. She gave a nervous chuckle. "I don't think that will be a problem." She hesitated. "But out of curiosity, how old is he?"

"He turned thirty-one in July. And to answer your next question, he's in the process of a divorce. He went to college out in Montana, and as soon as he graduated, he joined the rodeo circuit. He got married out there, but according to family scuttlebutt he recently caught her with another man. He's good about hiding his feelings, so no one knows how he's taking it, but he did admit the rodeo life was hard on a relationship."

"Really. Did you ever meet his wife?"

Jennifer scrunched up her nose in distaste. "Unfortunately, yes."

"That bad?"

"Honestly, I could never understand Dillon's attraction to her. She was extremely obnoxious. She had big boobs, big hair, and no brains."

Diana burst out laughing. "No way."

"I'm not kidding. All she needed was a bubble over her head saying Bimbo. 'Buckle Bunnies' is what rodeo riders call women who follow them around, and I think she was one of them. She was from some small town in Texas and latched onto Dillon like a leech. I think Dillon must have finally seen her for the slut she really was."

"Jennifer," Diana exclaimed.

"I know that sounds awful, but I love Dillon and can't stand to see him taken advantage of."

"I just met Dillon, but I honestly can't picture him with someone like that."

"Tell me about it. All I can say is she must have driven him crazy in bed. And here we are." She stopped the Jeep in front of a large two-story log home with a long, covered porch.

"Wow," Diana exclaimed. "That's quite a house."

"Wait until you see the view from the back." Jennifer grabbed her duffel bag from behind the seat. "Come on, I'm starving."

The smell of wood smoke filled the air as Diana followed Jennifer onto the wide front porch. A red-painted swing hung at one end, and a scattering of rocking chairs invited you to sit and relax. The aroma of fresh baked bread wafted through the house as they stepped into the great room.

"Besides my grandparents' room, there are four other bedrooms, so until we know which ones Gran wants us to use, you can leave your bag here," Jenn said, motioning to a nearby bench.

Diana placed her bag next to Jenn's and laid her jacket on top. "It smells wonderful in here," Diana said. "And I love this room." On the far wall, to Diana's left, a crackling fire roared in a stone fireplace big enough to roast an entire steer. Above it hung a landscape of the mountains and valley.

A scattering of oval rugs lay across the pine plank floor topped by comfortable worn leather furniture. Along the far wall, wide shelves held a flat screen television, a stereo system, books, and family photos.

"That's a beautiful painting," Diana said.

"My sister Shannon is the artist," Jenn replied. "She loves painting pictures of the ranch."

To Diana's right, an oak staircase led up to an open hallway which overlooked the room.

"Did you grow up in this house?" Diana asked as Jenn headed toward the kitchen.

Jennifer shook her head. "My mother, my uncle Dan, who's Dillon's father, Uncle Will, and Aunt Augusta all did. When I was really young, we lived in one of the cabins."

"Jennifer, is that you?" a female voice called. "Get on back here before the soup gets cold."

Jennifer smiled. "That's Gran. And her homemade soup is a real treat."

The kitchen was as homey and welcoming as the great room. The largest butcher-block table Diana had ever seen dominated the center of the floor. Glossy white cabinets and slate blue countertops lined one wall opposite another stone fireplace. Sliding doors led out the back onto a screened porch with the view of the valley beyond.

Next to the stove stood a tall, striking, gray-haired woman with Jennifer's green eyes and a ladle in her hand. Mouthwatering steam wafted from the pot in front of her. At the end of the counter, a bear of a man with rugged features and Dillon's sky-blue eyes was cutting thick slices of home-made bread.

"Gran, Gramps, I'd like you to meet my friend, Diana Thompson," Jennifer said. "Diana, my grandparents, Ada and Chester McCoy."

"It's nice to meet you, Diana," Ada said.

"Welcome to the Lazy M ranch, young lady," Chester added. "Come on in and make yourself at home."

"Thank you," Diana said while Jennifer hugged her

grandparents. "And thanks for having me. Your house is beautiful."

"Ah, it's only a house," Chester said. "But I appreciate the compliment."

"I'll bet you girls are about half starved," Ada said. "Sit yourselves down, and I'll bring you a bowl." She turned to Diana. "It's only vegetable soup. I hope you'll like it."

"Mrs. McCoy, if it tastes as good as it smells, I'll love it."

Smiling with pleasure, Ada carried bowls to the table along with a basket of bread. "And it's Ada and Chet. No need for formalities around here. There's iced tea in the pitcher, home-churned butter there on the dish, and salt in the shaker. Chet isn't supposed to have a lot of sodium, so I tell everyone to add their own."

"Hell's fire, Ada, a little salt isn't going to hurt me," Chet grumbled.

"That's the problem. You don't know how to use a little."

Chet, sitting across from Diana, winked, and she smiled.

Diana took one taste of the soup and groaned with pleasure. The broth was thick and rich with chunks of tender beef mixed with an array of vegetables. "This is delicious, Ada," Diana said. "I have to admit, the vegetable soup I'm used to eating comes out of a can."

Ada made a frown of disapproval. "It's a wonder you girls made it through college on the junk you ate. A person needs a full stomach to do well in school. How can a body be expected to study if their stomachs are growling?"

Diana smiled. "You've got a point." She didn't

want to tell Ada that even when she was growing up, "homemade" wasn't a word in her mother's vocabulary. It was all about convenience.

"I love to watch cooking shows and try recipes in magazines," Diana said.

Ada smiled. "I only make down-home dishes, nothing fancy."

"You're the best cook ever, Gran," Jennifer exclaimed. "As for me, I have no interest. Restaurants or frozen dinners are more my style."

"Did you see Dillon on your way up?" Chet asked as he defiantly sprinkled salt in his soup.

Jennifer nodded. "I wasn't sure if he'd make it. When did he get here?"

"He drove in a couple of days ago," Chet replied. "Said he had some time off and decided to come home."

Ada frowned. "I think there's something troubling that boy. He's been too quiet."

"I wonder if it has something to do with Tonya and the divorce?" Jennifer asked with concern.

Ada's frown deepened. "I don't like to judge people, but that girl rubbed me the wrong way the first time Dillon brought her home to meet us. All she did was ask me questions about the ranch and snoop around. And talk about lazy." Ada shook her head. "Diana, don't get me wrong. I don't expect house guests to do chores, but at least they can pick up after themselves and make their bed. Wherever she'd drop something, that's where it would stay. That girl thought since we rented out cabins, we would have cleaning people come in. Now, I have help with the cabins in the busy months, but I do a lot of the work myself. And I certainly don't have maid service in the house."

"Ada, she's out of his life," Chet said. "Let it go."

"I can't help it. Knowing she hurt Dillon riles me to no end." Chet shook his head and sighed.

"What do you girls have planned for the day?" Ada asked.

"I'm going to show Diana around the ranch," Jennifer replied. "Then I think we might drive down into town and do some shopping at Country General."

"Country General? What is that?" Diana asked.

"It's a wonderful old-fashioned general store with everything from clothing to cookware to barrels of candy. Trust me, you'll love it."

"Sounds great," Diana said as she and Jennifer rose and took their bowls to the sink. "Ada, thank you for a delicious lunch. Can we help you clean up?"

"That's okay. You girls go on and have a good time. Dinner will be on the table at six. Jennifer, I put Diana in the back bedroom. Make sure she has everything she needs."

"Thanks, Gran," Jennifer called as she and Diana left the kitchen, grabbed their bags, and headed up the stairs. "Your room is next to mine and we'll share a bathroom," she said as she led Diana down the hall.

Diana smiled with delight at the sunny room. The exposed log walls were painted butter yellow with white trim around the windows. An antique maple dresser and chest of drawers sat against one wall. Across from them was a four-poster bed covered with a beautiful hand-made quilt.

"Check this out," Jennifer said, opening French doors onto a screened porch, letting in the chill air. "This runs along three sides with stairs leading down on each end." She grinned. "When my cousins and I were young, we used to sneak out this way to the fire pit and smoke cigarettes."

"Did you ever get caught?"

"No, but I think my grandparents knew what we were up to."

Diana turned her attention to the vista spread out before her. In the distance, snow-capped mountains encircled the valley below. Sunlight sparkled off a stream as it wound its way through the trees. "I'll bet this is beautiful in the spring."

"It is. You'll have to come back." Jenn cocked her head. "Listen." Far off, the whistle of a train echoed. "I love that sound."

Diana nodded. "Me too."

"Let's unpack," Jenn said. "I'll be ready in a few minutes. Then we'll go for a walk."

Diana glanced at her boots. "Um, will we be mostly on the road?"

Without a word, Jennifer opened the closet and rummaged around, coming up with a pair of lady's cowboy boots. "These belong to Shannon. She's petite like you, so hopefully, until we can get you some in town, these will fit you. Also, that jacket of yours is gorgeous, but for tramping around in the woods, this might be better." She handed Diana a heavy corduroy coat.

"I suppose I have Shannon to thank for this as well?"

Jennifer grinned. "Thank goodness she's the runt of the family. Diana, do you own anything that didn't come from Neiman Marcus?"

Diana's eyes opened wide. "Certainly—some come

from Saks."

Chapter Three

Dillon, riding along the far eastern edge of the ranch, halted in disbelief at the gap in the white painted fence. He slid off Flame, a tall chestnut, and stared at the cut. He glanced around, but other than chattering squirrels, everything was quiet. He hunkered down and studied the ground. The latest snow had coated the area with a light dusting, but he thought he could make out hoof prints. Here the ranch bordered the Duffy property, neighbors of the McCoys for decades. Open land led to the ski lodge higher up the mountain. What the hell was going on? He doubted his friend Kevin Duffy would cut the fence, so who would? Dillon's mouth formed a thin line. The only reason would be to have access to McCoy land. But why? He knew when the snow got deep, people from the ski lodge rode snow mobiles in this area, but people usually didn't carry tools to cut fences while out having fun. He shook his head. He'd ask Kevin if he knew anything about this. He spotted the cut boards stacked near the fence. Thankfully he did carry a few tools with him. He'd temporarily block the opening and come back to fix it permanently.

A short time later, Dillon swung his leg over Flame, squinted into the sun, and inhaled the clear crisp air. He'd enjoyed living out west, but this land and these mountains would always be home. As he crossed the pasture toward the barn, memories of carefree days growing up here played in his mind. How in the hell had his life become so damn complicated? From the first time his father placed him on a pony, he and horses had been as one. At a young age, he'd gone to every small rodeo that was close by and watched television broadcasts of rodeos out west. He'd sit, eyes glued to the television, as his favorite riders, the coiled pigging string between their teeth, waited for the calf to be released. From the moment the rider shot from the chute, his lasso sailing through the air, Dillon silently counted. Under ten seconds, he'd shout, as the rope easily dropped over the calf's head, the rider flipping him onto his back and tying three of his legs. For hours afterward, he'd practice lassoing everything from his grandmother's goose yard ornament to his younger sister as she ran away.

His parents were disappointed when instead of going to UNC, he chose Rocky Mountain College in Montana, where he earned his degree in equestrian studies. His rodeo buddies called him the College Cowboy. Three years ago, he won his first gold buckle. That's when his life began to spin out of control.

He met Tonya at a rodeo BBQ in Texas. Intoxicated by both his fame and Tonya's advances, he fell for her beauty and her body. A few months later, in Las Vegas celebrating another win, they got married in the Elvis chapel. Why hadn't he seen Tonya for what she was? She'd use him until something better came along. While he was a winner, she loved him and his fame.

As he rode along, in his mind's eye, it wasn't the

beautiful mountain landscape that lay in front of him, but a low-end motel on the outskirts of Austin, Texas.

He wasn't sure if it was more rage or humiliation which seized him as he'd sat in his pickup truck in front of the Dew Drop Inn. *They say love is blind. Yeah, well, if that's true, lust must paralyze the brain.* How else could he explain his stupidity not realizing Tonya was making a fool out of him? Dillon clenched and unclenched his fists. He'd seen Cliff Walker, the rich son-of-a-bitch hanging around Tonya, but it took his rodeo friend Stew to make him grasp the truth. She was nothing but a beautiful buckle babe, and he'd fallen for her body and her lies.

He probably shouldn't have threatened the kid behind the front desk to get the room number where his cheating wife was lying in another man's arms, but nothing was going to stop him from confronting her. Dillon knew he should have driven away and never looked back, but as he'd stared at the door of room Seven, he allowed his anger to propel him forward.

He honestly couldn't believe he'd kicked in the door where Tonya lay in the bastard's arms, but he'd never been so fucking pissed off in his life. Dragging him from the bed, he planned on beating him to a pulp. Thankfully, Tonya's screams brought him to his senses. Before he'd done something which would have landed him in jail, he told Tonya what he thought of her and walked out.

The next day he filed for divorce, threw his gear into the truck, and headed east to NC. The ranch was the one place he could lick his wounds and clear his head.

Now he found himself wondering if he'd actually

loved Tonya as much as he'd thought. Was his hurt more over her betrayal than the divorce? If he were honest, since he'd been back on the ranch, he felt a sense of contentment he hadn't known in quite a while. Sure, riding the rodeo circuit was still exciting, and he enjoyed every minute. But at home, there'd been tension below the surface he hadn't realized until he'd put space between himself and Tonya. One thing he knew for sure—the next time he got involved with a woman, he'd make damn sure she was the right one. He wouldn't make the same mistake twice.

In the spacious barn, he removed Flame's saddle and blanket and rubbed him down. He tied a feedbag around his neck, checked the other horses, then closed the barn door.

The gravel path to his cabin led from the corral and into the woods where he passed thick stands of red oak and maple, their branches heavy with snow. Perhaps Tonya's betrayal and his buddy Stew's riding accident were omens telling him it was time to come home. The older you got the harder the ride became—and the harder the ground when you landed on your ass.

Dillon frowned. Come home and do what? Even though his grandparents had hired help, they were getting older. His aunts, uncles, and cousins used to pitch in, but now they were scattered all over the country. When he was here, he loved caring for the horses and taking guests out on trail rides. Even maintaining the cabins didn't bother him. The business aspect of running the ranch is what he'd shied away from.

The path turned, and his cabin came into view. Jennifer and Diana stood on the porch. Diana sure was a pretty little thing. He recalled how well her hand seemed to fit with his and how her smile made his heart beat a little faster. *Back up, cowboy. Another relationship is not what you need. Besides, she's engaged.* She'd had a strange expression in her eyes when he'd indicated her ring. He'd try to get Jenn alone and find out what was up with that.

"There you are," Jenn called as he neared the cabin. "I wanted to show Diana inside and figured you'd be back by now."

"Fence took longer than I expected," Dillon replied. "Besides, I thought you were going into town."

"We got distracted, and now it's too late," Jenn said.

Dillon stepped onto the porch and opened the door. "It wasn't locked. You could have gone on in."

"I didn't want to invade your privacy."

Dillon snorted. "Really? Since when?"

Jennifer grinned. "Well, you might have some girl stashed in here."

"Yeah, right." Dillon wiped his boots on the mat, placed his hat on a rack by the door, and slipped off his jacket. "I'm having a beer. Can I get you ladies something to drink?"

Jennifer took Diana's coat and hung theirs next to Dillon's. "We'll both have a glass of wine. I'll show Diana the cabin while you get it."

Dillon grinned. "Yes, Ma'am."

"Jenn, he doesn't have to wait on me," Diana said. "We can get our own wine."

"Oh, I know. He and I go back and forth at each other all the time. Now, as I said, this was the first cabin my great grandparents built. As the family grew, it was added on to, but they kept it as original as possible. There're now four bedrooms and three baths."

In the main room, heavy wood-framed couches and chairs with dark-red and cream plaid cushions sat on the worn hardwood floor. A brick fireplace dominated one wall, while shelves overflowing with books, games, and family photographs filled the other. Two doors led from the room, one leading to the kitchen, the other to a hallway and bedrooms.

"I love this," Diana said. "Your grandparents' house is fabulous, but this makes you want to kick your shoes off, curl up, and read a book." She thought of the modern house she grew up in. Her parents showered her and her brother with love and affection, but their house didn't have that cozy homey feeling. For one thing, her mother was a neat freak, so nothing was ever out of place. There weren't many knickknacks, and toys and games were always put away.

Diana noticed a framed drawing of the McCoy family tree. "This is quite something. There really are a lot of you."

"Someday, if you're really interested, I'll tell you who they all are." She pointed to the bottom of the drawing. "Gran made sure to leave room for the new babies." Jenn led Diana in the direction of the kitchen.

"Oh!" Diana gasped. Warm and welcoming were the words she thought of as she stepped through the door. Wide wood beams stretched across the ceiling. A large hand-hewed table and rustic chairs occupied the center of the wood-planked floor. In the far corner, a glass-fronted cabinet held an array of dishes. A wood-burning cook stove was opposite an L-shaped granite counter surrounded by rich maple cabinets. Converted antique gas sconces hung on the log walls.

"This is wonderful," Diana said, imagining herself cooking on the stove while happy children gathered around the table. She blinked. Whoa, where in the world had that come from? She glanced at Dillon taking a beer from the refrigerator, and her stomach did a little flip. Coming here was supposed to help sort out her feelings for Trent, and Dillon McCoy was throwing her emotions into total turmoil.

"Red or white?" Jennifer asked, as she removed wine glasses.

Diana jerked her mind back from how great Dillon's butt looked in his faded jeans. "Um, red please."

Jennifer poured each of them a glass and handed one to Diana. "Let's go sit in the living room. Dillon, can I light the fire?"

He nodded. "Make yourself at home. I need a shower. I'll join you in a few minutes."

Jenn soon had the fire blazing, and she and Diana were seated on one of the couches. "What do you think of the ranch so far?" Jennifer asked.

"I love it. I've never experienced anything like this. Trent took me to some of the North Carolina wineries, but we stayed in modern B&B's. When my family went on vacations, we always stayed in—" She hesitated. "—hotels."

Jennifer smiled. "Such as the Ritz or the Plaza?"

A blush spread across Diana's cheek. She didn't think about growing up wealthy. Her life was what it was—a house in a well-to-do neighborhood, private schools, expensive clothes, and world travel. She'd accepted it all because that's what she knew. But if she thought about it, none of those things seemed important. She desired a comfortable life certainly, but she could be perfectly happy living simply. *Like in a cabin in the woods? Could I?* a little voice in her head asked. *Well, damn, if this keeps up, I'll be more confused when I leave than when I got here.*

"Don't be embarrassed," Jennifer continued. "We don't have any say as to what lifestyle we're raised in. You grew up wealthy. So what? You're definitely not a snooty snob."

Diana grinned. "Well, I'm glad you don't consider me a snooty snob."

Jennifer lifted the bottle of wine from the pine coffee table and refilled their glasses. "My plan is to make a country girl out of you before we leave. Starting tomorrow. We don't usually eat Thanksgiving dinner until four or five o'clock. That gives anyone who's coming time to get here. So, you can have your first riding class in the morning."

Before Diana could reply, Dillon was back. The sight of him left her speechless. His damp hair was thick and fell across his forehead. His gray-and-white cowboy shirt emphasized his wide shoulders, and his black jeans rode low on his lean hips.

"That works for me," Dillon said, opening another beer and sitting on the couch across from them. "Because it's Thanksgiving, Gran doesn't make a big breakfast," he said to Diana. "We can start as early as you'd like."

"I really don't want to impose on you," she replied. "I feel as if we've put you on the spot."

He shook his head. "I don't mind at all. If I'm around horses, I'm happy."

"Dillon has one gold and one silver buckle from rodeo riding," Jennifer said.

"Congratulations," Diana said. "Although, to tell the truth, I don't know much about rodeos."

Dillon smiled. "Few people do."

"Great. While you two are riding, I can help Gran with Thanksgiving dinner," Jennifer said. She turned to Dillon. "I never asked Gran—who all is coming?"

"I honestly don't know where most of the clan are, but I do know your parents are with Shannon, and mine are spending it with Christy—my sister. Ben is in the Keys fishing with friends, and Zack is somewhere in Europe. So other than us, I think it will be Uncle Will, Aunt Martha, the twins, and Suzanna, who's bringing Aunt Augusta. None of them are arriving until tomorrow."

"Ben and Zack are Dillon's brothers," Jenn said. "The twins, Sally and Sam, live in Lexington with Aunt Martha and Uncle Will. They just graduated from UK and are a lot of fun. Augusta is another story. The family legend is her husband died to get away from her."

"Jenn, that's awful," Diana exclaimed.

"Sad, but true. My cousin Suzanna still lives in Charlotte, but her sister attends SCAD in Savannah."

Dillon grinned. "Augusta really is that bad. Her opinion is always the right one, and she loves to tell everybody how they should run their lives."

"One summer night when we were all teenagers," Jennifer said, "she caught my girl cousins and me sneaking out of the house. We were on our way to the pond to go swimming. She didn't believe us. She woke up the rest of the house to tell our parents that she knew we were going off to meet boys. Her two daughters were with us, and she smacked the crap out of them. The other parents did their best to calm her down, but she was sure she was right."

"Well, um, I'll make sure I'm on my best behavior—and don't sneak off to meet any boys."

Chapter Four

That evening, after a delicious dinner of fried pork chops, mashed potatoes and gravy, home-canned green beans, and a carrot cake for dessert, Ada and Chet hit Dillon and Jenn with a bombshell.

"We're planning on telling the rest of your cousins, but since you two are here, we thought it would be a good time to talk to you," Chet began.

A perplexed expression shown on both Dillon and Jenn's faces, but Dillon spoke first. "Okay, what's up?"

"We're ready to retire," Chet said. "Running the ranch has kept us tied down, so while we have some time left, we want to travel."

Jenn opened and closed her mouth before she found her voice. "You want to leave the ranch?"

"That's right," Ada said with delight. "We bought a motor home. "And in the spring, we're going to buy a little Jeep to pull behind it, and we're taking off."

Jenn sat speechless.

Dillon was the first to recover. "You did what?"

Chet nodded. "That's right. The motor home is a beauty. It has a motorized awning so we can sit outside and a flat screen TV for when it rains. Our first destination is Key West."

"But," Dillon began, "what about the ranch?"

"That's where you two come in," Ada continued.

"We thought one or both of you could take over."

"What?" Dillon and Jenn said as one.

"Take over running the ranch," Ada repeated. "Both of you are capable of doing so."

Jenn and Dillon exchanged glances, then Jenn spoke. "I'm honored you have that much confidence in me, and I love the ranch, but I work for a hotel chain. I want to do some traveling of my own."

Ada frowned. "I thought that was only until you finished school."

"No, Gran, I hope to make my career with Huntington."

All eyes turned to Dillon. He held up his hand. "Whoa there. I have a career of my own. What about the aunts and uncles? Wouldn't one of them be interested.?"

Chet scowled. "Not one of our children has any desire to take over the ranch. When they were old enough, they couldn't get away from here fast enough. They wanted to go off to college, then live in the city." He shook his head. "As for the other grandchildren, they like to visit, but I can't see any of them wanting to live here." He hesitated. "There's also the option of you buying us out."

"Buying you out," Dillon exclaimed. "Gramps, again, what about the aunts and uncles? I assume they all expect to inherit everything."

Chet's congenial face took on a hurt expression. "We told each of them our plans, and not one protested. If we left the ranch to them, they'd sell it and split the proceeds. This land has been in our family for more than a hundred years, and we'd like it to stay that way."

Ada shook her head. "It breaks my heart none of

my children care about their heritage, and I can't stand the thought of someone else owning the ranch." She scowled. "I don't know how he knew of our plans, but that realtor Martin Patrick came here and told us he had an interested buyer. The idea of a stranger owning McCoy land makes me sick to my stomach."

"Martin Patrick the creep?" Jenn asked.

Ada and Chet nodded.

"Yuck," Jenn said, scrunching up her nose. She turned to Diana. "He's a couple years older and hung around with Dillon's friends. He used to try to kiss me. When I was eighteen, he even asked me out. He's not bad looking, but there's something about him that screamed slime ball."

"If I remember correctly," Ada interjected, "he doesn't take rejection well."

"No, he doesn't," Jenn said. "He pestered me until Dillon and Sam had a talk with him." She smiled at Dillon. "I don't know what was said, but he left me alone after that."

"Chet asked him who the buyer was, and he said they want to remain anonymous," Ada continued.

Dillon frowned. "I don't like the sound of that."

"Chet thinks it's someone who wants to build houses or condos," Ada said.

Chet nodded. "Everyone around here knows how we feel about raping the land to build expensive houses."

"That can't happen," Jenn exclaimed. "Dillon, you have to do something."

"Me? What about you?"

Jenn flapped her hand. "Other than Gran and Gramps, you know more about running this ranch than anyone. You're the logical one to take over."

Dillon ignored Jenn and asked Chet, "What about Kevin Duffy? Could he be the buyer?"

Kevin, a childhood friend of Dillon's, inherited the adjoining property when his parents passed away. He and Kevin, along with other boys from the area, would spend hours roaming the woods and trails playing cowboys and Indians, and Rebels and Yankees. But after Dillon left for college, they saw each other less often. While home at the ranch, Dillon would run into Kevin, and they'd have a couple of beers together. Kevin married Bonnie Calhoun, a dark-haired beauty Dillon had dated the summer after high school. Although he and Bonnie had a good time, she was way too possessive and clingy for Dillon's taste.

"I stopped into Kevin's sporting goods store in town and he said he wasn't," Chet said. "Although his property isn't anywhere near as large as ours, someone owning both could make quite a killing selling off lots."

Diana stood. "I'm going to sit by the fire and let you continue with your family discussion. Ada, thank you for a wonderful meal. Jenn, when you're done, I'll be happy to help with the cleanup."

Jenn rose. "We can do the dishes later. I'll come with you and tell you more about awful Martin." She smiled at Dillon. "This one is all yours."

Dillon scowled. "Thanks." He studied his grandparents while absorbing all they'd said. Was he ready to pick up his life, move to North Carolina, and start over? If he were honest with himself, besides riding, there was nothing to keep him in Texas. Until they decided where they wanted to settle, he and Tonya rented a house near her parents. After he'd told her he was divorcing her, Tonya moved back home, and he'd allowed the lease to run out. As for his rodeo buddies, they were spread all over, and he could make trips out to see them. So now it was just him and his horse.

"I want to make sure I understand," Dillon said. "By taking over, you mean for me to live here permanently?"

Chet leaned back in his chair. "That's right. Of course, until you purchased the property, we'd pay you a salary. Your grandmother and I have a nice amount set aside for retirement, and with the guest income from the ranch, we should be fine."

"Gramps, you have to give me time to think about this."

"Dillon, you know as well as I do, you can't keep riding forever. You've won championship buckles and haven't had any bad accidents, so why not quit while you're ahead?"

Visions of Stew's crumpled body lying in the chute flashed in Dillon's mind.

"You don't have to make up your mind right now," Ada said. "We just wanted to let you know our plans."

"Answer me this. If I don't say yes, what will you do?"

Chet and Ada exchanged glances before Chet spoke. "I suppose we'll close things down while we travel and open for a few months when we're home. Although that will mean hiring more people to take care of the horses and the property."

"Not to mention checking on the cabins and the house," Ada added.

Dillon studied his grandparents' solemn faces and sighed. They'd set him up and reeled him in. They knew he wouldn't want strangers taking care of the horses or the ranch. He ran his hand through his hair. "Let me think about it."

His grandparents smiled. "Good enough," Chet said. "After Thanksgiving, we'll go over the books and the day-to-day operation."

"When do you plan on telling the rest of the family I might be taking over?" Dillon asked.

"Oh, sometime during Thanksgiving," Ada replied.

"Great," Dillon mumbled.

"Now, I'm going to help your grandmother clear the dishes. Then I think it's time for a game of euchre," Chet said.

****

Diana wasn't much of a card player, but she knew cut-throat was the only way to describe Jenn's style.

"I guess we're partners," Dillon said.

Apprehension turned Diana's palms damp. "I have to warn you, I'm not very good at cards."

He gave her a reassuring smile. "Don't worry. I'm not like Jenn. I play to have fun."

Instantly she relaxed, and even when she made mistakes, he'd laugh and say, "it's only a game." Diana thoroughly enjoyed herself, and when she and Dillon finally won a round, to her amazement, she clapped and jumped up and down. Afterward they made popcorn over the fire and watched a Christmas movie, which had all the women crying.

****

Now, snuggled down in her warm bed, for the first time in a long time, Diana was relaxed and carefree. The boisterous activities of the McCoys would never have been allowed in her own family home. Only quiet conversation, never lively discussions of politics or current events. No loud music, only classical played softly in the background. Games were played in the finished basement, and television was watched in the family room. She loved her parents, but escaping all that structure is why she and her brother didn't go to college closer to home. He chose Michigan and she picked NC.

Trent's family wasn't quite as reserved as hers, but his mother, born a southern belle, required proper decorum at all times. Diana sighed. Trent expected that of her as well. Could that be what was wrong with their lovemaking? She thought he'd been disappointed that she wasn't a virgin. She buried her face in the pillow. Dillon's handsome face swam through her mind. His sensuous mouth could probably kiss a girl senseless, and his sky-blue eyes, hot with passion, could turn any woman's resistance to desire.

Diana sat up and held her head in her hands. *You have to get your mind off Dillon.* A tear rolled down her cheek. She'd come to work out her feelings about Trent, and now it was perfectly clear she couldn't marry him. If she could have sexual fantasies about another man, she had no business going through with the marriage. Her thoughts should be all about her fiancé, not some cowboy she just met.

She took a deep breath. Fantasizing about a man isn't a reason for calling off a wedding. As long as it was only that, a fantasy. Women fantasize over movie stars and athletes all the time. That doesn't mean they're going to have an affair with one.

That's right. Dillon is a man I'm attracted to, nothing more. Seriously, Diana, what in the world do you think you'd have in common with a cowboy? And could you truly see yourself living in the country, miles from civilization? And what about teaching? You've been offered a position at a prestigious college. Could you turn that down, to do what?

Trent and the lifestyle she'd have with him were what she was used to. They both enjoyed Shakespeare, the Brontes and Dickens, classical music, and BBC. To Diana's delight, he'd accompany her while she rummaged around in antique shops. She and Trent were perfect for each other. Her mind on the right track, she lay back down. But as she drifted off to sleep, a cabin in the mountains and a pair of sky-blue eyes filled her dreams.

Chapter Five

The next morning, Diana showered then dressed in crisp blue jeans, a dark pink cashmere turtleneck sweater, and warm socks. She pulled on the boots Jennifer let her borrow and glanced at her own Italian leather ones in the closet. She didn't have many obsessions, but shoes were one of them. She bit her lower lip. Other than sandals and running shoes, she didn't own any footwear that weren't heels. She turned her foot this way and that studying the scuffed worn boots and grinned. Her mother would be horrified, but she thought they were perfect.

When she entered the kitchen, Ada was placing a breakfast of maple oatmeal, toast, and fruit on the table. Chet, Dillon, and Jenn were already there.

"Good morning. Happy Thanksgiving," Ada said, greeting her with a warm smile. "I hope you slept well."

"Yes, thank you, very well, and happy Thanksgiving to all of you," Diana replied.

"Coffee is in the pot on the stove. I don't have a drip coffee maker. I prefer my old percolator."

Diana smiled. "I don't blame you. I've never found one that doesn't drip all over the place." Diana filled a cup and sat down at the table. "I hope I haven't kept everyone waiting."

"Nope," Jenn replied. "I just got here myself."

"Hand me your bowl, and I'll fill it for you," Dillon said. "The oatmeal pot is too hot to pass."

As she did so, their fingers touched. It was over in a second, but once again the sensation of butterflies taking flight filled her stomach.

"Diana, I understand Dillon is going to give you riding lessons this morning," Ada said.

"That's right," she replied, hoping her voice didn't give away how nervous she was. "I'm afraid I might be quite a challenge."

Chet gave a dismissive wave. "Nonsense. If you can sit on a horse, Dillon can teach you to ride."

Diana couldn't help but smile. "That might be a challenge in itself."

"Don't worry—if you start to fall off, I'll catch you," Dillon quietly added.

The low, husky sound of his voice sent a tingle up Diana's spine. Unable to meet his eyes, she busied herself buttering a piece of toast.

"The rest of the family should arrive around noon," Ada said. "I plan on having a light lunch, then dinner at five. This will give everyone time to settle in and visit."

"This morning, I'll help you in the kitchen, Gran," Jenn said. "Then after I introduce Diana to Sally, Sam, and Suzanna, we might do some exploring to show her more of the area."

Dillon rose and took his dirty dishes to the sink. Diana followed. "If you're ready, let's go," he said.

Once they were outside, Diana breathed deeply of the crisp morning air. "Where is that wonderful smell coming from?"

"That's the Fraser firs." He pointed to a stand of twelve-foot trees. "They're the number one choice in

Christmas trees."

"Don't tell me you're going to cut down those beautiful trees."

"Not those. There are smaller ones we grow specifically for Christmas."

"I always wanted a real tree, but my mother said they made too much of a mess."

"Mine was the opposite. She'd hang real garland all over the house, and there were needles everywhere."

They made their way down the gravel road toward the barn. "Sorry, I could have driven up here so you wouldn't have to walk," Dillon said.

"I might be a city girl, but I think I can make it that far. Besides, I'm enjoying the exercise. Are those dogwoods?" She pointed to a small group of trees.

"Yeah. They're scattered throughout the property. Beautiful to see in full bloom."

"I can imagine. Oh, look." Diana smiled with delight as two rabbits peered at them from under a bush. "They're so cute." She took a step closer, and the rabbits flashed their cotton tails at them and vanished into the woods. "Darn, I was hoping for a picture."

****

"They normally don't stay around people for very long." At the barn Dillon slid open the wide door. Inside the aroma of horse and hay greeted them. "Have a seat while I saddle the horses." He indicated a bale of hay. "I've already been here this morning, so they've been fed and watered."

Diana sat and cleared her throat. "Um, Dillon, I have a confession to make."

He raised one brow. "What's that?"

"Actually, I have been on a horse before. My

parents sent me to some riding school when I was six. I was so terrified of the pony, when they sat me on his back I froze. I couldn't make him move. All we did was sit there until the teacher gave up and lifted me off."

Dillon's lips twitched with suppressed laughter. "Well, you're not six, and I promise I'll put you on a gentle mare. If you can't make her go, I'll lead you behind me."

He opened the stall door and led out a black horse with four white stockings and a white streak down her nose. "This is Flora. We use her for all our beginner riders."

"Oh, she's beautiful," Diana exclaimed. She hurried over to stroke the mare's nose. "Do you have an apple or some sugar I can give her?"

From his coat pocket, he withdrew a sugar cube.

Diana held the sweet in the palm of her hand and laughed with delight when Flora gently took it from her. "That's a good horse," Diana crooned. "You and I are going to get along fine, aren't we?"

"Would you like to saddle her?"

"Sure, what do I do?"

"The first thing is to place the blanket on her back. Fold it in half, then smooth it out." He nodded. "That's right. Next, comes the saddle. Once it's in place, you tighten the girth strap." He took her hands in his. "Here, like this. You don't want to get it too tight. Now, the bridle. When you put it on, be careful not to smash or scrunch her ears."

Diana shook her head. "I'm too nervous. You do it."

"It's easy." He secured the bridle and reached for the bit. "First, make sure not to bang their teeth, and in the winter, you want the bit warm." He handed it to her. "Place it beneath your coat for a few minutes."

Diana unbuttoned the top two buttons of her coat and held the bit against her chest. His gaze followed the motion of her hand. The sudden heat in his eyes made Diana's breath catch in her throat. The desire in their blue depths held her incapable of movement. For what seemed like an eternity, they stood staring at one another. Flora snorted and nudged Dillon with her nose, and the spell was broken.

Shaken, Diana took a step back and, hoping her fingers weren't trembling too badly, handed Dillon the bit, then quickly buttoned her coat.

Dillon secured the bit in Flora's mouth. On his face, traces of his desire lingered. "Okay, well, she's ready to mount," Dillon said. "Let's go outside. There's a block you can stand on." He led Flora out and gave Diana the reins. "Hold on to her until I bring out Flame."

Diana leaned against the horse and whispered, "Flora, I think I'm in deep trouble. If I'm not mistaken, he almost kissed me. And I almost let him."

****

Dillon cursed under his breath. What the hell was wrong with him? She was engaged, and until the divorce was final, he was still married. He hadn't been involved with a woman since he left Tonya, but that was no excuse. He was thirty-one, old enough to tamp down his sexual desires. What was it about Diana that made him lose his self-control?

He had Flame saddled and was leading him from the barn when the sight of Diana bent over, her nice little ass clearly revealed in her well-fitting jeans, stopped him in his tracks. He gritted his teeth. Was the woman trying to drive him crazy?

She stood upright, turned, and smiled. Her eyes were lit with excitement and her cheeks rosy from the cold. A light breeze lifted her long hair.

"Look what I found." She held out the pointed triangular stone. "Is this an arrowhead?"

Dillon took the small stone from her hand. "Yep. There were Indians all through these mountains. I'd say it's Cherokee. Now you have your first souvenir."

Diana smiled and placed the stone in her pocket.

"Are you ready to mount Flora?"

"Sure. Let's give it a try." She slipped on her gloves, stepped up on the wooden block, and swung her leg over the horse's back, slipping her feet into the stirrups. She grinned down at Dillon. "So far so good. I haven't fallen off."

Dillon handed her the reins. "This part is pretty simple. If you want her to go left, pull the left-hand rein, same for the right."

Diana nodded.

"I'll take you on the trail we use for the beginners. Flora knows the way and should follow me. You won't have to worry about directing her."

"Will we be going up into the mountains?"

"Not today. The trail is a little rough in spots, but it's gradual. It leads through the woods and along a small stream that runs through the property. We'll end up at a meadow where you can see the Smoky Mountains in the distance."

"Sounds wonderful. I'm ready. Let's go."

Dillon adjusted his Stetson, flung his leg over Flame, and took his place in front of Diana and Flora.

"We're going to pass a few of the cabins we rent out to guests," he called back over his shoulder.

****

Diana, apprehensive but determined, tightened her hands on the reins, and Flora fell into line behind Flame. The sky was brilliant blue and crystal clear. As they entered the woods, there were oak, maple, and pine trees all along the trail. The snow was a little thicker on the ground, and the air chillier.

"In the summer, rhododendron bloom all through here," Dillon said. "You'll have to come back."

****

By next spring I'll be married, Diana thought. Could she picture Trent on the back of a horse riding through the woods admiring flowering shrubbery? She inwardly scoffed. *Not at all. Trent's idea of rustic is staying at a comfortable five-star B&B, or a chalet overlooking a ski resort.* And what about her? If she hadn't come with Jennifer, could she have ever seen herself riding on a trail in winter through the woods? Probably not. Because they didn't snow ski, in winter her family vacationed in the Caribbean or the south of France.

As they neared one of the cabins, the trail widened, and Dillon slowed Flame so Diana could come up next to him.

"You doing okay?" he asked.

Diana nodded. "Flora is doing all the work. I'm sitting here enjoying the ride. I haven't once felt like I'm about to fall off."

Dillon grinned. "That's good to hear."

"I assume the cabin ahead belongs to the ranch?"

Dillon nodded. "We have eight cabins scattered

throughout the property. One of my favorites, Red Oak, sits high up on the ridge. The view from there is of the valley and mountains."

"Can we go there?" Diana asked.

"Let's see how you do today. It's more of a climb to get to Red Oak."

"Is this cabin pretty rustic?" Diana asked, as they passed the log structure.

"Rustic on the outside, modern inside. There's only one cabin left on the property that doesn't have satellite TV or Wi-Fi. It's nestled in the woods and basically one room with a fireplace, a small kitchen, and a porch with a comfortable rocker. It's truly my favorite."

"Really. Why?"

"The quiet and privacy. I can be alone and think things through."

"Sounds like that's the place for me," Diana whispered.

"This is none of my business, and you can tell me so, but you seem like a lady who's troubled, and something tells me it has to do with your fiancé."

If he detected her inner turmoil, did he also feel her attraction to him? Mortification reddened Diana's cheeks. If he noticed, hopefully he would attribute it to the cold, but his next words told her he'd seen the truth.

"Sorry, I didn't mean to make you uncomfortable. And as I said it's none of my business."

Diana didn't know what to say. She was a pretty private person only sharing her feelings with her cousin Claire and Jenn. Diane and her brother were close, but other than things to do with their parents, she kept her private life to herself. So why did she have the urge to share her innermost feelings with this man who was practically a stranger?

Before she could respond, he reached over and lightly squeezed her hand. "Sometimes talking about what's troubling you helps put things in the right perspective." He gave her a slight smile. "The trail is going to get steeper and narrower after we pass this next cabin, and you'll have to stay behind me. Soon after that, we'll come to the meadow, and we'll take a break. The snow might be too deep to cross, but you'll still be able to see the mountains."

Diana nodded and Flora fell into step behind Flame. They passed the last cabin, and the meadow spread out before them. Dillon drew Flame to a halt and motioned for her to quietly come next to him. When she did so, he pointed to three deer standing near some pine trees, and in the distance were the snow-crested ridges of the Smoky Mountains.

Diana caught her breath. "It's magnificent," she whispered.

"I never get tired of this view. Because of this." He indicated their surroundings. "The last cabin we passed is another favorite of our guests."

"It all reminds me of a Christmas card." Diana patted her pockets. "Damn," she murmured. "I don't have my phone to take a picture."

Dillon gestured. "They're leaving anyway."

For a minute, the deer stared at them, their ears alert, then bounded off into the woods. "Oh, I must have made too much noise," Diana exclaimed.

"You didn't do anything. They could smell us. I'm surprised they stayed as long as they did. If it wasn't so slippery, we could go out onto that outcropping of rocks." Diana glanced to where he pointed and shuddered.

"It's smooth on top, and you can see the stream that runs through the valley below," he continued.

She shook her head. "I don't mind heights if I'm a safe distance away. Out there, I'd go into a full-blown panic attack. In fact, that's why I never learned to ski. You'd have to drag me kicking and screaming onto one of those chair lifts."

Dillon smiled and Diana thought it the sexiest smile she'd ever seen. There was a slight cleft in his chin, and fine lines formed at the corners of his eyes. Diana inwardly groaned. The butterflies were back.

"I'd hold onto you. I wouldn't let you fall," he softly said.

With his slow southern accent, the words sounded like warm honey rolling off his tongue. The depth of his eyes and the sound of his voice mesmerized her.

The horses stood side by side. Her and Dillon's legs touched. He leaned toward her, and the light aroma of wood smoke, hay, and his spicy cologne filled her nostrils. Diana knew what he was about to do but had no willpower to stop him. He cupped her cheek and their lips met.

Gentle at first, his lips glided over hers. He increased the pressure until she opened her mouth and his tongue slipped in. Diana moaned and wrapped her arms around his neck. His arms around her waist, he deepened the kiss. Before she realized what he was doing, without breaking their kiss Dillon lifted her from Flora and placed her across his lap.

Cradled in his arms, Diana clung to him, delicious sensations filling her. Her body came alive in a way that surprised her. The only thing that mattered was this man and this moment.

Flame moved, bringing her back to reality. Diana's eyes fluttered open, and she stared into Dillon's, deep with passion and need.

Oh, dear God, what was she doing? She barely knew Dillon, and there she lay sprawled across his lap. What would he think of her? "Dillon, I..."

He placed a gloved finger over her lips. When he spoke, his voice was low and husky. "It's not your fault. You're engaged, and I shouldn't have done that.

She swallowed hard and touched his cheek. "I'm just as guilty." She should tell him about Trent, and why she was here, but now wasn't the moment. She needed to be alone, where she could process what just happened.

"You don't have to explain." He glanced away, then back. "I should promise that won't happen again, but I can't. All I can promise is I'll try to behave."

She gave him a slight smile. "We're adults. We should be able to control ourselves."

Dillon cleared his throat and easily set her back on her saddle. "Whatever you say."

Chapter Six

As they made their way back through the woods, Diana's guilt threatened to consume her. Not only did she enjoy every second of his kiss, she didn't want him to stop. One terrible truth she had no doubt about—if they hadn't been sitting on a horse, she'd be in his bed. What a complicated mess her life had become. If she had her own car, she'd make some excuse and leave, but she couldn't do that to Jenn. Until she could make sense of her emotions, she'd try her best not to be alone with Dillon.

Dillon suddenly pulled Flame to a halt, jarring Diana from her thoughts. "What's wrong?"

"I'm not sure. There are horse tracks going off the trail into the woods." Dillon frowned. "I don't recall seeing them when we passed here earlier."

Diana glanced around. "We're near one of the cabins. Perhaps you were distracted describing the ranch to me."

"I suppose. But that doesn't explain what they're doing here."

"Do other riders use this trail?"

"No. This is all McCoy land. Our closest neighbor, the Duffys' property, is in that direction. They have a few cabins, and it's possible one of their guests wandered over here by mistake."

"Isn't the ranch surrounded by fence?"

"No. Only the areas that border public land." Still frowning, Dillon resumed riding toward the barn. When they were almost there, once again Dillon stopped. "There's someone ahead of us."

"Jenn?"

"I don't think so. If it were her, she'd come to meet us." He started forward. "Stay behind me."

The trail widened, and in the distance a man in a parka stood. "I don't think there's a problem," Dillon said. "But stay back a little way."

Curious, Diana nodded.

The snow muffled the sound of Flame's hooves as Dillon pressed him forward. When he got within thirty feet of the man, he called, "Hello, can I help you?"

The man turned and Dillon quietly cursed. "Martin, what are you doing here?"

Martin Patrick stood still and waited for them to approach. He was stocky with attractive features and a smile that reminded Diana of a used car salesman.

"Hey, Dillon, how ya doin'?" Martin replied.

"I'm fine. I'll ask again, what are you doing here?"

At the sharp tone of Dillon's voice, Martin's smile wavered. "Actually, Dillon, I heard you were in town, and I wanted to have a word with you." His gaze shifted to Diana, who had ridden up beside Dillon. "That's if you have the time."

Dillon urged Flame in the direction of the barn. "It depends on what you want to talk about. If it has anything to do with selling the ranch, it's not happening. Besides, it's Thanksgiving. Don't you have somewhere else to be?"

Martin fell into step next to the horses. "My family

49

is getting together for dinner later with friends. Now I think it would be worth your while to hear me out."

At the barn, Dillon swung his leg from Flame's back, then lifted Diana down. "Martin, I can't imagine that anything you have to say would be worth my while."

For a second, anger flickered across Martin's face. "Well, you won't know until you hear it."

"If you want to talk while I put the horses up, I'll listen."

"Diana, would you mind going to the house without me?" Dillon asked. "If you'd rather drive…" He pointed to a pickup truck parked next to the barn. "You can use the truck. I'll be there as quick as I can."

"After being on the horse, I think I'll walk," Diana said. "I'll see you later."

****

Dillon led both horses into the barn and removed their saddles. Martin followed him in and leaned against a stall.

"I'm listening," Dillon said, as he rubbed Flame down.

Martin cleared his throat. "Dillon, I'll get right to the point. We all know your grandparents can't wait to head out in their new motor home. They're getting older, and this place is becoming too much for them to take care of. I need you to convince them selling is a good idea. I have a buyer who is offering a damn good price for the land and business. Think about it. They could travel anywhere they choose and never have to worry about finances."

"As far as I know, they don't have to worry about finances now."

Martin waved his hand. "You know what I mean. Selling would give them a fantastic nest egg to fall back on."

Dillon leaned his arm on Flame's back. "Answer me this. If they sell, where are they supposed to live when they aren't traveling?"

"With the money my buyer is offering, they could buy or build anywhere."

"But they like it right here." Dillon led Flame into a stall and began brushing down Flora. "Tell me, Martin, who is your buyer?"

"Um, well, for the time being, they asked to remain anonymous."

"Why is that? Do they have something to hide?"

Martin shook his head. "Not at all. They prefer to keep their transactions low key. They don't want everyone knowing their business."

"Is that right? Then can I know what your buyer plans on doing with the ranch?"

Martin hesitated. "I'm not sure."

How dare the son-of-a-bitch come here and lie to my face. Dillon stopped what he was doing and glared at Martin. "That's a damned lie and you know it. This is a prime piece of real estate, and I'll bet you know as well as I do that your buyer plans on tearing down the cabins and building houses or condos. Trust me, that will never happen. You know what? I had a decision to make, and after talking to you, I've made it. You can tell your buyer the Lazy M is definitely not for sale. I'm staying, and I'm taking over the ranch."

"You? You're a rodeo rider. What do you know about running a tourist ranch?"

Dillon stepped from the barn. "Perhaps I know a

little about running this ranch because I grew up here."

"Think about it. Do you want to prevent your grandparents from that kind of financial security?" Martin asked, following after Dillon.

Dillon stopped, narrowed his eyes, and set his mouth in a grim line.

Martin took a step back. "You know I'm right. Besides, do you really want to give up your cowboy life out west to run a weekend dude ranch?"

"My decision stands. Tell your buyer the property is not for sale. Now, I think it's time for you to leave."

Martin stomped off, slammed his car door, and drove away. Dillon sighed. *Well, I guess I'm moving to North Carolina.*

Chapter Seven

A bright red cardinal flew from branch to branch and chattering squirrels darted in and out of the trees as Diana made her way slowly up the road to the house. A jumble of emotions swirled in her mind. It was obvious she couldn't be in love with Trent and lust after another man. Diana let out a long sigh. Lust wasn't a word she'd normally use when it came to sex, but lust was the only word to explain her reaction toward Dillon.

But was that all it was? Was she about to break her engagement and hurt a wonderful man for something that might disappear as quickly as it had come? Perhaps if she got it out of her system, she'd find out the fantasy of Dillon in bed was only that—a fantasy. She mentally shook her head. If his love-making was anywhere near as good as his kiss promised, it would be fantasy come to life. So, after a night in bed with Dillon, what would she say to Trent? *By the way, I really lusted after this cowboy, so I spent the night with him, but it was only sex.*

Yeah right. How would I feel if he told me that about some woman? And what about Dillon? He isn't divorced. What if his feelings toward me are purely sexual? What if he still loves his wife? Would I want to get into a relationship with such insecurity? Diana pursed her lips. *Listen to me, I don't even know if*

Dillon would want to have a relationship. Maybe all he wants is a night in bed.

She thought about how disappointed her mother would be if she were to call off the engagement. Well, she wasn't going to marry someone just because her parents approved. She rubbed her temples. Instead of her life becoming less complicated, it was more complicated than ever.

"Diana, finally, you're back."

Diana glanced up to see Jennifer and three other people standing on the porch of the house.

"We were about to go searching for you," Jennifer continued as Diana paused at the bottom of the steps. "These are my cousins, Sally, Sam, and Suzanna. They arrived about an hour ago."

Diana guessed the three were around her and Jennifer's age. Sam and Sally, the twins, truly had similar features—attractive with sea-green eyes, slightly turned up noses, and blond hair the color of Jennifer's. Suzanna, not as tall as Jennifer and Sally, was striking with long red hair and big blue eyes.

"We've decided to have a bonfire tonight, so we need to go make sure the fire pit is ready, and there's wood cut," Jennifer said, as she peered around Diana. "Where's Dillon?"

"He said he'd be right up," Diana replied. "That Martin guy met us as we were heading back to the barn."

Jennifer scowled. "What was he doing here?"

"I don't know. I think it had something to do with the ranch. I tell you, Dillon wasn't happy to see him."

"I don't blame him," Sam said. "The guy is a jerk."

Jennifer flapped her hands. "Let's not talk about

Martin. We'll probably run into Dillon along the way." She turned to Diana. "How was your riding lesson?"

Remembering Dillon's kiss, Diana hoped her cheeks weren't turning pink. "Well, I didn't fall off. We went up to the meadow, and it was beautiful. We also saw three deer."

"That's one of my favorite spots," Suzanna said.

"Mine too," Sally added.

"Jennifer tells us this is your first time here," Suzanna said. "What do you think?"

"I love it," Diana replied. "It must have been wonderful spending summers here."

Suzanna nodded. "But I could never live here. It's too far from civilization for me."

"Jenn tells me you're from Charlotte," Diana said.

"That's right. I work for Preston Books."

"I enjoy reading mystery novels," Diana said.

Suzanna grinned. "Me too. In fact, Preston has a contest going on for the managers of all their stores. We have a chance to win a trip on a mystery cruise."

"Wow, that would be great," Diana replied. "Good luck."

Sally pointed. "There's Dillon."

Sally, Sam, and Suzanna hurried ahead to meet Dillon, while Jennifer hung back with Diana.

"Okay, before he gets here, spill it," Jennifer said. "What happened between you and Dillon?"

Surprised, Diana cleared her throat. "What makes you think something happened?"

"Because it's written all over your face. When I asked you how the riding lessons went, you turned as red as my sweater."

"I was hoping you wouldn't notice."

"Well, I did notice, so I say again, spill it."

Diana debated on how much to tell her friend. She decided to tell as little as possible. "Nothing much. One little kiss."

"Dillon kissed you?"

Diana nodded.

"Holy crap, Diana, where were you? What happened afterward?"

Diana hesitated. Jenn didn't need to know she was sprawled across Dillon's lap on top of his horse. She cleared her throat. "We were in the meadow."

"Okay, so how was it?"

"It was a kiss. It meant nothing."

"By the expression on your face, it did mean something. Diana, I'm sorry I talked you into coming here with me. All I've done is make things worse. Dillon is my cousin, and I love him, but I wasn't kidding when I said he could leave a string of broken hearts. Please don't become one of them. Don't get me wrong. He doesn't do it intentionally. It just happens. I guess because he's never met the right one. He must have thought Tonya was it, but obviously he was wrong. When I saw the way he was looking at you, and knowing your own emotional state, I should have never left you alone with him."

"I'm a big girl and was perfectly capable of telling him no."

"Damn, there he is," Jennifer said, as Dillon approached. "We'll talk more later," she whispered.

****

Irritated over his conversation with Martin and angry with himself for trying to seduce Diana, Dillon stomped more than walked up the road. He'd wait until he could get his grandfather alone before informing him of his decision to run the ranch. What to do about Diana was a more pressing matter.

He couldn't help but wonder how far things would have gone if they hadn't been on the back of a horse. She certainly reacted to his kiss. Damn it to hell, he had to stop thinking about her. She wore an engagement ring. He didn't know the circumstances surrounding the troubled look in her eyes, but one thing he did know, engaged or not, she was attracted to him.

And what about him? Why did he feel as if he'd been hit with a thunderbolt when his lips had touched hers? He'd been with a number of women, and he and Tonya had a wild time in bed, but even she hadn't affected him the way Diana did. She really wasn't even his type. He was usually attracted to tall curvy women. Diana, small, and though well-proportioned, wasn't well-endowed, but he'd bet her firm breast would fit his hand nicely.

He gritted his teeth. Thankfully, the ranch would be full of people for the next few days. Because with thoughts like that, he knew damn well he shouldn't be alone with Diana Thompson.

"Hey, Dillon."

Startled from his thoughts, he smiled as Sally, Sam, and Suzanna hurried toward him. Diana and Jenn following behind. "Damn," he muttered, seeing Diana and Jenn's heads close together. Was she telling Jenn about the kiss? Jenn's narrowed eyes spoke volumes. He silently groaned. Well, what was done was done. He couldn't take the kiss back.

Chapter Eight

Martin seethed as he drove his BMW down the mountain. *Damn Dillon McCoy.* Why wouldn't he listen to reason? Sweat coated the palms of his hands as he gripped the steering wheel. He had to convince the McCoys to sell. His life literally depended upon it.

Things had been going so well. He thought he'd been careful, only occasionally over-pricing an appraisal. Everyone came away with a little extra, and everyone was happy. So what if the house or condo later ended up in foreclosure. But he hadn't been careful enough. His blackmailer was constantly on his ass. If he had the nerve, he'd tell them to go to hell, but he couldn't afford to lose his license or go to jail. He had a wife and baby son.

He turned off the mountain road and headed for town, deciding to stop and have a quick drink before going home. He entered The Stag's Head pub and took a seat at the bar.

"We're closing early because it's Thanksgiving," the bartender said.

Martin nodded and ordered a beer. He'd taken one sip, when a voice behind him spoke.

"Hello, Martin."

Mug in hand, Martin froze. He muttered a curse. He hadn't seen the car in the parking lot, but his thoughts had been on the McCoys. He swallowed the bile burning his throat and glued a friendly smile on his face. "Hey there. Happy Thanksgiving."

The other's smile was without warmth. "I have a table. Why don't you join me."

Martin licked suddenly dry lips. "I'd like to, but I only stopped in for one. The wife is at home." He chuckled. "Don't want to keep her waiting."

"Oh, I'm sure Meg wouldn't mind if you were a little late. Tell her you were with me."

There was no way out, so Martin picked up his beer and followed.

Once seated, his companion, with cold eyes and a menacing voice, asked, "Have you spoken with Dillon?"

Martin needed to play for time. "Yes, but we didn't have a chance for a private conversation."

"I told you I'm running out of patience. If the old folks won't listen to you, Dillon has to convince them."

"For God's sake, it's Thanksgiving, and there's a house full of people. I couldn't get him alone, but…" Martin thought of the girl on the horse with Dillon. "Dillon has some girl up there. By the look of him, the only thing on his mind is her." The fury in his companion's face sent sweat trickling down Martin's back.

"I don't give a damn how many women Dillon McCoy has. You get him alone and convince him it would be in his best interest to sell. I don't think you really want me to go to the board of realtors, do you?"

Martin swallowed hard before he spoke. "Why is it so important for you to have the Lazy M? There are other properties for sale close to the same acreage."

"That's none of your business. I told you what I want you to do. If you can't get Dillon to cooperate, then get him out of the way. I don't care how you do it. Once he's no longer an obstacle, Chet and Ada should be easy to convince. Now, do it." Without a backward glance, his companion got up and left the pub.

Martin, eyes blazing with hatred, signaled for another beer. What the hell was he going to do? He'd invested heavily in a revitalization project that Meg, his wife, knew nothing about. The outdoor shops and restaurants near Asheville should have been a sure thing, but the money had run out and the deal had collapsed. He'd needed to make some quick money, so he'd fudged the assessments on a few houses, taken kickbacks from the borrowers, and it was his bad luck he'd been snared by this blackmailer.

Dillon's smug expression filled his mind and he scowled. Always the man who got the ladies. That entire family acted as if they were better than everyone else. He'd asked Jennifer out once, and she'd stared at him as if he'd had two heads. And now his entire future was in their hands. *Well, bullshit on that.* Martin slammed his glass on the table and rose. He would find a way to get Dillon McCoy to sell, no matter what he had to do.

Chapter Nine

Diana stared in awe at the Thanksgiving feast laid out before them. Dominating the array of dishes sat the largest turkey she'd ever seen. Heaping bowls of buttery mashed potatoes, thick brown gravy, herb dressing, sweet potato casserole, corn pudding, and cranberry sauce filled every square inch. Her own family's Thanksgiving dinners usually consisted of her and her brother, their parents, and sometimes grandparents—at a restaurant.

Diana thoroughly enjoyed meeting the rest of Jennifer's family. They were friendly and welcoming and made her feel comfortable. Unfortunately, Ada put Diana between Jennifer and Dillon. His cologne was playing havoc with her senses, and each time their legs touched, memories of his lips on hers and the feel of his arms around her flashed through her mind.

"Diana, Ada tells us your family is from Philadelphia," Dillon's uncle Will, a tall, heavy-set man who resembled Chet, said.

Diana brushed away thoughts of Dillon and cleared her throat. "Yes, that's right."

"Nice city," he continued. "My architectural firm had a couple of conferences there. I enjoyed sightseeing. Lots of history."

"We certainly get a lot of tourists," Diana said.

"You wouldn't get me anywhere near those big cities on the east coast," Augusta interjected. "I'd be afraid of being mugged or murdered." Augusta, tall like Ada, was heavier, with blonde hair streaked by silver, blue eyes, and a face that could be attractive if her expression wasn't so stern.

Before Diana could reply, Will turned to his sister. "Ah, Augusta, they're no worse than anywhere else."

"Those cities are certainly more dangerous than Asheville or Charlotte," Augusta declared. "Why, they're always in the news with one awful thing happening after another."

Chet cleared his throat. "Tell us, Diana, did you enjoy your riding lesson?"

Diana hoped her cheeks weren't glowing pink as they had earlier. "Yes, very much. Dillon is a wonderful teacher." She could feel Dillon shift in his seat. Again, their legs brushed, and her body reacted. Dillon let out a long low breath, and Diana wondered if he was as aware of her as she was of him. "The trail and scenery were beautiful, and we actually saw some deer," Diana continued. "I've never spent much time in the country."

"I enjoy living in Lexington," Will's wife, Martha said, "but I do miss the mountains."

"Charlotte is one of the most up and coming cities in the south," Augusta stated.

"Lexington is a modern city as well," Martha replied, with a slight edge to her voice.

"What do you young people have planned for this evening?" Chet asked, obviously trying to defuse the tension.

"After dinner, we thought we'd play a game, then we're going to have our bonfire," Jennifer replied.

"Is the pit ready?" Will asked.

Dillon nodded. "I cut some wood earlier."

Augusta scowled. "Don't you think it will be way too cold?"

"Mama, we've done it millions of times," Suzanna said. "Besides, we aren't children."

"You can make plenty of hot chocolate to take with you," Ada said.

"And anything you'd like to add to it," Chet said with a wink.

"Great," Jennifer said. "We also thought we'd make some hot spiced wine."

Augusta frowned. "I hope you're not planning on staying out late and drinking too much."

Suzanna's cheeks turned pink. "Mama, please."

"Who's ready for dessert?" Ada asked. "We have apple and pumpkin pies with vanilla ice-cream."

A collective groan circled the table. "How about if we get the dishes cleaned up, then have dessert?" Martha suggested. "I think we're all too full from all this wonderful food to appreciate those homemade pies right now."

"We'll handle the cleanup," Jennifer said, getting to her feet.

Sam and Dillon also rose. "That's right, and while the girls are doing that, we'll set up the Wii."

Jennifer frowned. "Why is it the girls have to do the dishes while the boys have fun?"

"We'd be happy to help," Sam said, "but you always say we get in the way."

Sally smiled and stacked dishes. "He's right, Jennifer."

"If you're planning on playing Wii, you'll have to

go to the guest cabin," Chet said. "We moved everything so we old folks could visit without all the noise."

"Since the fire pit is over there, that will work," Dillon said, as he and Sam headed for the door. "We'll get everything ready and make the hot chocolate and spiced wine."

The older relations retired to the living room, and the girls were left in the kitchen. Diana, in amazement, took in the mound of dirty dishes, glassware, and pots and pans. They'd be here for hours, she thought.

Jennifer placed a hand on her shoulder. "Don't worry, it's not as bad as it looks. Gran has a super-duper dishwasher, and we have a routine. One scrapes the food off, one rinses, and one places them in the dishwasher. Trust me, it will take no time."

Diana nodded. "Okay, put me to work." Soon Diana was busy rinsing, and Sally said, "Diana, that's a beautiful engagement ring. Shouldn't you take it off?"

"Yes, I meant to mention it earlier," Suzanna said. "It's lovely. Do you have a date for the wedding?"

Diana hesitated. Should she tell them she spent the afternoon kissing their cousin, and there wouldn't be a wedding? Thankfully Jennifer came to her rescue.

"Speaking of engagements," Jennifer said. "You'll never guess who I heard is marrying Tim Bambury—Tammy Isaac." At the gasps from both Sally and Suzanna, Jennifer nodded. "That's right. As soon as Tim's divorce is final."

Diana, grateful for Jennifer's distraction, tuned out the conversation and concentrated on Trent and the mess she was in. Was she overreacting to her and Dillon's kiss? Was it spontaneous and soon forgotten?

Was she crazy to break the engagement over a kiss? She inwardly sighed. Or was the kiss an excuse to do something she already knew she should do?

"See, Diana, I told you it would go quickly." Jennifer broke into her thoughts. "The dishes are done, and we can head over to the guest cabin."

Amazed, Diana glanced around the spotless kitchen.

"Make sure you have a hat and gloves," Jennifer continued. "The fire pit has a tendency to keep your front warm while your backside freezes."

A short time later, the four girls were bundled up and ready to leave.

"I have flashlights, but I don't think we'll need them," Jennifer said as they headed out into the night.

The air was crisp and the sky velvet black. A thousand stars twinkled above, and the moon was full and easily lit their way.

"They're calling for more snow," Sally said. "I hope it holds off."

"Me too," Suzanna added.

Jennifer sniffed. "I smell wood smoke. They must have the fire going." She turned to Diana. "Have you ever sat around a campfire?"

Diana shook her head. "I always wanted to."

"Didn't you go on camping trips when you were in the scouts?" Sally asked.

"I was never allowed to join. I'm sure my mother expected to have to volunteer to help. I think the idea of dozens of girls she couldn't control scared the life out of her."

"I have to warn you, Dillon and Sam love to tell awful spooky stories, which I think they make up as

Debby Grahl

they go along," Suzanna said.

Diana laughed. "I love spooky stories."

They turned off the road onto a path where the glow from a fire led the way.

"Hello," Jennifer called as they approached. Seeing no one, they headed for the cabin.

"Perfect timing," Sam said as the girls entered. "Dillon has the drinks made."

"What will you have?" Dillon asked Diana.

The sight of him quickened Diana's pulse. His hair was slightly mussed, and he'd changed into a soft sweater the same color as his eyes.

"I'll, um, have some of the spiced wine," Diana replied.

From a large metal urn with a spout, Dillon filled her mug. "Jenn, Sally, Suzanna, how about you?"

Sally chose hot chocolate spiked with an Irish cream liqueur, while the other two chose the wine.

They carried their full mugs out to the blazing fire.

"We normally sit on hay bales," Jennifer said. "But we could bring a chair from the porch?"

"No, the hay is fine," Diana replied.

"Great. We'll share," Jennifer said.

Soon they were all seated around the fire, and Diana took her first sip of the hot spiced wine. "Oh my, this is delicious."

Dillon, seated across the fire from her, smiled. "I'm glad you like it."

"So, Diana, did Jennifer tell you about the witch who lives in the woods?" Sam asked.

Sally groaned. "Here we go."

"Sam. There's no witch who lives in the woods." Jenn turned to Diana. "This is one of the horrible stories

66

we were telling you about."

"It's not a horrible story," Sam said indignantly. "It's true."

Diana grinned at Sam. "No, she didn't tell me. Why don't you."

"God, Diana, don't encourage him."

Sam ignored Jenn, lowered his voice, and began. "Over a hundred years ago, there was a beautiful girl named Wilhelmina, who had long blonde hair and big blue eyes and lived all alone in a log cabin here in the mountains. The townsfolk said she appeared sweet and kind but was really an evil witch. Children were told to stay away from her, and men were warned not to go near her because those who did were never seen again. But there was one who didn't believe the story, Simon Bellows. Simon claimed the rumors about her were wrong, and he'd been to see her many times, and she was no witch. He told everyone he was in love with her, and they were going to get married. On the day before the wedding, Simon couldn't wait to see his love, so he snuck up to her cabin to surprise her. But the surprise was on him, for what he found was a horror come to life. Her beauty and the picturesque cabin were nothing but illusion. The cabin was actually a falling down shack and Wilhelmina, glimpsed through an open window, was an ancient hag. Enraged that he'd been taken for a fool and heartbroken over her betrayal, Simon slipped away.

The next day the townsfolk gathered at the base of the mountain to watch Wilhelmina and Simon take their vows. The bride was beautiful in white lace and pearls. She stood alone, in a green meadow surrounded by blooming dogwoods waiting for her groom, but Simon never came. As time passed, people drifted away, but Wilhelmina refused to leave. Finally, as the last rays of the sun filled the sky, Wilhelmina turned and made her way back up the mountain. The townsfolk say that night an awful keening sound echoed through the valley. Simon had left, and ever since Wilhelmina, vowing revenge, walks these mountains and kills any man she comes upon."

After Sam concluded his story, the little group sat quietly, the only sound being the crackling flames from the fire pit. As Jenn was about to speak, a rustling noise came from the woods beyond them.

"What was that?" Sally asked.

"I'll bet it's Wilhelmina," Sam replied.

Jenn snorted. "Then you and Dillon had better go inside. Sally, Suzanna, Diana and I are perfectly safe."

"No, you're not," Sam stated. "I didn't tell the rest of the story." Once again he lowered his voice. "You see weeks later Simon returned with a beautiful bride and Wilhelmina went berserk. One night as Simon and his love slept, Wilhelmina slipped into town and with a hatchet hacked both Simon and his wife to death. No one in the town had the nerve to go after Wilhelmina, so to this day she still roams these woods with her bloody hatchet."

Sally scowled at her brother. "Sam, you made that up."

Sam shrugged. "Nope, it's all true."

Laughing, Dillon rose and placed more wood on the fire. "I've heard the same story. In fact, I've seen Wilhelmina."

"You have not," Jenn exclaimed. "Because, according to Sam, if you had, you'd be dead."

"I said I saw her; I didn't say she saw me."

Jenn shook her head. "You're full of it. Diana, don't believe anything he says."

Diana, who had thoroughly enjoyed Sam's story, said teasingly, "I believe every word."

Dillon, who now sat on a bale of hay to Diana's right, refilled her mug. "It's nice to have at least one person who believes me."

"Okay, where did you see her?" Suzanna asked.

"Last spring up at Red Oak. I went to check the cabin, and it started to rain. I decided to stay the night. I fell asleep on the couch, and something woke me. I looked out the window and she was standing at the edge of the woods."

"Was she beautiful or a hag?" Sam asked.

"I only saw her from the back. She was wearing a long cape with a hood and was heading away from me."

"Could you see through her?" Sally asked.

Dillon paused. "I don't think so."

"Then how could it have been her?" Suzanna stated.

Dillon shrugged. "It definitely was a woman. Who else other than Wilhelmina would be in the woods late at night?"

"I still say you're full of it," Jenn said, rising and brushing hay from the back of her jeans. "I'm ready for some pumpkin pie. Who wants to go with me?"

Sam, Sally, and Suzanna all stood, but Diana hesitated. She was enjoying herself, and she didn't want to go. But if everyone left, she'd be alone with Dillon, and that was asking for trouble. Sighing, she started to rise, but Jenn's words stopped her.

"I'm not ready to call it a night. We'll go get some

dessert and bring it back. Afterward we can play some Wii.

"Sounds good," Sam said, and the others agreed.

"Dillon, is that all right with you? We don't want to keep you up," Jenn asked.

Dillon nodded. "Sure, bring me a piece of apple pie. How about you, Diana, would you like anything?"

"Pumpkin sounds good to me, no ice cream," she said as she rose. "I can come along and help."

Jenn waved her away. "We can get it. Stay here and enjoy the fire and your wine."

"Okay, tell me the truth," Diana said to Dillon after they'd all disappeared into the darkness. "Did you really see Wilhelmina?"

Dillon sipped his wine and shrugged. "I saw something. Who or what, I can't be sure." He grinned. "I enjoy getting Jennifer riled up."

Diana grinned back. "I kind of guessed that. You two are pretty close, aren't you?"

"Yeah, we are. Growing up she was always following me around. She was quite the tomboy, wanting to do what I was doing. Except for riding. She never had the knack for it."

As he spoke, firelight played across his handsome face. His features grew serious, indecision in his eyes. Exhilaration and anticipation filled Diana as she gazed into their blue depths. She knew exactly what he was thinking. What she wasn't prepared for was the longing that gripped her as he spoke each word, his voice a low sultry whisper.

"I want to kiss and hold you again."

Diana's heart raced and her head spun. Later, she'd blame the romance of the fire and the heady wine she'd drunk for her inability to stop him.

He took her mug from her hand and placed it on the ground. She sat mesmerized as his lips drew closer. When his mouth covered hers, Diana sighed. She tightened her arms around his neck and luxuriated in his kiss. His lips were gentle as they coaxed and teased, bringing her body to fever pitch. As his tongue danced with hers, Diana made little whimpering sounds.

She tangled her fingers in the hair at the base of his neck and tugged. He smelled like wood smoke and tasted like wine.

His kiss deepened and Diana surrendered to her need for him.

He ran his hand under her jacket and caressed her breast. For a second she stiffened, knowing she should stop him. But it felt so good. Through her sweater, he ran his thumb over her nipple. As the tiny bud hardened, a low moan escaped her.

"I know, darlin', I know," he murmured.

Breathless, Diana lay in his arms. Reluctantly she opened her eyes and gazed into his. Despite his heated desire, common sense thankfully overruled her impulse to go further.

She cleared her throat, and with a voice that wasn't too steady said, "Dillon, I, I…"

That's all she managed to say before he gently kissed her. "It's okay, Darlin'. I wish you'd been naked in my bed, and I could please you properly."

Her self-control was slipping away. It was warm and wonderful here in his arms. She struggled to gather her wits. "Dillon, the others will be back soon."

He let out a long breath and sat her beside him. "I want to say to hell with the others and take you into the cabin and make love to you until the sun rises."

Diana closed her eyes and willed herself to stay strong. If she were honest, that's exactly what she wanted him to do. Before things went any further, she had to tell him the truth about Trent. Not knowing how to begin, the words came out in a rush. "Dillon, I need to explain. As you know, I'm engaged. I'm here because of my doubts about the marriage. Jenn thought it might help if I got away to think things through. I know now I can't marry Trent, and I feel terrible about doing this to him, but marrying him would be worse."

Dillon ran his hand down his face. "Diana, I'm sorry I had a part in all this. I knew there was a man in your life, and I should have kept my distance. I hope I'm not the reason you're calling off the marriage."

She touched his arm. "You're not the reason, but you did help show me I don't love Trent the way I should."

His expression seemed more hopeful than contrite. He gave her a slight smile. "Does this mean you'll come into the cabin with me?"

Diana laughed. "No, it does not." She hesitated. If this was to go any further, she wanted to make sure his marriage was truly over, but would asking him be too intrusive? She took a deep breath and said, "Jenn told me you're in the middle of a divorce. That must be tough."

He was silent for a minute before replying, "I met Tonya during the height of my career. I was caught up in the excitement of winning championships, and we had a lot of fun. But after the excitement died down, she got bored. I caught her in bed with another man."

The pain in his voice broke her heart. She touched

his cheek.

"Dillon, I'm sorry. How awful."

"I guess I went a little crazy. I actually pulled the son-of-a-bitch out of bed and punched him. Tonya started screaming, and I thought I'd better leave before the police showed up. I called Tonya a few unkind names and left. I can have a little bit of a temper, but I've never been that angry. On my drive here from Texas, I had a lot of time to think. I'm not sure I loved Tonya as much as I thought. Yes, her betrayal hurt, but walking away isn't as hard as I expected. Besides, I could never trust her again. Once that's gone, the relationship is over."

Diana nodded. "I agree. If I could kiss you and let you touch me intimately, I could never marry Trent and live with that secret."

"So now what do we do?" Dillon asked.

The firelight showed the hope in his eyes. Diana knew she should tell him they needed to resolve their other relationships before they entered one of their own, but once again, the words wouldn't come. Instead she whispered, "I don't know."

He bent his head to kiss her. "I do."

The snap of a branch made Diana pull away. "What was that?"

"Probably the others coming back." He gave her a quick kiss and whispered, "We've got two more nights." He handed her the mug of wine and stood to place more wood on the fire, then froze. In a calm voice he said, "Diana, get up and slowly go to the cabin."

"Why? What's wrong?"

"Something's out there, and it's not Jennifer and the rest. It could be a black bear or some other animal, but I don't want to take any chances. So please do as I say. I'll be right behind you."

The night was still, the only sound the crackle and pop of the fire. Diana stood and strained to see what Dillon was looking at and whispered, "I don't see anything."

Then, beyond the firelight, a shadow moved. She eased her way toward the cabin. When she'd reached the porch, Dillon cautiously headed toward her.

As he stepped onto the porch, he removed his cell phone from his pocket. "I don't know if I'll have a signal, but I'll try. I want to let Jennifer know there might be a bear. I don't want them walking back here carrying food. He punched in her number, and to Diana's relief Jenn answered.

Dillon quickly explained, paused, then said okay and disconnected. "They were about to leave and were going to drive over anyway, so there's nothing to worry about."

"I never thought about bears," Diana said. "Aren't they dangerous?"

"If you keep your distance, they normally keep theirs." A scowl crossed his face as he stared into the darkness. "Most of the black bears around here are already hibernating. And as I said, I'm not sure that's what I saw." He arched one brow. "Perhaps Wilhelmina is lurking in the dark."

Diana shuddered. "Not funny."

****

Dillon smiled and took her hand. "Let's go inside and wait for Jenn."

As Diana stepped through the door, Dillon glanced uneasily over his shoulder toward the woods. In the darkness, it was hard to distinguish one shape from another, but he wasn't convinced that what he saw was an animal, but rather was human. If he were alone, he'd get one of the rifles kept in the cabin and investigate. He couldn't imagine who would be lurking in the trees, but there was the cut fence and the horse tracks he'd seen with Diana. From now on, he'd make sure he was more aware of his surroundings. If someone was trespassing on McCoy land, he'd find out why.

Chapter Ten

Diana lay in Dillon's arms and he was kissing her passionately. His hand was sliding up her leg when Jennifer abruptly awakened her by bouncing on her bed.

"Get up sleepy head," she called. "We're going to have breakfast, then go into Pine Bluff for some shopping before it gets too late."

Diana blinked a couple of times to erase Dillon's face from her mind. God, what a dream. Talk about realistic. She slowly sat up and brushed the hair from her eyes. "What time is it?"

"Six-thirty."

"What? Jenn, we didn't get to bed until after two."

"I know, but if we don't get an early start, all the good stuff will be gone. Remember, it's Black Friday.

Diana groaned. They'd eaten their pie, then played games until they were all yawning. Sam was staying with Dillon, so the girls drove back to the house alone. Exhausted, Diana had tumbled into bed.

"Okay, give me a minute to shower, and I'll be ready," she said, flinging back the covers.

"I've already showered," Jenn said as she stretched out on Diana's bed. "I'll wait here." She plumped the pillows behind her. "I can't wait to hear what happened between you and Dillon when we left to get the pie."

Diana, gathering clean clothes, froze. She knew if she and Dillon had been alone, she'd have ended up in his bed. Best to keep that to herself. There were some things even your closest friend didn't need to know. She shrugged. "Not much."

"Bullshit. I noticed the way he kept staring at you when we were sitting around the fire pit. I honestly was concerned about leaving you with him, but I could tell you were enjoying yourself, and it would have been silly for you to go with us to get pie, so I left it in your hands, or maybe his hands?"

Diana sighed and sat on the edge of the bed. "I told him about Trent and why I came with you."

"Really, what did you say?"

"That I was having misgivings about the marriage and decided I can't go through with it." She ran her finger over her engagement ring, and a tear ran down her cheek. "Jenn, I feel awful doing this to Trent." A little sob escaped her. "Now how am I going to tell him?"

Jenn sat next to Diana and placed her arm around her shoulders. "I'm so sorry. I know this is tearing you apart. If you want to leave today, I'll be happy to drive you."

Diana shook her head. "Trent isn't due back from his ski trip for another week. There's no sense sitting in Chapel Hill. At least here, I can stay distracted and not dwell on what I have to do."

Jenn rose. "That's true. I'll let you get ready." She squeezed Diana's arm. "Hang in there."

After Jenn left, Diana headed for the bathroom. Decorated in gray and rose, there was an old-fashioned pedestal sink and a modern walk-in shower. While shampooing her hair, Diana rehearsed different ways to break the news to Trent all of which would result in the same outcome, hurt.

And what about the rest of her life? Could she still accept the job at the school of Science and Math and be so close to Trent? She let the warm water flow over her. She knew one thing; she wasn't going home to Philadelphia. She couldn't take the disapproval and disappointment in her mother's eyes. She turned off the shower and reached for a fluffy towel. *For now, I'll be a coward and play Scarlett and think about it tomorrow.*

By eight o'clock, Jenn, Diana, Sally, and Suzanna were on their way down the mountain to Pine Bluff. "We'll stop at Country General first, then go to Asheville and the shops at Biltmore," Jennifer said. "You'll love those stores, Diana. They're all high-end."

Upon entering the store, Diana stared in total delight. In front of her were shelf after shelf and barrel after barrel of candy—gum drops, hard candy, peppermint sticks, chocolate bars, truffles, turtles, licorice, suckers, orange slices, and fireballs.

Jennifer grinned. "Diana, you look like the proverbial kid in the candy store."

"I can't take it all in. My parents weren't big on my brother and me having candy, but there's nobody to tell me no now."

Jennifer took her by the arm. "Come on, you can get candy on the way out. Wait until I show you the clothes."

Before Diana knew what hit her, she was in a dressing room surrounded by jeans, western and flannel shirts, sweaters, and a couple of suede vests. She stood in front of the mirror shocked at the change in her appearance. She muffled her laughter. Her mother would be horrified. The flannel shirt had light and dark blue checks, and the jeans were slightly faded. The vest was deep blue with fringe on the pockets, and the belt had a small rearing horse on the silver buckle.

"So, what do you think?" Jenn asked from the other side of the dressing room door.

"I love it all," Diana replied.

"Good. I found a great jacket for you to try."

Diana opened the door, and the other three girls gasped.

"Oh, my God, you look great," they said as one.

"Try this on." Jenn handed her a chocolate brown suede jacket with fake fox fur around the collar and cuffs. "Perfect. I think you should buy it all."

Diana hesitated. She had to admit, she really liked the clothes, but how often would she wear them? "Perhaps a few things."

"Okay, but keep what you have on," Jenn said. "We'll snip the tags off after you've paid. Now, we need to find you some boots without three-inch heels."

Two hours later, after visiting more stores, they'd stashed their purchases in the SUV and were seated in a quaint café, eating salads and drinking cappuccino.

"I'm exhausted," Suzanna said.

"Me too," Sally agreed.

"You can't poop out on us yet," Jenn said. "We haven't been to the Biltmore shops. I promised Diana we'd go there."

Diana shook her head. "Sorry, but I agree with Suzanna and Sally. I'm exhausted. Besides, I'm happy with the things I bought. I even found a scarf for my

Mom at Ellie's and an antique broach for my grandmother at the jewelry shop."

"If you're sure."

Diana nodded.

"I say we go home and see what Dillon and Sam are up to." Sally said.

"I thought after a while we could come back to town for dinner, and give the parents a break from us," Suzanna said.

Jenn smiled. "I was thinking the same thing. We'd better make reservations somewhere."

"How about the Stag's Head?" Sally suggested. "They usually have a good country band. We can do some dancing."

"Perfect." Jenn dug in her purse for her phone. "I'll call now."

As they sat finishing their coffee, a bit of sadness came over Diana. How she wished she had a fun, carefree family like the McCoys. Her household was so structured. They'd never do anything on the spur of the moment.

"Does that sound okay to you, Diana?" Sally asked.

"Sure." Diana hesitated. "Although, I'm not much of a dancer."

"Don't worry," Suzanna said. "We'll teach you how to do the two-step."

"Um, Diana, do you like country music?" Sally asked.

"I haven't heard enough of it to say one way or the other, but I'm willing to give it a try."

Jenn dropped her phone back in her purse. "All set. We've got seven o'clock reservations. Diana, you'll love the music, trust me." She gave her a wide grin. "You might even like riding the bucking bronco."

Sally laughed. "Jenn, stop teasing her. There's no bucking bronco."

A woman approached the table. "Hello, ladies. Out doing some shopping?"

She stood about five-foot-seven, with curly, light-brown hair, and big brown eyes. The cashmere sweater she wore showed off her impressive chest, and her wool pants a slim waist and long legs.

"Hey, Bonnie," Jenn replied. "We've been here since the stores opened. How about you?"

"I finished up here, and I'm on my way to Asheville."

Jen indicated Diana. "Bonnie, this is my friend Diana Thompson. Diana, this is Bonnie Duffy. She and her husband own the property next to ours."

Diana smiled. "Hi, nice to meet you."

"You too. Are you enjoying our little town?"

"Very much. And I love the ranch."

"Dillon's been giving her riding lessons," Jenn added.

"If anyone can teach you to ride, it's Dillon," Bonnie said. "Well, ladies, enjoy the rest of your day. Tell Ada and Chet I said happy Thanksgiving."

Bonnie's smile seemed forced.

After Bonnie left, Suzanna leaned in close. "Remember the time we caught Bonnie and Dillon at Red Oak?"

Jenn rolled her eyes. "I think all our male cousins used to take girls out there." She grinned. "And they thought nobody knew."

"I never thought she was right for him," Sally said.

A stab of jealousy shot through Diana at hearing Bonnie knew what it was like to have Dillon make love to her. For heaven's sake, she just met the man. She normally didn't have lustful thoughts about men. But since Dillon kissed her, she couldn't get images of them rolling around in bed out of her mind. In the time she'd known Trent, she'd never had fantasies about him.

"Diana, you okay?"

Diana blinked away Dillon's handsome face. All three girls were staring at her. "What? Yes, sorry."

Jenn laughed. "Girl, you definitely left the building. With that dreamy expression in your eyes, you must have been thinking about a man."

Diana felt her cheeks turning pink. "Actually, I was thinking about how much fun I'm having."

Jenn snorted. "Yeah, right." She reached for her coat. "Let's go, so we can find the boys and let them know they're taking us out tonight."

****

Dillon and Sam rode their horses through the snow until the cabin on the ridge, Red Oak, came into view. In the distance, a soft orange and pink sky spread across the jagged mountain peaks.

"Gramps wanted me to check on the cabin," Dillon said. "There hasn't been anyone up here since the snow started to fall."

Sam nodded. "I never get tired of the view. When the cabin wasn't rented, I used to bring Carly Jane Hadley up here."

Dillon snorted. "That's until Gramps caught you two and about skinned you alive."

Sam sighed. "Her daddy wasn't too happy either. I suppose making love on the deck wasn't a good idea."

Dillon laughed. "You think?"

"Yeah, well, we got caught up in the moment. Soon after that she left for college. I haven't seen her since." He frowned. "I really cared for her."

"Do you know where she is now?"

"Not really, but I think Jenn keeps in touch with her."

"Is her family still in the area?"

"I think so."

"Why don't you give her a call and find out."

Sam shook his head. "I haven't talked to her in four years. She might be involved with someone."

"So, if she is, she'll tell you."

Sam shrugged. "I'll think about it." He grinned. "Speaking about summer romances, I wasn't the only one who used this cabin. Didn't you and Bonnie come up here?"

Dillon grinned back. "You're right. The difference is, I never got caught."

The A-frame sat in a clearing surrounded on three sides by tall evergreens. A deck off the back gave a breathtaking view of the valley.

They tied their horses beneath one of the evergreens and stepped onto the covered porch. In the summer, rockers and a swing invited guests to sit and relax.

Dillon placed the key in the lock and opened the door. They stomped the snow from their boots and stepped in.

"If you'll go upstairs, I'll look around down here," Dillon said. The living room, kitchen, and dining room were combined, with a half bath and laundry off the kitchen.

Something wasn't right. No one had been here in a couple of months, but the room seemed lived in. Pillows on the sofa were mussed, and crumbs lay on the kitchen counter. He checked the trash and found beer cans and a wine bottle.

"Hey, Dillon," Sam called. "I thought you said no one's been staying here."

"That's right. What did you find?"

"I think the king-size bed has been slept in, and towels in the bathroom used."

Dillon's mouth formed a grim line. "Damn it to hell."

Sam came down the stairs. "Is it possible someone is using the cabin without Gramps knowing?"

"Sure. When the snow gets deep, he doesn't come up here."

"They'd have to live close and know the cabin wouldn't be checked on."

Dillon nodded. "That could be anyone in the area. I'm tempted to camp out up here to see if I can catch them."

"I'm not leaving until Sunday. I can stay with you."

Dillon looked thoughtful. "Sam, there's been other peculiar things going on." He told him about finding the cut in the fence, seeing the horse tracks, and thinking someone was in the woods during their bonfire. "And now this."

"Who could it be?" Sam asked with incredulity.

Dillon shook his head. "I have no idea."

"There were two dirty towels. Could someone be using the cabin as a place to meet?"

"Great. We've got a love nest."

Sam frowned. "How did they get in?"

"Good question. The front door was locked when we got here, so let's check the windows."

"Here we go," Sam called. "The sliding door leading onto the deck isn't locked."

Dillon shook his head. "I'll bet the cleaning crew forgot to check it."

"But how would someone know they could get in?"

"Another good question."

"Perhaps they were hiking up here, tried the door on a chance it was unlocked, and got lucky."

"Could be. But that doesn't explain the cut fence and the tracks I saw."

"If they've been staying here, they could keep their horse in the enclosure out back. But again, I ask, why?"

"I wish I knew." Dillon headed for the door. "Make sure everything is locked, and let's go. We want to get back before dark."

The four girls were seated around Dillon's fireplace when Dillon and Sam entered the cabin.

"There you two are," Jenn said. "We wondered if you'd ever get here. We're going to The Stag's Head for dinner and dancing, so get cleaned up."

"Glad you made yourselves at home," Dillon said with a laugh. "Do you mind if we have a beer first?"

Jenn rolled her eyes. "Only if you're quick about it."

Dillon and Sam took off their coats and hats and headed for the kitchen. Once they were seated with the girls, they told them what they'd found at Red Oak. Dillon hesitated before deciding to tell them everything. "I'm not going to say anything to Gramps right now.

There's no reason to get him and Gran upset. We all need to keep our eyes open for anything unusual."

"Holy crap," Jenn exclaimed. "Why would someone stay at Red Oak and sneak around in the dark?"

"Who knows," Dillon replied. "After everyone has gone, I thought about camping up there to see if I can catch them."

"Won't that be dangerous?" Diana asked.

"We think it might be two people rendezvousing," Sam said.

"It must be someone local," Jenn added.

Sam nodded. "Probably."

"That's incredible," Suzanna exclaimed. "I wonder who it is?"

"And how did they know they could get in?" Sally asked.

"Perhaps it was just by chance," Diana suggested.

"Yeah," Suzanna said. "They were snooping around and found the unlocked door."

"That's what we thought," Sam said.

"If the cabin wasn't rented, wouldn't cars parked up there draw someone's attention?" Diana asked.

"Not necessarily," Dillon replied. "If the snow is deep, cars can't get up there. If the roads are clear, the cabin is so far up, unless you purposely went there, no one would know, and the road goes out at the north gate. I'll ask Gramps when the cabin was rented last."

Hands on hips, Jenn scowled. "I think we should go stay up there and catch them."

Dillon sipped his beer. "How would we all get there? The snow is too deep to drive. If we rode the horses, where would we shelter them? There's only that small enclosure that holds two horses."

"Damn, you're right," Jenn said. "I'll bet it's two married people fooling around, and they can't take a chance checking into a motel."

Sally nodded excitedly. "Who do we know that could be secret lovers?"

Dillon instantly pictured Diana in his arms seated by the campfire and glanced at her. By the flush on her cheeks, he knew she'd had the same thought. Secret lovers. He grinned to himself. He liked the sound of that.

"Two people sneaking around explains Red Oak, but what about the fence and the tracks Dillon saw?" Suzanna asked.

"Maybe whoever it is needed a secluded way in, so they cut the fence." Sally suggested.

"Yes, but that area isn't easily accessed," Sam said.

Dillon got to his feet. "We can speculate all night, but I'm hungry and need a shower."

Sam also rose. "Me too."

****

"Shouldn't we go change?" Diana asked, after Dillon and Sam left.

"If you'd like, but what you're wearing is fine," Jenn said, gathering up the wine glasses. "I'll be ready as soon as I put these in the dishwasher."

After Jenn left the room, Diana glanced down at her jeans and flannel shirt. "I guess it's just me, but I'd feel better if I changed into something a little dressier for dinner."

"I understand," Suzanna said.

"Don't get too dressed up," Sally added. "The Stag's Head is just down-home country."

Diana gnawed on her lower lip. "I did buy that vest and western shirt."

"Perfect," Jenn said, rejoining them. "If Gramps lets us take the ranch van, we can all fit. Who will be our DD for the night?"

"I will," Suzanna said.

Chapter Eleven

A couple of hours later, they sat at a round table in the rustic ambience of the Stag's Head pub. Prints of western towns hung on wood-paneled walls. Wide beams crossed the ceiling, and polished hardwood covered the floor. A long bar stretched along one wall, and a stage filled another. Wagon wheel light fixtures hung overhead, and waitresses wore black jeans, white shirts, and string ties.

"I love this," Diana said.

"Have you ever been in a country bar before?" Dillon asked.

"No." She hesitated. "I suppose the closest would be when my family visited Lake Tahoe, and the car got a flat tire. We waited in a log cabin restaurant until the car was ready."

Dillon smiled. "Well, darlin', we're a long way from Lake Tahoe." He laughed and leaned close, lowering his voice. "I'm going to show you how much fun a country girl can have."

Diana's heart beat faster. When he smiled, Dillon McCoy was the sexiest man she'd ever met. His dark red western shirt showed off his wide shoulders, and his black jeans sat low on his waist and fit snugly along his thighs. To Diana's chagrin, they were almost dressed alike. Before they'd left, she'd decided to change into black jeans, a snap-front red and black western shirt, and a black vest.

She loved the smell of his cologne and wanted to run her fingers through his thick hair. *God, I have to stop thinking about him this way,* she thought, as her eyes traveled down his body. To Diana's relief, the waitress arrived to take their order.

"What would you like?" Dillon asked.

"Um, what is everyone else drinking?"

"Except for Suzanna, we're all having beer," Jenn replied. "But get whatever you want."

"Bring her a Light," Dillon said to the waitress. "We'll start her out slow." He turned to Diana. "If you don't like it, Sam will drink it."

"And for dinner?" The waitress, whose nametag read 'Patty', asked.

"The prime rib is incredible here," Sam said.

They all ordered the prime rib, and Diana sat back and took in her surroundings. Next to them, a group of young women were doing shots of something. Men lined the bar, and couples sat in booths. She smiled to herself. If her mother could only see her now.

"What are you smiling about?" Dillon asked.

"I'm having fun," Diana replied.

"Glad to hear it. I didn't tell you, but you look good."

"Thanks. Jenn, Sally, and Suzanna had fun today dressing me."

"And we did a great job," Jenn added.

"Here's the band." Sam said, as four thirty-something men stepped onto the stage.

"Oh, my God," Sally exclaimed. "It's Bobby Ray."

Jenn and Suzanna glanced from Sally's startled

face to the handsome man strapping on his guitar. Wavy dark hair reached below his collar. From where they sat, Diana couldn't see the color of his eyes, but his face was lean with a straight nose and a thick mustache above a sensual mouth. He had an athletic build and stood around six feet.

"I can't believe he's here." Sally said. "I thought he left the area to go to college." She paused. "University of Georgia, I think."

"Sally, are you okay?" Jenn asked.

Sally's face grew taut and she nodded. "The jerk broke my heart, but I'm over him. I'll be fine."

From the pain in Sally's eyes, Diana doubted this was true.

"To fill you in on what's going on," Jenn said to Diana, "Sally used to play keyboard with Bobby Ray's band."

"He sees you," Suzanna said.

Bobby Ray stared at Sally, then gave her a slight smile.

"Do you think he'll have the nerve to come over and speak to you?" Jenn asked.

"I don't know," Sally whispered back, her eyes never leaving Bobby Ray's.

"Thank God the drinks are here," Jenn said. "I think we could all use one."

Diana took a sip of her beer and was pleasantly surprised.

"Well, what do you think?" Dillon asked.

Diana nodded. "It's tastier than I thought."

Jenn laughed. "Next we'll have you doing tequila shots."

Their dinners arrived, and Diana was enjoying the

people around her and the delicious food. When another beer was placed in front of her, she hesitated, then shrugged. Why not?

The band started with a lively song about a Louisiana Saturday night. Some people got up to dance. Couples faced each other, while girls stood side-by-side.

Dillon bent close. "They're doing a dance called the two-step."

"Come on, Sam, we can do this," Jenn said, tugging on Sam's arm.

Diana smiled with delight as Jenn and Sam circled the floor.

"I can teach you," Dillon said.

Diana shook her head. "I'm not much of a dancer." Memories of hours of dreaded ballet lessons played through Diana's mind. She had wanted to learn tap, but her mother insisted ballet would give her grace and poise.

"We'll start with something slow," Dillon continued. He took her hand and pulled her from her chair.

"Dillon, I can't," Diana protested to no avail. Dillon wasn't letting go. The next thing she knew, she was in his arms on the dance floor.

"Come on up and hold your girl tight," Bobby Ray said and began to sing.

"This song is perfect," Dillon whispered in her ear. "It's called 'Feels So Right'. Listen to the words, darlin'."

Diana held onto Dillon as they swayed to the music, and he quietly sang along with Bobby Ray.

His right hand rested on her lower back. The gentle

pressure brought them intimately close. Her desire for him alarmed her. If he could do this to her dancing, what could he do in bed? Dillon ran soft kisses along her cheek.

Diana inwardly groaned. She was in big trouble. Thankfully, the song ended.

"Let's see what they play next," Dillon said.

When Diana opened her mouth to protest, he gently kissed her lips.

What are the others going to think? Diana franticly thought. *They know I'm engaged, and here I stand letting Dillon kiss me.* She glanced around. The dance floor was packed. Chances were Jenn and the rest couldn't see them.

"Dillon, you have to stop that. I'm supposed to be engaged. What will the others think?"

"Ah, well, you don't have to worry about that."

"What? Why not?"

"Because while you were changing earlier, Jenn explained the situation. I guess Sally and Suzanna picked up on our..." He hesitated. "...interest in each other."

Diana groaned. "I'm so embarrassed."

"There's no reason to feel that way. Everyone makes mistakes. Take me. I thought Tonya was the one for me, and see how wrong I was. Sally and Bobby Ray were crazy about one another until his band and partying meant more to him than she did. Sam used to date a great girl named Carly Jane, and he let her get away. So don't slam yourself for realizing your mistake before causing more hurt for both of you."

"I know you're right, but it's easier said than done."

Bobby Ray started to sing, "Hello, darlin'," and Dillon cursed.

"What's wrong?"

"Come on. We need to sit down. Sally is going to need us."

Confused, Diana followed. At the table, Sally sat white-faced, transfixed on Bobby Ray.

"The S-O-B," Jenn hissed. "What does he think he's doing?"

Diana turned questioning eyes to Dillon and mouthed, "What's wrong?"

"Listen."

"Oh," Diana murmured, as Bobby Ray sang of love he couldn't forget.

Sally took a long sip of her beer and blinked back tears.

"Well, this night is complete," Sam said.

Diana glanced to see what had caught Sam's attention. A pretty, petite redhead was joining the table next to them.

Dillon roared with laughter. "I'm beginning to think we're in the middle of some TV sitcom. Drama in Pine Bluff."

"Not funny," Sam replied.

Diana tugged at Dillon's arm. "Who is she?"

"That's Carly Jane. The girl I told you about."

Jenn flapped her hands. "Okay, everyone, we're here to have a good time, and no matter who else shows up, we're going to do just that."

Sally finished her beer and told Sam to order her a shot of tequila. "You're right. Come on, girls. Let's dance."

Jenn grabbed Diana's arm. "You're coming too."

Protesting the entire way, Diana found herself in a circle with Jenn, Sally, and Suzanna. Bobby Ray was singing something about God blessing Texas, and the floor was hopping.

"Feel the beat and move with it," Jenn called. Diana copied what the others were doing. Soon she was laughing and wiggling right along with them.

****

"They've got every guy in here staring at them," Sam said.

Dillon nodded. "I can see why." His cousins were damn pretty, but Diana, well, he only had eyes for her. He could tell his attraction to her made her uncomfortable, and he should stay away, but damn it, they both knew she wasn't going to marry that other guy. Although considering the mess his life was in, was this the time to become involved with Diana? She didn't seem the type to have a sexual relationship without some kind of commitment. Besides, her life was in Chapel Hill, and he was about to take over the ranch. He was interested, but could they build a relationship?

Dillon smiled as Jenn taught Diana the two-step. She'd told him about Diana's background, and he thought he was seeing a side of her she normally kept hidden beneath her proper, serious outer shell. She was coming alive before his eyes. No matter how messed up their lives were, he knew he wanted her.

The band played another fast song, and while the girls danced, Dillon scanned the room. To his surprise, his neighbor, Kevin Duffy, sat at the bar, an expression of pure misery on his face.

Sam finished his beer and placed the glass on the

table. "Well, I think I have enough liquid courage to go ask Carly to dance."

"Has she seen you?"

"Oh, yeah, she smiled a few times. I'm hoping that's encouragement and not the spider about to devour the fly."

Dillon chuckled. "Good luck. I see Kevin. I'm going to go say hi."

He skirted the crowded dancefloor and made his way to the bar. "Hey, Kevin, how's it going?" Dillon asked, leaning close to be heard over the music.

At the sound of Dillon's voice, Kevin jumped. "Dillon, hey, hi. I didn't see you standing there."

Dillon took in Kevin's beard-stubbled face, wrinkled clothes, and trembling hands. "Buddy, you don't look so good. Are you all right?"

"Sure, I'm fine. I've been a little under the weather. That's all. How you doing?"

"Not bad. It's nice being home." Dillon cocked his head. Kevin wouldn't meet his eyes. "I'm sorry to hear of Bonnie's daddy's passing. Is she okay?"

Kevin's fingers tightened around his beer glass. "Yeah, sure, but it's tough. She didn't feel up to coming out tonight."

"It must be hard to lose your last parent," Dillon said. "Especially when you're the only child. Tell her I send my condolences. The family is in town." Dillon pointed. "We're sitting over there. Why don't you come and join us?"

Kevin shook his head. "Thanks, but I have to get home. Bonnie will wonder where I am." He finally met Dillon's eyes. "Tell Ada and Chet..." He hesitated. "That I..." He swallowed and rose. "Tell them I said hey. Take care."

Dillon opened his mouth to ask him about the cut in the fence, but Kevin hurried from the bar. Something was seriously wrong. Dillon couldn't remember a time when Kevin wasn't immaculately groomed or ready to join him for a beer and catch up on their lives. He hoped Kevin's behavior had more to do with feeling poorly, and not with either of his businesses. The Duffy property wasn't as large as the McCoys'. They had a few cabins, but their land was mostly used as a campground. Bonnie, Kevin's wife, was in charge of the campground, while Kevin ran a small sporting goods store in Pine Bluff.

Dillon headed back to their table. On his way, he spotted Martin Patrick seated in a far corner glowering at him. He wanted to flip him off but decided to ignore him instead.

In the shadows, another pair of eyes, full of hatred, glared at Dillon's back.

The band started playing a slow song, and Dillon glanced around for Diana but didn't see her. Jenn, Sally, and Suzanna were dancing with men he didn't know, but where was Diana? The dance floor was packed. Could she be dancing with someone? The stab of jealousy that knifed through him rocked him with its intensity. Christ, he hardly knew Diana, and he was reacting as if they'd been together for years. He scanned the crowd. Sam was with Carly Jane, but still no Diana. When Dillon glimpsed a well-shaped jean-clad bottom with a male hand grasping it, he jumped to his feet.

"Where are you going?" Diana said from behind him.

Hearing her voice, relief washed over him. "Trying to find you," he replied. "When I got back to the table, everyone was dancing."

She studied his face. "I had to use the Ladies'. You were talking to someone at the bar, and I didn't want to interrupt." She frowned. "Did you think I was dancing with another man?"

Dillon grinned, hoping the truth didn't show. "I thought perhaps some cowboy swept you off your feet."

She cocked her head. "Actually, a cowboy did sweep me off my feet."

The heat in her eyes told Dillon everything he needed to know. Diana wanted him as much as he wanted her.

"This next song goes out to all the rodeo riders out there," Bobby Ray said.

When the first chords filled the room, Dillon smiled and took Diana's hand. "Darlin', they're playing my song."

****

Held in his arms, swaying to the music, Diana was happier than she'd ever been. She wasn't sure if the amount of beer she'd consumed contributed to her euphoria, but she didn't care. She tightened her arms around Dillon's neck and inhaled the smell that was only his. His thick chest hair showing above the undone top snap of his shirt tickled her nose as she pressed closer. He softly sang along as he twirled them across the floor. If she had a way of stopping time, she'd do it now. She let the silky strands of his hair run through her fingers. When he pressed his arousal against her, she practically moaned aloud, and her legs went weak.

"I want you," he whispered close to her ear.

Diana licked suddenly dry lips. Oh, how she wanted to ignore her guilt and abandon herself in his arms, giving herself to him completely. She knew without any doubt, Dillon McCoy could show her pleasure she'd never known. The song ended and Dillon kissed her lips. She prayed Bobby Ray would sing another slow song, but he announced they were taking a break.

"Damn," Dillon swore. "Darlin', stay in front of me. If the rest see the condition I'm in, I'll never hear the end of it."

Her eyes full of mirth, Diana did as he asked. When they got to the table, only Suzanna was there.

"Where is everyone?" Dillon asked, quickly sitting down.

"Jenn and Sally headed for the Ladies', and Sam is at the bar talking to Carly Jane."

The waitress appeared. "Another round?"

Diana was about to say no when Dillon nodded.

"Are you enjoying yourself, Diana?" Suzanna asked.

"Oh, yes. I'm having a great time."

Beneath the table, Dillon squeezed her knee.

When her beer was placed in front of her, Diana glanced toward Dillon. Was he trying to get her drunk, thinking her determination to talk to Trent before having a relationship with him would falter? Was he right? If they were alone, would she stop him? She silently shook her head. She'd better make sure this was her last drink. She couldn't trust herself if she didn't.

Jenn and Sally returned to the table. "Oh, no," Sally gasped. "Here he comes."

Bobby Ray, beer in hand, headed toward them.

"Do you want me to tell him to go away?" Jenn asked.

Sally frowned. "Nope, I can deal with him."

"Hey, how y'all doing," Bobby Ray said, pulling out a chair and sitting down.

Diana thought it took a lot of nerve, but his gray eyes never left Sally's face.

"We're fine," Sally replied stiffly. "What are you doing in North Carolina?"

Bobby Ray sipped his beer and shrugged. "The band has been touring some. Mostly Tennessee and Kentucky. We had some time off, so we decided to come home for Thanksgiving." He paused. "Sally, you look amazing."

Sally smiled. "Thanks."

Bobby Ray turned to Dillon. "How's the rodeo circuit?"

Dillon shrugged. "You win some, you lose some."

"Dillon's won championship buckles," Jenn said.

Bobby Ray nodded. "Congratulations."

"How long will you be in town?" he asked Sally.

"Until Sunday."

Bobby Ray shifted in his seat, seeming a little uncomfortable. He finished his beer and rose. "I'll catch y'all later. If there's anything you'd like to hear, let me know." He stared directly at Sally. "I'll be here until Monday."

After he left, Sally let out a long breath. Tears formed in her eyes.

Suzanna squeezed her hand. "You okay?"

Sally nodded.

"He was sure giving you the lost-puppy-dog look," Jenn said. "If I'm not mistaken, he was asking you to call him."

"When Hell freezes over," Sally replied.

But somehow Diana didn't think it would be long before icicles formed in Hell.

Sam stopped at the table with Carly Jane right beside him. "I'm, um, going with Carly. She'll give me a ride home." He placed bills on the table. "Here's my part of the tab."

"Sure," Dillon said. "I think we're about ready to go as well."

The others agreed, and Dillon motioned for the check.

"Well, at least one of us is going to get lucky tonight," Jenn said, with a smile.

Dillon and Diana's eyes met.

As they left the bar, Dillon's cell rang. By the tone of his voice, he wasn't happy with whoever he was talking to.

When Dillon let out a string of curse words, Diana glanced over her shoulder.

"It must be Tonya," Jenn said. "She's the only one who can make him swear like that."

Sally snorted. "She was the only blast from the past missing tonight."

Suzanna laughed. "I'm glad I don't have any past love who might rear their ugly head."

"Tell me about it," Jenn said. "All my past loves are glad they're rid of me."

Diana got into the farthest back seat of the van, expecting Dillon to sit up front with Suzanna. To her surprise, he climbed in next to her. She wanted desperately to ask him what had upset him, but knowing she shouldn't pry, she kept her mouth shut.

Suzanna turned on a country radio station, and the girls sang along with a tune Diana didn't recognize.

Dillon put his arm around her and held her against him. Before she could speak, his mouth covered hers. His kiss was anything but gentle. He kissed her as if she were the last woman he'd ever kiss. Surprised at first, Diana yielded to his demanding lips. When he pressed her down on the seat, for a second she almost acquiesced to him as he gently squeezed her breast. But no matter how much she enjoyed what he was doing, they were in the back of a van full of people. When his hand slid over her hip to cup her bottom, she broke their kiss and gasped, "Dillon, we can't."

His words were low as he whispered, "Yes, we can."

He ran his hand up her leg. Even through her jeans, his finger found and stroked the special spot that instantly dampened her panties. When his hand touched her bare skin, Diana snapped out of her lustful haze. Her zipper was down, and his fingers were about to get her to the point of no return. Diana grabbed his hand. "Dillon, stop. We can't do this here."

He let out a long breath. "Okay, okay, give me a minute."

She righted her clothing and still in his arms, sat up.

"Diana, I'm sorry. I should have never done that to you. The call I got was from Tonya. It seems she's no longer with the candy-ass cowboy, and she wants money. She was screaming that I left her broke and alone. Which is bullshit. I wanted to lose myself in something sweet." He ran his finger down her cheek. "You."

Diana's heart melted. "Dillon, I'd love to stay in your arms, but please understand." She smiled and leaned closer. "I can't say I didn't like what you were doing. I'd just rather not have an audience."

His white teeth flashed in the darkness. "I promise, the next time I lay you down, there won't be anyone for miles."

Diana's palms dampened at the picture that conjured in her mind.

****

Aspen, Colorado

Trent Sawyer sipped his scotch and water and smiled at the beautiful woman seated across from him. Belinda Alan had long red hair that hung in a mass of curls down her back. Her eyes were sky blue beneath delicately arched brows. Her cheekbones were set high in a heart-shaped face. Each curve of her incredible body was outlined in the soft sweater and wool slacks she wore. The restaurant, one of Aspen's finest, was candle-lit and looked out over the slopes.

"Have you decided what you'll have?" Trent asked.

When she replied, her voice was slightly breathless. "Everything sounds so wonderful. Why don't you order for both of us?"

Trent motioned for the waiter. "We'll both have the filet with béarnaise sauce. And bring us a bottle of pinot noir."

"I still can't believe that if I hadn't fallen going over that mogul, we would have never met." She smiled. "I could have lain out there for hours if you hadn't stopped."

"That tells me we were meant to meet." Trent

reached across the table and took her hand. "I'm only glad you weren't hurt."

"I should have known I wasn't ready to try an advanced slope, but I love a challenge."

Trent nodded. "So do I."

"This is my first time skiing here," Belinda said. "My friends and I usually go to Jackson Hole, but we heard the nightlife in Aspen was hopping."

The waiter returned and poured them each a glass of wine.

Belinda sipped hers and sighed. "Wonderful. Excellent choice."

For a moment, guilt threatened to overcome Trent. The first time he'd tasted this particular wine, he'd been with Diana. He inwardly sighed. He knew what he was doing was wrong, but damn it, he wanted some excitement in his life. And he thought the lady across from him was what he needed.

When his parents canceled their ski trip, Trent decided, since Diana was going off with Jenn, he'd go to Aspen on his own. He knew marrying Diana was a mistake, but his mother considered her the perfect match—beautiful, poised, rich, and always the proper lady. His mother was right. Diana was exactly that, and she'd be a good wife to him. She'd fit in with the country club crowd and know how to conduct herself with business associates and their wives.

It wasn't that he didn't care for Diana, but she didn't excite him the way he wanted or needed. Belinda sipped her wine. Something told him Belinda could be amazingly improper with her sexy mouth. He pictured her sumptuous body beneath him, and his desire grew.

Again, Diana's face flashed in his mind. Their sex

was satisfying at times, but he wanted a woman with more imagination. He knew his life with Diana would be pleasant enough as long as he could find true satisfaction in the arms of a woman like Belinda.

Chapter Twelve

Diana stood in her bedroom at the ranch house gazing out into the dark sky. When they'd dropped Dillon off at his cabin, "Stay with me" was clear in his smoldering eyes. She wasn't experienced enough to handle the sexual charge between them. Could she get through the next couple of days and not end up in his bed? Picturing his irresistible smile, Diana groaned aloud. The answer was probably no. She leaned her forehead against the cool glass. The other question— did she want to tell him no? The answer was also no.

What was happening to her? It was as if one Diana stayed in Chapel Hill and another came here. If someone would have told her she'd lay in the back of a van and let a man, who's practically a stranger, almost make love to her, she would have looked at them like they were crazy.

Diana rubbed her temples. Dillon's sexual promise attracted her, but he was also fun to be with. She loved his sense of humor and his easy-going outlook on life. A quiet cabin in the mountains made him happy. He didn't need constant entertainment. She frowned. Unlike Trent who preferred a fast-paced lifestyle. Although Trent did enjoy rummaging around in antique shops with her. Her frown deepened. Or did he? The more she thought about it, she realized he'd come into the shops but soon after tell her he'd wait for her outside. She'd usually find him down the street sitting in a bar.

How much did they truly have in common? He definitely liked to party more than she did, but she'd had a good time tonight. It was more Trent's rowdy friends' idea of having fun she didn't care for than the party itself.

She glanced at the digital clock. Aspen's time was two hours behind them. She could call Trent. Perhaps talking to him would snap her out of this desire for Dillon. But what if her voice gave her away? Could she hide her guilt? She'd better not take the chance. She definitely wasn't going to break up with him over the phone. The question was when and how. She knew she couldn't postpone it very long. Should she wait until after Christmas? She shook her head. Even though her parents, his parents, and Trent were all going to despise her, the sooner she broke it off the better. She needed to do it when he got home from Aspen. As for Dillon, she'd better try and make sure they were never alone.

Diana awoke to the smell of coffee. To her surprise, Jenn, Sally, and Suzanna were seated around her in their pajamas, coffee cups in hand.

"Wake up, sleepy head," Jenn said, picking up the coffee pot and pouring her a mug. "We thought we'd have a girls' powwow and discuss men."

"My part of the conversation will be short," Suzanna said.

"Mine too," Jenn added. "That leaves Sally and Diana."

Diana sat up and blinked the sleep from her eyes. Sally and Suzanna had flopped down on the foot of her bed while Jenn took the chaise longue. Diana took a sip of the fragrant brew and smiled in pleasure.

"I'm glad you prefer strong coffee," Jenn said. "When Suzanna makes it, you can stand a spoon up in it."

Suzanna snorted. "Not like the colored water you brew."

Jenn flapped her hand. "On to more interesting subjects. Dillon and Bobby Ray."

Sally yawned. "We might as well move on to Dillon, because there's nothing to say about Bobby Ray."

"Sure there isn't," Jenn said, smiling. "You two looked as if you could eat each other up right on the spot."

Sally rolled her eyes. "Not hardly. I'm sure the man is still more interested in his band than me."

"That's why he told you he'd be here until Monday?" Suzanna added.

"The jerk probably thinks he can sweet talk me into bed. Well, it's not going to happen."

"You told us he was one wild man in the sack," Jenn said. "Don't you want to see if he still is?"

Sally sighed. "Hmm, that he was."

"I only had one man who ever made me scream," Jenn said, "But he moved to Alaska, and I didn't want an orgasm badly enough to follow him to the North Pole."

Suzanna cupped her chin in her hand. "There's never been a man who made me scream."

"What about that guy from town who used to hang around with Dillon?" Jenn asked. "He had the hots for you. Didn't you go out with him a couple of times?"

Suzanna nodded. "Dustin Chambers. He was nice enough, but he seemed kind of sly and calculating. I'm not sure how to explain it. I always thought he was hiding something." She smiled. "Although, I have to admit, he was a damn good kisser. I heard he decided to go up north to college."

Diana couldn't believe how open they were with one another discussing their sex lives. When their attention turned to her, visions of her laying across Dillon's lap by the campfire and in the backseat of the van swam before her eyes and her cheeks burned. "I, ah, um."

Jenn burst out laughing. "Diana, you should see your face. It's okay. We're all your friends. Whatever is talked about in this room, stays in this room."

Sally and Suzanna nodded.

"Come on, tell us, has a man ever made you scream?"

Dillon and she hadn't had sex, but if his kiss could almost make her have an orgasm, God help her if he ever got her into his bed. She cleared her throat and sipped her coffee. "No," she finally managed to say.

Jenn grinned. "Things were pretty hot between you and Dillon on the dance floor and in the back seat of the van."

Mortified, Diana opened and closed her mouth in silence.

"Jenn, stop it," Sally said. "Can't you see you're embarrassing her?"

"It's all right," Diana said. "I'm not used to having girl talk like this."

"Yeah, Diana knows I'm kidding her. Although, Dillon is clearly interested, and that makes me nervous."

"We all love our cousin, but he's had women following after him since he was a kid. We don't want you to get hurt," Sally added.

Suzanna shook her head. "I think you're both wrong. There's something different about Dillon when he looks at Diana. I don't recall ever seeing him go all gooey at Tonya."

"I know what you mean," Sally said. "There was a softness in his eyes."

Jenn's brows drew together. "Well, I'll be damned. Could Dillon McCoy have finally found the right woman?"

Diana held up her hand. "Dillon and I have just met. I'll admit there's an attraction between us, but we're both still obligated to other people, and until that's resolved, it can't go any further."

Suzanna touched Diana's leg. "Jenn told us about Trent. Anything you'd like to talk about, we'll listen."

Diana gave a wan smile. "I appreciate that. There's not much to say. Trent is a nice guy whom I don't love enough to spend the rest of my life with. And now I have the hurtful task of telling him, his parents, and my parents, who are all going to hate me." To Diana's embarrassment, a tear slid down her cheek.

All three girls hurried to put their arms around her. "You're doing the right thing," Jenn said.

"You'd be hurting Trent worse if you went ahead with the wedding," Sally agreed.

"Sometimes you have to stop thinking about other people," Suzanna quietly said. "And think about yourself."

Diana was so touched by their kindness and

compassion, she hugged them while her tears flowed.

"Okay, enough," Jenn said, wiping a tear from her own cheek. "Let's plan what to do today."

"Suzanna and I thought we'd go skiing," Sally said. "Yesterday, Sam mentioned he'd like to go, but that was before Carly Jane appeared. He might have forgotten all about it."

"I'd go," Jenn said, "but Diana doesn't ski."

This was the opening Diana needed. Dillon would probably join them. "That's fine. I'd be happy to curl up with a book."

"If you're sure?" Jenn asked. "I don't mind staying with you."

Diana shook her head. "Please go. You know me— I love to read."

"Okay, well then, Diana, we'll meet you downstairs for breakfast."

A half hour later, Diana entered the kitchen to find the room full of people.

"Come on in, Diana," Ada said. "There's a place next to Dillon."

With her traitorous heart skipping a beat, Diana sat. The table was laden with sausage, biscuits, gravy, eggs, fried potatoes, and grits.

"What would you like?" Dillon asked.

"There's so much to choose from," Diana said.

"When family is here, Ada loves to fix a big country breakfast," Chet said.

Diana filled her plate and sighed with pure pleasure as she bit into the homemade biscuit. "Ada, these are delicious. I'd love to learn how to bake."

"You have Jenn bring you back when the house isn't full, and we'll spend the day cooking."

Diana smiled. "Really? I'd enjoy that."

"Speaking of the house being empty," Chet continued. "Ada and I decided since Dillon is staying, we're going on a cruise before Christmas."

Silence filled the room until Augusta spoke, "What on earth are you talking about, Daddy. You can't just up and take off."

"And why not?" Ada asked. "The family isn't coming back until the day before Christmas. The ranch is closed until March. So, I'll ask again, why not?"

Before Augusta could respond, Will spoke up. "I think it's a wonderful idea. If I could take time off work, Martha and I would join you."

Augusta's mouth formed a thin line. "I don't know what's gotten into everyone. First Mama and Daddy buy a motor home to head off to who knows where. Dillon's moving back to run the ranch, instead of it being sold. And now you're talking about cruises during the holidays."

"Your mother and I aren't getting any younger," Chet said. "We want to enjoy the time we have left. You're more than welcome to come with us on the cruise."

"No, thank you. I'm a widow and don't have money to spend on frivolous things."

"I'm sure we could help with your ticket," Ada said.

Augusta scowled. "I'll think about it."

Suzanna glanced at her mother, then winced as if in pain.

"What do you all have planned for today?" Martha asked.

"Sally, Suzanna, Sam, and I are going skiing," Jenn

replied.

"Carly Jane is joining us," Sam added.

"Isn't she that nice girl you used to date?" his mother asked.

Sam cleared his voice. "Yeah, Mama, that's her." Before his mother could ask any more questions, Sam asked, "What about Diana?"

"She doesn't ski," Jenn replied.

As Diana opened her mouth to say she planned to curl up with a book, Dillon said, "Great. Diana and I can continue with our riding lessons."

She started to protest, but what could she say that wouldn't sound rude? "If you'd rather ski, I'll be fine here."

Dillon shook his head. "I don't have any qualms about riding a bronc, but strapping sticks to my feet and sliding down the side of a mountain isn't happening. Gramps, does Buddy Clark still own the ski area?"

"No, he sold out a year ago. Some Yank from Ohio or Wisconsin bought it. I understand he's really sprucing the place up. Not only is he upgrading the lifts, he's remodeling and adding onto the chalet."

"Well, coming from up there, they should know something about making snow," Augusta added.

Chet shook his head. "It was fine the way it was. People always want to make things bigger and better. This isn't Aspen or Vail, for goodness sakes."

"If they attract more people to the ski area, that might bring more business to the ranch," Sam added.

Will nodded. "Good point." He pushed his chair from the table. "There are a couple of football games Dad and I plan to watch."

"I thought Martha and Augusta could help me pick

out clothes for the cruise," Ada said. "You kids go on and have fun. We'll do the cleanup. Remember, dinner is at six."

"I'll wait for you to change into warm clothes," Dillon said as Diana rose.

Seeing the mirth in his eyes, Diana gritted her teeth. He'd known she'd try to avoid him, and he'd made sure that was impossible.

Diana forced a smile. "It might take me a while. I can meet you at the barn."

He smiled back. "I'm in no hurry. I'll wait."

Chapter Thirteen

Thirty minutes later, Diana and Dillon made their way down the road to the barn. Not knowing quite what to say, she began with a general topic. "The snow is beginning to melt. I hope they'll still be able to ski."

"They blow fresh snow onto the slopes, so they'll be all right."

"How far away is the ski area?"

Dillon opened the barn door. "Not far. Just over the ridge. In the summer, it's a nice hike."

The barn was pleasantly warm. Diana inhaled the smell of hay, fresh oats, and the horses and found it comforting. She was so nervous the last time she was here, she hadn't really taken in her surroundings. The cleanliness of the barn was the first thing she noticed. The floor was swept, and the feed was kept in closed containers. Saddles, bridles, and other tack hung on the wall. Folded blankets were stacked neatly on a shelf. A ladder led to the loft above the stalls. Movie scenes of couples making love in the hay flickered through her mind. What would it be like to have Dillon making love to her in a mound of soft hay? He must have read her thoughts because he gave her his killer grin and said, "Do you want to climb up?"

Heat crept up her cheeks, and she quickly shook her head. "I was, um, admiring the neatness of the barn."

His grin widened. "I used to climb up there all the time and fall asleep. Hay makes a great bed."

The image of the two of them rolling around in the loft grew more explicit in her mind. She cleared her throat. "Which stall is Flora's?"

"The third one. Do you want to saddle her?"

Diana nodded. "I'll give it a try." Soon, Flora was saddled and ready to go. Pleased with herself, Diana led her to the mounting block. She was seated when Dillon rode out of the barn. "Where will we go today?"

"I thought we'd ride out to the other cabins. After what Sam and I found at Red Oak, I'd like to make sure no one's been using them as well."

"Can we go as far as Red Oak?"

Dillon glanced at the sky. "It might snow again. I don't want to take a chance of being caught up there. Once we get to the last cabin on the trail, you'll see Red Oak in the distance."

For a while, the path was wide enough for them to ride side by side. "Are there roads that lead to all the cabins?" Diana asked.

"Yeah, but they're either dirt or gravel. And some are pretty narrow. In the summer, getting cars up isn't a problem. In the snow, it's almost impossible. In case of an emergency, we have a couple of snowmobiles."

Diana fell back behind Dillon. She breathed the clear, crisp air and sighed. When was the last time she'd been this content? If anyone had told her she'd be so happy in such a tranquil setting, she would have laughed. Raised in the suburbs of Philly, here she was, thoroughly enjoying herself.

"The first cabin is coming up," Dillon said.

"Are they all made of logs?" Diana asked.

Dillon nodded. "Except for Red Oak."

"They must have taken years to build."

"That they did. My great grandparents started the ranch, and we've been adding onto it ever since. Up ahead is our oldest cabin, and the one I told you was my favorite."

They stopped, and the cabin, situated in a stand of evergreens, was charming. A porch stretched across the front with multi-paned windows on either side of a screened door. A brick chimney stood at one end with a small picnic area laid out on the other.

"Want to go in?" Dillon asked.

Diana knew exactly what he was up to, but she really did need to relieve herself. She should have never drunk so much coffee before they left. "Would it be possible to use the bathroom?"

"Sure." He slid from his horse. "It might be a little chilly inside. We keep the heat on low in this cabin in case one of us wants to use it."

As he helped her off Flora, their body contact sent alarm bells clanging in her head. She needed to put a stop to whatever ideas he might have. "Dillon, I'm only going to use the bathroom, nothing else."

His eyes widened innocently. "Sure thing." He held open the screen and placed the key in a heavy oak door.

The smell of wood smoke greeted Diana as she stepped in. To her left, a couch and chair faced the stone fireplace. To her right, a quilt-covered brass bed, with nightstands on either side, sat upon a braided rug. Along the back wall was a small L-shaped kitchen with a table and chairs. Between the bed and the kitchen, a short hall led to the bathroom on one side and a closet

Debby Grahl

on the other.

"It's certainly cozy," Diana said.

Dillon nodded. "I come out here and hike, read, nap, and sit on the porch."

"I'll only be a minute." Diana headed in the direction of the bathroom. It was larger than she had expected. . There was a decent-sized shower and a vanity sink. She quickly did her business and washed her hands. As she headed into the living area, she carefully avoided the inviting bed. She found Dillon, his coat off, sitting on the couch drinking a soda.

"Where did you get that?" she asked.

"I always keep a supply in the fridge. Would you like one?"

"No thanks."

"Have a seat."

"No thanks."

Dillon grinned. "You don't have to be afraid of me."

"Yes, I do."

Dillon's grin widened. "Diana, I'm not going to attack you. Come sit down."

She chose to sit in a chair instead of next to him on the couch.

He crossed one booted foot over his knee and studied her. "I don't bite."

"Yes, you do."

He set his can on the pine coffee table and held out his hand to her. "Diana, come here."

She sighed. "Dillon, if I come over there, we're going to end up in that bed. I can't go back to Trent with that kind of guilt. Breaking the engagement will be hard enough. Knowing I've been with another man will make it worse."

He finished his soda and rose. "Fair enough. But even though I've never brought another woman here, I will have you in that bed."

A thrill of anticipation tingled Diana's senses. She licked suddenly dry lips. "You've got a date."

"In order to see Red Oak, we'll have to ride a little further," Dillon said. They'd mounted their horses, and Diana glanced back, regret in her eyes. Should she have given into her desire and allowed Dillon to make love to her? It took everything she had to tell him no and walk out of that cabin. She felt different with Dillon, alive and unrestrained.

Had there always been this other side of her waiting to be set free—one who drank beer and did the two-step, who thought about having wild sex with a man who made her heart race and her body crave his touch? She kept telling him she needed to wait until she broke her engagement, but when would that be? How long until she'd be back in Dillon's arms? Was she wasting precious time when she could be in his bed? Diana opened her mouth to tell Dillon to stop when the gun blast shattered the silence.

Chapter Fourteen

In the seconds it took Diana to comprehend what she'd heard, Dillon was off his horse and lifting her off Flora.

"Get in the cabin." He shoved the key into her hand. "I'm going to secure the horses."

"Dillon, was that a gunshot?"

He nudged her toward the porch. "Do it."

On trembling legs, Diana did as he asked. She had the door open when Dillon joined her. "Answer me, was that a gunshot?"

"Yes."

"Oh, my God, who?"

"I don't know," Dillon replied. "No one should be firing a rifle up here. Hunting isn't allowed on our land or on the Duffys' property."

Shaken, Dillon stepped to one of the windows and peered out. What the hell was happening? He was glad Diana didn't know the bullet had flown directly past him, barely missing his head. No Hunting signs were posted throughout the property, but Dillon would bet the shooter wasn't an illegal hunter. Seated on a horse, there's no way he could be mistaken for a deer. So who the hell shot at him and why? He didn't carry his cell phone when he rode because chances were there wouldn't be a signal. But right now, he wished he had it with him. "Diana, do you have your phone?"

"No. I didn't think I'd need it."

He turned and cursed beneath his breath. Her face was chalk white, and her hands shook. He took her in his arms and held her close. "I don't know who might be out there. There are no firearms in the cabin, and until I know what's going on, I don't feel safe riding all the way back."

She clung to him. "What are we going to do?"

"Wait here until the family comes looking for us."

"How long will that be?"

"Until we don't show up for dinner. I told Gramps we were heading this way, so they'll drive the four-wheel truck up here."

"What time is it now?"

Dillon glanced toward the digital display next to the bed. "Two o'clock."

"That means we've got four hours until someone might come."

Dillon nodded. "We'd might as well settle in. Are you hungry? I can see what canned goods are in the cupboard."

She shook her head. "I'm too nervous to eat. But I could use something to drink."

"I'm not sure what's here." He opened the cupboard above the stove. "Sorry, all I have is a bottle of bourbon."

She hesitated. "Sure, why not? Thanks." Still trembling slightly, she rubbed her arms.

"Are you cold?"

"A little."

"I could turn up the heat, but I think I'll light the fireplace. The smoke will help them find us."

"Dillon, are we safe in here?"

He didn't think whoever it was would come to the cabin, but he couldn't be sure. Considering where the shot came from, the shooter had to have been above him. The trail became steeper as it winded toward Red Oak. Dense thickets of trees lined the way, and there were plenty of places for cover.

But how did the shooter get up there? Dillon hadn't seen any truck or horse tracks in the snow. Although most of the snow and ice had melted on the road, tire marks would still be visible. Could he be overreacting? Could the shooter be some lost hunter who saw Flame and thought he was a deer? Or could this all be related to the other strange happenings? If he were alone, he'd take his chances and head for home, but he wasn't about to risk Diana getting hurt. He let out a long sigh. "I'm pretty sure whoever it is won't come to the cabin. In fact, they're probably long gone."

He poured Diana's bourbon and handed it to her. "Drink this and try to relax. I'll light the fire. It should be warmer in here soon."

She removed her coat and sat on the couch. Dillon silently cursed at the fear written on her face. When he discovered the identity of the shooter, he was going to pound the shit out of him.

By the time Dillon had a fire blazing, Diana had emptied her glass and was pouring more. He topped off his and looked out the front windows. Snow had begun to fall, covering any tracks the shooter would have made. He sat down next to Diana.

"Could this have anything to do with the other peculiar happenings on the ranch?" she asked.

"I question that as well. It's one thing to trespass.

Shooting a gun is quite another matter."

"Dillon, if someone drives up here to get us, how will you get the horses back?"

"I'll ride Flame, and if Sam is with them, he can take Flora. If not, I'll guide her behind me."

"What if the shooter is still here? Won't it be dangerous?"

"I don't think so. Whoever that was won't be hanging around where there's a number of people."

"What about the horses? Will they be okay?"

"They're in a couple of stalls behind the cabin. They'll be fine."

She sipped more of her drink and leaned close to Dillon. "If all these instances are related, shouldn't you notify the police?"

"I suppose I could tell Sheriff Dunn, but I'm not sure what he can do. My hope is to catch whoever it is red-handed."

"Dillon, that scares me. You could get hurt."

He held her close and kissed the top of her head. "I'll be fine."

"You see all those needless shootings on TV and wonder what could be going through someone's mind to kill innocent people."

"I know. I can't imagine what drives a person to do something like that."

"When I heard the shot, I'm not sure if I was more surprised or scared. The sound echoing around us was eerie."

"Diana, you have to stop thinking about it." He set their glasses on the coffee table. He lifted her onto his lap. "How about this?" He bent his head and pressed his lips to hers.

****

For a second, she resisted, then she let out a little sigh, wrapped her arms around his neck, and opened her mouth to him.

Safe and secure, cuddled there in his arms, Diana allowed the masculine strength of him to comfort her. His kiss sent waves of warmth throughout her body. His tongue teased while his hand stroked down her back to cup her bottom. As his kiss deepened, Diana marveled at how her body reacted to him. She grew damp between her legs, and her need for him grew. His hand slid under her sweater and found her breast. He stroked and squeezed until she thought she'd go mad.

He broke their kiss and their eyes met. He reached for the hem of her sweater. His voice was low and husky. "If you're going to stop me, do it now."

She should tell him no, but she was tired of fighting her desire for him. She lifted her arms and allowed him to remove her sweater.

He ran his finger along the lace trim of her bra. "Nice." He reached behind and undid the hooks. When the silky fabric fell away, Dillon smiled. He cupped her small, firm breast in his palm. "Perfect." He bent his head and took her nipple into his mouth.

She arched her back to give him better access. He squeezed, suckled, and circled her nipple with his tongue. Her breath caught as pleasure pulsated through her.

In one swift move, he lifted her up and headed for the bed. "We're going to do this right." He laid her down on the quilt and removed her boots, jeans, and bikini panties.

Slightly self-conscious, Diana lay naked before

him.

"You're so beautiful," Dillon said, as he unbuttoned his flannel shirt.

Diana's mouth watered at the sight of his bare muscular chest covered in thick hair. He quickly pulled off his boots and undid his belt. He unbuttoned his jeans, and his flat stomach came into view. Her eyes opened wide as his full erection was revealed.

She swallowed and whispered, "Oh, my."

Dillon grinned. "Will I do, darlin'?"

Diana could barely breathe. "Oh, yes."

"I'm sure liking what I see," he said, coming down on top of her. This time when his mouth covered hers, his kiss, full of his need, let her know he wasn't holding anything back.

Diana fisted her hand in the hair at the nape of his neck and tugged. The pressure between her legs built, aching for release.

Dillon drew his lips from hers and rasped, "Darlin', I've thought of nothing but having you beneath me. I want to watch you come, but this time I'll be inside you."

Half crazed with lust, Diana finally managed to gasp, "Yes."

He lowered his head, and once again took her nipple into his mouth. As he sucked, his hand slid over her hip and between her legs

She cried his name as his finger rubbed her swollen bud.

"God, you're so wet. That's it, darlin', enjoy what I'm doing." He slid two fingers into her and stroked.

The erotic sensations his touch created had Diana incapable of speech. Panting, she clung to him.

"Let it come, darlin'." He circled her bud with his thumb, while his fingers slowly glided in and out.

"Oh, sweet heaven, Dillon," she screamed as the strongest climax she'd ever experienced shot through her body. At that moment, she couldn't have said a coherent word if her life depended upon it. Ripples of orgasm flowed through her as Dillon settled himself between her legs. Paper tore, then he eased into her. His blue eyes were dark with passion as he thrust himself deep.

This was the most erotic experience she'd ever had. She dug her fingers into his shoulders as she arched upward. She could have sworn he let out a low growl.

Diana lost all self-control. She raked her nails down his back as she demanded more.

"I'll give you all I've got, darlin'." Sweat coated their bodies as he thrust harder and harder. The climax coiling inside of her grew to such intensity she lost all conscious thought.

Dillon cupped her bottom. "Diana, you've got the sweetest little—"

"Dillon," Diana shouted as the orgasm rocked her body.

"That's it, darlin'. Let me feel you come. Christ," Dillon shouted as he thrust into her one last time with his own release.

When Dillon collapsed on top of her, Diana wrapped her arms around his neck and held him tight. Talk about explosive sex. She'd definitely seen stars. She smiled. *Or perhaps a laser show*. Had she screamed? She grinned. *I believe I did, twice*.

Dillon raised his head and gazed into her eyes. "What are you smiling about?"

"The fact that I feel wonderful."

He grinned back. "I hope I'm responsible for your happy state."

She slid her fingers down his back. "Oh, yes."

He lightly kissed her lips. "I'm sorry I came at you like a wild bull, but I couldn't stop myself."

"Hmm. I think I like wild bulls."

Dillon laughed. "Is that right. Well, darlin', you sure made the eight-second ride."

Diana's cheeks turned pink, and he laughed harder. "I love it when you blush."

He once again kissed her lips, but this time the kiss deepened. Her body craved more of him.

****

When he spoke, desire was clear in his voice. "I want you again."

Diana, slightly breathless, replied, "I want you too."

He rose. "I've got to get rid of this damn condom." He hurried to the bathroom and was back in seconds. "Diana, by any chance are you on the pill?"

She nodded. "Why?"

"Because the condom broke."

She lifted her arms to him. "Come here."

This time, he planned on taking it much slower. He usually had a little more finesse, but her trim little body was driving him over the edge. Even now, her beautiful face, with her hair flowing across the pillow, her eyes dark with need, her lips swollen with his kisses, and her arms welcoming him back, made him want to thrust himself into her and send them both flying again.

Instead, he lowered himself on top of her and gently kissed her. His self-control threatened to snap.

When she made little whimpering sounds and whispered his name, Dillon lost himself in the taste and feel of her.

Chapter Fifteen

The tall man gazed out across the valley from his office window taking in the splendor of his surroundings. He'd grown up here, traveled all over the world, but this would always be home. He'd accomplished much, but there was still one prize for him to win. He glanced at the map of the county hanging on his wall and smiled. There were those who dismissed him as insignificant, different from them. He would show them, one in particular, how they had underestimated him. He intended to have it all, no matter how he had to go about getting it. Money and power were wonderful tools.

A knock sounded at his door and he frowned. He wasn't expecting anyone. He opened the door and scowled. "What are you doing here? It isn't safe."

"We might have a problem." His visitor slipped past him and stood in the center of the room.

The man closed the door, folded his arms across his chest, and waited.

His visitor took a deep breath before stating in a rush, "I just did something that could cause problems."

He narrowed his eyes. "Explain."

"I thought I lost something the last time we met. I went to check, and I saw Dillon and the girl out riding. I never go that far without a rifle. I don't know what came over me. I shot at Dillon and missed."

The man headed for the mini-bar and poured himself a tumbler of Kentucky's best. "What did he do?"

"I don't know. I left as quickly as possible. Because he was with the girl, I didn't think he'd come after me."

"Now your stupidity has alerted him, and he'll become cautious. What were your intentions, to kill both of them? How would that be explained?" He could tell by the expression on his visitor's face that the harshness in his tone had an effect. Good. If his plan was to work, he couldn't afford mistakes.

"It's hunting season. Perhaps it will be blamed on a hunter," his visitor stammered.

The man scoffed. "One dead body? Perhaps, but two?"

"I know, I'm sorry. I reacted without thinking."

"If we're to achieve our goal, any harm that comes to Dillon McCoy must seem like an accident." He sighed. He knew involving another person in his plan was risky, but he had no choice. Their knowledge and standing in the community were vital to his success.

The man smiled, and the tension left his visitor's face. "Plan your next move with caution. When Dillon is alone, strike."

After his visitor left, the man paced the floor. This new development could complicate everything. It might become necessary to adjust his plans. He wasn't about to allow stupidity to ruin all his hard work. No, if he had to eliminate the problem, so be it.

Chapter Sixteen

As darkness settled around them, the only illumination came from the glowing fire. Diana lay beneath the quilt drowsing in Dillon's arms. Her nose pressed against his chest, she breathed in the spicy scent of him. She was so incredibly happy. The guilt was just below the surface, but for this moment she'd enjoy the man who had awakened her desire and shown her true passion. She yawned, and her eyes drooped. The sound of an engine broke the silence, and Diana's eyes flew open. "Oh, my God, Dillon, get up."

Dillon's hand, which was resting on her backside, squeezed and murmured, "I like it right here."

She wiggled from his embrace. "Dillon, I hear someone coming."

He opened his eyes and cursed. "That's the ranch truck. I'd recognize the sound of it anywhere."

"Oh, my God, oh, my God," Diana exclaimed as she jumped from the bed, grabbed her clothes, and headed for the bathroom. "Hurry and get dressed and make the bed."

Diana first slipped her sweater on backwards, then couldn't get her jeans buttoned. She finally managed to dress and studied herself in the mirror, and she groaned. Her hair was a tangled mess. Her lips were red and swollen from Dillon's kisses, and her cheeks were bright pink. Whoever was in that truck would know exactly how she and Dillon spent the last few hours. She splashed cold water on her face and, finding a comb in the vanity, attempted to untangle her hair.

When Jenn and Sam's voices reached her from the other room, she tamped down her panic. She closed her eyes and took slow calming breaths. *Get a grip, Diana. Dillon and you are adults. What you did wasn't right, but it also wasn't a crime. It was a natural act between two people who are attracted to one another. It will be fine. Perhaps Jenn won't even notice you look as if you've been having screaming multiple orgasm sex for hours.* Diana laughed. *Yeah right.* Jenn didn't miss a thing. Diana took another deep breath and opened the bathroom door.

When she entered the main room, she glanced toward the bed and let out a sigh of relief. Thankfully Dillon had straightened the quilt. He stood dressed, leaning against the sink drinking a soda. Either she was in the bathroom longer than she thought, or he moved like lightning.

Jenn and Sam were near the fireplace listening as Dillon explained what had happened. When Jenn glanced at her, Diana knew there was no doubt in Jenn's mind what she and Dillon had been up to.

"Do you think it was a hunter?" Sam asked as Dillon finished.

Dillon shook his head. "If it was, he has really bad eyesight, or extremely poor aim."

"Are you saying you think they intentionally shot at you?" Jenn asked.

Dillon shrugged. "I don't know. I had no idea what was going on, so I didn't feel safe riding home with

Diana." He turned to Sam. "Will you help me get the horses to the barn?"

Sam nodded. "No problem."

"This is all getting too weird," Jenn said. "Dillon, I think you should tell the sheriff."

"I agree, but like I told Diana, I don't know what he can do."

"At least he'd be aware of what's going on," Sam added.

"Okay, I need to get Diana back. Everyone is worried to death," Jenn said. She paused and took in the room. "I haven't been in here in ages. I forgot how cozy it is."

"We made do," Dillon said.

Jenn rolled her eyes. "I'll bet you did. Come on, Diana. Let's go."

"I'm going to make sure the fire is banked and everything is off before we leave," Dillon said. "We'll be there shortly. Tell Gran not to wait dinner on us. Sam, there should be a rifle under the truck seat. Please go get it."

Diana climbed into the truck and braced herself for the questions she knew were coming. Jenn didn't disappoint her. She'd barely had the truck door closed when she turned to Diana. "Okay, spill it. What happened?"

"Exactly what Dillon told you. We heard a rifle shot."

Jenn waved her hand. "Don't play dumb, Diana. You know what I mean. What happened between you and Dillon? And don't tell me nothing, because sex is written all over both of you."

Diana let out a long sigh. "Okay, yes, we made

love."

Jenn snorted. "Made love."

Diana couldn't help but grin. "Okay, we had wild sex, and, yes, I screamed."

Jenn grinned back. "Good for you. With the chemistry sizzling between you two, it was bound to happen."

Diana ran her finger over her engagement ring, then slipped it from her finger and placed it in her pocket. "Jenn, I know what we did was wrong, but it was the most fantastic experience of my life. I don't know what will happen between Dillon and me, but if it doesn't work out, I'll always have this afternoon to remember."

"I saw the way he looked at you as we were leaving the cabin, and Suzanna's right. I've never seen such caring in his eyes. Have you decided what you're going to tell Trent?"

"That I love him, but not enough to spend the rest of my life with him. I'd only end up hurting both of us."

"Are you going to tell him about Dillon?"

Diana shook her head. "He'll be hurt enough. That would be like rubbing salt into the wound."

"What about your parents?"

"My mother will probably disown me, or she'll tell me I need to see a psychiatrist."

Jenn let out a long breath. "Hopefully it won't be that bad. I would think your happiness comes first."

"My mother's idea of happiness is a well-organized life where everyone does as expected. Breaking an engagement to a man who has his life planned out and has a stable job with a six-digit salary amounts to insanity." *Not to mention running off with a cowboy whose life is as messed up as mine.*

They were in front of the ranch house, and Jenn turned off the truck. "We'll tell everyone about the shooter and that you held up in the cabin playing cards."

"Will they believe us?"

"I doubt it, but we'll stick to that story anyway. Besides, you're a guest. They can't be rude."

****

Dillon swung his leg over Flame and headed down the path, the rifle held securely across his lap, with Sam and Flora right behind. Images of the last few hours spent with Diana wouldn't leave his thoughts. Christ, what was the woman doing to him? He'd spent many an hour in bed with women, but none had satisfied him or made him half-crazed with lust. He should have kept his hands off her, but damn it to hell, she wanted him as much as he wanted her. They both knew she wasn't going to marry that other guy. He felt sorry for him, but better he found out now than after the marriage. He wondered how much Diana would tell him. All he needed was some jilted fiancé coming after him. He sighed. Diana would never involve him. She'd place the blame on herself. What if the guy got royally pissed? What if he took his anger out on Diana? What if he hurt her? Dillon's hands balled into fists. If he touched her, he'd have to break a few of his bones. What a fucked-up mess. As for him, he had Tonya to deal with. If she knew he was involved with another woman, she'd do everything she could to make his life miserable.

The path widened and Sam rode up next to Dillon. "Do you really think someone took a shot at you?"

Dillon, thankful for Sam getting his mind off Diana

and Tonya, nodded. "I didn't want to say anything in front of Diana and Jenn, but the bullet went right over my head."

"Son-of-a-bitch," Sam swore. "In that case, you need to call the sheriff."

"The problem is the new snow has filled in any tracks, and I can't be positive he was aiming at me. I thought I'd ride up here tomorrow and see if I can find anything."

"Do you want me to come with you?"

"Sure. Two sets of eyes are better than one."

"Do you think he'll be back?"

"Who knows. If he did shoot at me, I sure as hell would like to know why."

"Could this have something to do with selling the ranch?"

Dillon brought Flame to a halt and stared at Sam. "Christ. With all the other strange happenings, I totally forgot about the ranch. But who would want the land enough to kill for it?" Dillon paused. "Martin?"

Sam nodded. "I saw him last night at the Stag's Head. He was sitting in a corner and was pretty drunk. The scowl on his face when I passed said it all. I assume he's still pissed at us for convincing him to stay away from Jenn, but what if it's something more?"

"I saw him too. He wasn't giving me a warm friendly smile either." Dillon shook his head. "I can't see Martin having the balls to shoot at me. Skulk around in the dark, yes. Perhaps we should pay him a visit."

Sam grinned. "Cousin, I'm right with you."

Chapter Seventeen

When Dillon and Sam arrived at the house, Ada was setting out leftovers. They all filled their plates and took seats around the table.

"Dillon, do you think it's worth calling Sheriff Dunn?" Chet asked.

"I suppose we can report the shooting," Dillon replied. "As for the sheriff coming out, I don't think it will do any good. If there were tracks, chances are the snow will have covered them. Just in case, though, Sam and I thought we'd ride out in the morning and see if we find signs of someone being out there."

"Will that be safe?" Martha asked.

Will gave his wife a reassuring pat on the hand. "Whoever it was isn't going to hang around."

"You don't know that," Augusta stated. "I think this should be left to the sheriff to deal with."

Chet nodded. "I agree with Will. Whoever it was is long gone. But I think we should still report the incident."

"I have to believe it was a hunter who wandered onto our land," Ada said.

"We have No Hunting signs posted all over the property," Chet said. "And, unless the Duffys have changed their policy, they do too. Dillon, have you heard different?"

Dillon shook his head. "We can also ride over there tomorrow and find out."

"If not a hunter, then who?" Ada asked. "Other than the main road leading up from town, this property doesn't exactly have easy access."

"They could come by way of the ski area," Sam suggested.

Chet knitted his brows. "In the summer, yes. It would be quite the trek in all this snow."

"Not if they were wearing cross-country skis," Suzanna added.

"My god," Sally exclaimed. "Suzanna, you've got it."

"A hunter on skis?" Augusta said with astonishment. "You can't be serious."

"Are you sure it was a gunshot?" Will asked. "Or if it even came from our property? You know as well as I that sound travels in these mountains. Perhaps it was nothing but a car backfiring."

Dillon hesitated. Should he say that the bullet just missed his head? No. There wasn't any reason to get everyone more riled up than they already were. He'd play it low key until he had more information. "Uncle Will, you might be right. We can't ignore any possibilities."

"Dillon, I think it's time to tell everyone about Red Oak and the rest," Jenn said.

Dillon gave Jenn a thanks-a-lot look, let out a long breath, and explained. "So, you see, someone's been trespassing for who knows how long."

Chet's face turned thunderous. "The hell you say. Well, I'll put a stop to this right now. I'll hire men to ride the perimeter of the ranch. I'll be damned if I'll allow someone to break into my cabins, shoot a rifle on my property, or damage my fence."

"Chet, calm down," Ada said. "Think of your blood pressure."

"Gramps, Gran is right," Dillon said. "Don't get yourself all worked up. I'll explain everything to Sherriff Dunn."

"That's right, Daddy," Augusta interjected. "Let Dillon handle this."

Hoping to decrease the tension, Dillon said, "Actually as far as Red Oak, I think it's two people meeting up there."

"What?" his grandmother and both aunts said at the same time.

"Who the hell would that be?" Chet asked.

Dillon shrugged. "Someone who knows the cabin is empty in the winter, which could be anyone in the area."

"They'd have to be able to get to it," Aunt Martha suggested.

"When there's no snow, it's not a problem," Chet said. "Dillon, do you honestly think you'd be safe staying here? Your grandmother and I don't want to worry about you while we're gone."

"I'm sure they're not dangerous. Besides, we locked the doors. It won't be easy for them to get back in."

"Will you be able to repair the fence?" Chet asked.

"I did. Although it's temporary. I'll take care of it soon." He rose. "I don't know about y'all, but I'm ready to do something fun."

****

Diana, not wanting to intrude on this family

conversation, sat quietly and listened. She'd paid special attention to the expressions that crossed Dillon's face. Then there was the glance that passed between Dillon and Sam. Surely they shared something they weren't telling the others. Perhaps she could persuade him to confide in her. When Dillon suggested they find something to do, she rose and followed the group from the room.

"You know what sounds good to me," Jenn said. "A movie."

"Yes," Sally agreed. "I love going to the show here. Diana, the theater was built in the twenties right after talkies started, and it hasn't really changed."

Suzanna nodded. "They usually show classics. Let's see what's playing."

Jenn brought up the website. "Perfect," she exclaimed. "White Christmas."

Dillon and Sam groaned.

"Oh, come on," Suzanna said. "It will be fun."

"What do you think?" Dillon asked Diana.

"I'd like to go."

"Okay. I'll see if Gramps will let us use the ranch van again."

"I'm going to call Carly Jane and ask her if she'd like to join us," Sam said.

Diana headed for the stairs. "I'm going to take a quick shower."

An hour later, Jenn, Sally, Suzanna, Diana, and Dillon were on their way down the mountain in Dillon's extended-cab truck.

"I'm glad Sam is picking up Carly Jane, and we didn't have to use the van," Jenn said. "In the snow, the truck has more traction with those sand bags in the back."

"My thought exactly," Dillon said, stopping in front of the theater. "I'll drop you girls off and go park."

The Spirit Theater lit up Main Street, a pile of cream-colored blocks rising to a pink pillar of neon, a marquee of glowing orange with yellow lights declaring "White Christmas" above the ticket booth.

"Oh, my, it's wonderful," Diana said, staring up at the theater's facade. She'd attended a number of Broadway theaters with her parents, but none could compare to the charm of the Spirit.

"Dillon gave me money for all our tickets," Jenn said.

Pure delight filled Diana's face as they entered the gray and white tiled lobby. To her right stood a popcorn machine and candy display case. To her left, a coat check counter. Posters of actors and actresses from the twenties, thirties, and forties lined the walls. The women employees wore dropped hip dresses and Mary Jane shoes, while the men had white shirts with bow ties.

Dillon, Sam, and Carly Jane came through the double glass doors. Sam introduced Carly Jane to Diana while Dillon purchased popcorn and sodas for them all.

"If we want to sit together, we'd better find seats now," Jenn said.

They made their way down the aisle past dimly lit wall sconces which illuminated rows of plush burgundy chairs. Diana sat between Dillon and Jenn, a smile of contentment on her face. She munched popcorn as the opening credits filled the screen.

"Having fun?" Dillon whispered as he placed his

arm across her shoulders.

Diana nodded and leaned toward him. "I haven't seen this movie in years," she whispered back.

Afterward, they all decided to stop for ice-cream. Diana, full from the popcorn, shared a coffee mocha cone with Dillon. As they took turns licking the creamy chocolate, Diana became more aroused by the minute. *Thank goodness we're in a public place surrounded by others, or I'd be jumping his bones.* When he leaned forward and handed her the cone, the heat in his eyes told her he'd been thinking the same.

Good grief, what was the matter with her? She was acting like some sex-starved maniac.

Dillon leaned even closer and in a low tone said, "Stay with me tonight."

Every cell in her body was screaming yes, but she shook her head. "It wouldn't be right," she murmured.

Dillon glanced to where Sam and Carly Jane sat in deep conversation. "I doubt Sam is coming home, so we'd be alone."

"Your family would know."

"Not if you snuck out the upstairs porch."

Diana's eyes opened wide with incredulity. She'd never snuck out to do anything in her life. She shook her head. "I couldn't do that."

"Then I'll come to you."

Diana was practically speechless. The thought of making love with Dillon while the rest of the family slept was inconceivable. What if they were discovered? Her humiliation would be unbearable. "Dillon, don't even think about it," she hissed.

"Are you two ready to go," Jenn asked with a yawn.

Diana jumped to her feet. "Yes."

Chapter Eighteen

Sunday morning, Ada made blueberry pancakes, sausage patties, and eggs. "I like everyone to leave on a full stomach," she said as they took their places around the table.

Diana poured syrup on her pancake and thought, *If I keep eating like this, I won't fit in my clothes.* As she gazed at all the friendly faces, sadness overtook her. She would miss this warm, welcoming family. She was again seated next to Dillon. The night before, she'd tossed and turned with dreams of Dillon making love to her. She would miss him madly.

Would she ever see him again? Until his divorce, Dillon was still a part of Tonya's life. Besides, she didn't know if he even wanted a relationship with her. The possibility of never seeing him again turned her stomach into knots. Thankfully she'd finished eating, for she no longer had an appetite.

"Suzanna and I will be leaving right after breakfast," Augusta said, breaking into Diana's thoughts.

"Martha, Sally, and I are as well," Will added.

Jenn turned to Diana. "I promised Gran I'd help her organize her clothes for their cruise, so we'll leave a little later if that's okay?"

Before Diana could reply, Dillon spoke. "Diana, if

you'd like to go for one more ride, we'd have time to do so."

This might be her last chance to be with him for quite a while, or ever. Diana knew what she should do, but instead she did what she wanted to do. "Sure, that would be great."

"Considering what happened yesterday, do you think it's safe?" Ada asked.

"We won't go far," Dillon replied.

After saying goodbye to those who were leaving, Diana and Dillon headed to the barn.

"Sam wasn't at breakfast," Diana said

Dillon hesitated. "He came in late last night mad as hell. I think he and Carly Jane had a fight. He told me this morning he wasn't up to family questions, so he stayed in the cabin. I didn't ask, and he didn't offer to tell me what happened."

"Oh, that's too bad. They seemed to get along so well."

Entering the barn, Diana inhaled deeply. She found she enjoyed the smell of oiled leather, horses, and fresh hay. She hurried to Flora's stall and stroked her nose as she whinnied in greeting.

Diana grinned. "I think she likes me."

Dillon's voice was low. "So do I." He cupped the back of her head and tilted her face upward.

He was going to kiss her, and she had no willpower to stop him. When his lips touched hers, she wrapped her arms around his neck and opened her mouth to him.

His tongue gently slid in and out of her mouth while he pressed himself against her, moving his hips in rhythm with his tongue.

She mimicked his every move, rubbing herself

against his erection.

Without breaking their kiss, Dillon guided her to the ladder leading to the hay loft. "Climb up." He murmured.

Diana, in a lust-filled haze, blinked. "What?"

"The ladder, climb up." Dillon gently turned her, placed his hands on her bottom, gave her a boost, and helped her up.

Diana found herself lying in a mound of hay with Dillon on top of her. "This is crazy. What if someone finds us?"

He unzipped her coat and ran his hand under her sweater. "The horses are the only ones who will know what we're up to." He unhooked her bra and exposed her breast, and his tongue ran across her nipple.

Diana wiggled beneath him. What was it about him that caused her to ignore all her proper upbringing? "Dillon."

"I know, darlin'." He removed her boots, unzipped her jeans, and slipped them down over her hips. His hand slid between her legs, and his fingers found her slick bud. "You're always so wet and ready for me. That's it, Baby, come for me."

After her climax subsided and her thought process somewhat returned, Diana tugged at the snaps of his shirt. "I want you."

"Darlin', nothing is going to stop me from being inside you." Within seconds, he'd removed their clothes and his hot mouth was kissing down her body. When he reached her soft mound, Diana opened for him. Dillon was the only man who ever touched her so intimately, and the sensation of his mouth on her drove her mad. "Dillon, I..." When his tongue touched her heat, Diana didn't care if every resident in the county came through the barn door. Anything else she was about to say died on her lips. She dug her fingers into the hay and arched her back to give him better access. "Oh, sweet heaven, don't stop."

****

Dillon couldn't get enough of the taste of her. He placed his hands under her bottom and raised her to him. He made love to her with his mouth until she screamed with her release.

He was so hard, he didn't know if he'd last long enough to slide inside her. He rose above her and plunged himself in deep. His voice was low and husky. He demanded, "Diana, move with me." As his thrusts became faster, she tightened around him. "Come with me, Diana," he growled. When her orgasm began, he thrust into her one last time and followed her over the edge.

With her in his arms, Dillon rolled onto his back. "Darlin', you're going to kill me."

Diana, slightly out of breath, gazed into his eyes and smiled. "Ditto."

Dillon chuckled and brushed back her hair. "You look as if you've had a roll in the hay."

Diana frowned. "And whose fault is that?"

His hand drifted down her back to stroke her bottom. "Are you saying you didn't enjoy what I was doing?"

She pursed her lips in thought. "I suppose it was pleasant enough."

"Is that right?" He nuzzled her neck. "I guess I'll have to try and do better."

"Dillon, stop."

"Hmm. If my memory is correct, a few minutes ago you were hollering for me not to."

Diana's face turned bright red, and she stammered. "I did not holler."

Dillon's eyes lit with amusement. "Darlin', you probably scared the horses."

"Oh, for heaven's sake, let me up. We need to get dressed. Jenn is going to wonder what's happened to me."

At that moment, the sound of cars coming down the gravel drive reached them. Dillon placed his finger on her lips. "If they stop, lay still."

The sounds receded, and soon there was silence. Dillon let out a long breath. "They're gone." He ran his finger along her lower lip and whispered. "I wouldn't mind if Jenn left without you."

A lump formed in Diana's throat, and tears threatened to fall. She whispered back, "I wouldn't either."

"Diana, I don't know what this is between us, but I do know I want you in my life. I only wish things weren't so damn complicated."

"So do I."

He rolled her onto her back and gave her a long kiss. "We'll work it out. But for now…" He slid his erection into her. "We'll do this."

A while later, Diana reluctantly reached for her clothes. "We need to go. What am I supposed to say when Jenn asks where we rode the horses?"

He gave her a wicked grin. "Darlin', you can say you didn't have to leave the barn.

She gave him a playful slap. "Stop that." She quickly dressed and climbed down the ladder.

Dillon, chuckling, followed.

Diana scowled. "What are you grinning at?"

He plucked a piece of hay from her hair. "You need to let me clean you up."

She studied him more closely. Hay clung to him. She shook her head. "Dillon, we might as well put signs around our necks declaring we've been messing around in the barn."

"Oh, it's not that bad. Turn around, and I'll brush you off."

She then did the same to him.

"Am I presentable?" she asked.

He lightly kissed her lips. "Perfect." Amusement left his eyes. "Diana, I know you need to take care of business with Trent, and I've got to deal with Tonya, but I want to see you again. When you feel the time is right, call me. I'll be here."

****

Joy filled Diana's heart. He wanted to see her again. Could she hope his feelings for her were more than sexual attraction? Could they possibly have a future together? She hesitated. "I'll call. Perhaps I can come back sooner than I thought."

He held her in his arms. "I don't know what the future will bring, but for now taking care of the ranch is my responsibility. Do you understand what I'm saying?"

Diana nodded. "Your life is here. Mine is in Chapel Hill, but Trent's parents are well known in the community. Staying there might be impossible for me."

Dillon cocked his head. "Teachers are needed everywhere."

Visions of a small classroom in the country filled

her mind. Getting hired at a prestigious school was her mother's goal, not hers. As long as she was teaching, she'd be happy. *Reality check, Diana. You have a lot to deal with before you can consider a drastic lifestyle change.* She hugged him and stepped away. "I know we have to take this slow, but I'm going to miss you."

"I'm only four hours away." He zipped her fur jacket. "I liked you in your new clothes."

She swallowed the lump in her throat. "I did too."

He took her hand and led her from the barn.

When they passed the trail they'd taken the day before, Diana turned to Dillon. "What are you going to do about the gunshot?"

Dillon glanced at the bright sun in the clear sky. "Some of the snow will melt. I'm going to ride around and see if I can find any sign of someone being there."

"Please be careful. Are you taking Sam with you?"

Dillon shrugged. "I don't know." He put his arm around her shoulders. "Don't worry. I'll be fine."

****

An hour later, Dillon stood on the porch as Jenn's Jeep disappeared down the drive. If someone had told him he'd be attracted to a wealthy city girl whose background couldn't be more different from his, he'd have laughed. Could that be it? She was fresh and new. She didn't care how many gold buckles he'd won or for the excitement of the rodeo circuit. He pictured her shapely little body coming to life beneath him, and his body reacted. Christ, if he didn't stop thinking about her, he'd have a permanent hard on.

"I'm beginning to think women are put on earth to drive men crazy," Sam said, coming up beside Dillon.

Lost in thought, Dillon jumped.

Sam grinned. "Sorry, didn't mean to startle you. By your expression, I thought Diana might be on your mind."

Dillon nodded but didn't respond.

"Do you still want to ride up the trail and see what we can find?"

"Yeah, but you don't have to stay. Gran and Gramps will be here, and I'll take my phone with me."

"Are you sure? I don't mind staying."

Dillon shook his head. "I'll be cautious. So, tell me, what's up with you and Carly Jane?"

Sam scowled. "Not a good subject."

Dillon patted his shoulder. "Cousin, I hear you. I'm going to ride out. I'll see you at Christmas."

Sam nodded. "Let me know if you discover anything."

"Will do," Dillon called as he headed for the barn.

****

Diana stared out the window as Jenn drove down I-40 toward Chapel Hill. Her emotions fluctuated between already missing Dillon and rehearsing how she'd explain her reasons for canceling the wedding to Trent and her parents.

"Hey, you okay?" Jenn asked.

Diana sighed. "I'm mentally rehearsing what I'll say to Trent. He'll be hurt and angry, and I can't blame him."

"Are you sure what you're doing is right?"

"Oh, yes."

"Then all you can do is tell him how you feel. And don't lay a guilt trip on yourself."

With the traces of love-making still on her body, Diana couldn't ignore her guilt. "That's easier said than done."

"This really isn't any of my business, but since you're my best friend, I'll ask. Did Dillon talk to you about a future together?"

"Kind of. We did discuss the fact we both have other people in our lives we have to deal with."

"Well, Tonya is about out of his, and hopefully Trent will go without causing you trouble."

Diana snorted. "Are you forgetting my mother? I can't begin to imagine what she'll say."

"Just make sure she says it from four hundred miles away."

"No kidding. Actually, I plan on postponing that conversation for as long as possible." Diana was quiet for a while before saying, "You know what will surprise you? I really enjoyed the ranch. I loved the seclusion, the scenery, the horses, and the fact no one cared how I was dressed or how I acted."

Jenn arched her brows. "This coming from a city girl who always looks like she stepped from a fashion catalog and could sound as if she was giving a lecture at Harvard. Yeah, I'm surprised. But I have to ask, did your attraction come from those things you mentioned, or was it Dillon who made them attractive?"

Diana paused before replying. Jenn had a good point. Was it her feelings toward Dillon or the fact the lifestyle was so out of her norm? No, she could see herself living in Pine Bluff and teaching at a local school. Amazed at this admission, Diana grinned. "Honestly, I could give up my old life in a minute for a cabin in the woods."

Jenn gaped. "Holy crap, you're serious. What about your teaching career?"

"As Dillon said, teachers are needed everywhere."

Jenn let out a long breath. "Make sure this is truly what you want, and not lust talking."

"Oh, lust is talking all right, but it's not the only voice I hear."

Chapter Nineteen

Dillon scanned the trail as he rode Flame up to the ridge. He found plenty of animal tracks in the snow, but no human footprints. As long as he was this far, he'd go check Red Oak. He rounded a bend in the trail, and the cabin came into view. Dillon halted Flame when he spotted a horse and rider near the top of the ridge.

He realized it was Kevin Duffy and frowned. What the hell was he doing way up here? Could he be the one using the cabin? He'd certainly acted strangely the other night in the Stag's Head. Dillon coaxed Flame forward, then stopped. Had Kevin taken a shot at him? He had his own property. Why would he want the Lazy M? Dillon led Flame from the trees and called, "Hey, Kevin."

"I'll bet you weren't expecting to see me," Kevin said when Dillon rode up next to him.

Dillon shrugged. "The property line is nearby. Besides, we've been neighbors for years."

Kevin nodded. "I was out riding and, without paying attention to where I was going, ended up here."

Dillon hesitated before he said, "Kevin, I need to ask you something, and I'd appreciate a straight answer. Have you been using this cabin to meet someone?"

Surprise, then unease showed in Kevin's eyes. "No, why are you asking?"

"Sam and I discovered the door unlocked and evidence someone had been inside."

"And what makes you think it was me?"

"I'm not accusing you, but whoever it was knew the location of the cabin." The expression on Kevin's face tightened.

"Dillon, if you're insinuating I'm fooling around on Bonnie, you're way off base. I happen to love my wife."

"I'm not insinuating anything. The way I see it, they knew where to go, and they had to have come across your property or ours."

Kevin shook his head. "Not necessarily. They could cross over from the ski area or come up one of the trails from below."

"Perhaps, but that's quite a ways. If they drove, where did they park? Do you have anyone camping or staying in your cabins?"

"Not camping, but two cabins are occupied. When was the last time Red Oak was rented?"

"The end of October."

"And no one has been up here since?"

Dillon shook his head.

"Sounds like hikers found the cabin unlocked and decided to make themselves at home."

Dillon studied Kevin as he spoke. He had the feeling Kevin knew more than he was saying. Could he be lying about an affair? This was certainly a secluded spot. "I made sure the cabin is locked, and I plan on keeping an eye on things." Dillon paused. "There's something else. Have you had any hunters on your property?"

"No, why?"

Dillon told him about the gunshot. "The damn bullet came close to killing me."

The color drained from Kevin's face. Seconds passed before he whispered, "Good God." He let out a long breath. "I can ask if anyone staying with us has a gun, but I can't imagine it being one of them. Both cabins are rented by a large family for Thanksgiving."

"I'd appreciate that," Dillon said.

"Did you contact the sheriff?"

"Not yet."

"Will you?"

"I don't know if it would be worthwhile. I've searched the area and haven't found anything to identify the person."

"Who in the hell would take a shot at you?"

Dillon shrugged. "I have no idea."

"Maybe kids wandered up here, and you being there was a coincidence."

Kevin had a point. In the past, during hunting season, Dillon had come upon teenage boys with rifles who claimed they didn't realize where they were. "That's a possibility. Has Martin Patrick talked to you about selling your property?"

Kevin looked surprised at the question. "Not Martin specifically. We're always getting letters from realtors wanting to know if we're interested in selling. Why?"

"He told my grandparents he has a buyer for the ranch but won't say who. I told him the Lazy M wasn't for sale."

"He always was an ass. Anyone who knows Chet and Ada knows how much the ranch means to them."

"Yeah, well, he wasn't pleased when I told him I'm

taking over."

"You're staying? What about your rodeo riding?"

"I'm putting it on hold. My grandparents want to travel, and I don't want anyone else running the ranch."

Kevin nodded. "I understand." He eased his horse around. "I'd better be getting back. Take care."

"We'll have to get together for a beer," Dillon called.

"Yeah, sure, sounds good."

Kevin rode away and Dillon frowned. Something was definitely wrong. He knew Kevin pretty well. As teenagers, they were nearly inseparable. They'd spent many nights camping on Kevin's property, drinking his dad's beer, and fantasizing about dating girls at school. They boasted to one another about the first time they got laid and laughed over the ass-chewing Dillon got when he'd been caught with Brenda James in the barn.

He stared at the tracks Kevin's horse had left in the snow. Could Bonnie have told him about their past relationship? God, he hoped not. It took place after high school, and Kevin had already left for college. It was a summer fling and meant nothing. Could that be why he was acting so odd? Whatever was wrong with the laid-back guy he'd known, Kevin was stressed and, if Dillon was reading him right, hiding something.

Dillon took the key for the cabin from his pocket and unlocked the door. He wanted to do a thorough search for any clue to the intruder. He straightened the cushions on the couch, checking under each. He looked under chairs and tables. Nothing. In the kitchen he wiped off the counters and took out the trash. Would hikers carry beer and wine? He shook his head. Probably not.

Upstairs, he gathered the dirty towels and glanced at the shower, vanity, and sink. All clean. Whoever it was, they were neat. In the bedroom, the comforter was mussed, and the blinds closed. He pulled the comforter back to remove the sheets. Under one of the pillows lay a gold hoop earring. He opened the window blinds for more light. The thin gold hoop had a tiny blue stone. Dillon frowned. Something about it seemed familiar. But who? He shook his head. One of his girl cousins must have worn one similar. Downstairs in the kitchen, he found a sandwich bag and placed the earring inside. He gathered the sheets and towels and tossed them in the washer, checked the refrigerator, found a beer, and sat down to think.

There was a chance the intruder and the shooter weren't connected. Hikers very well could have come upon the cabin and taken advantage of the unlocked door. But how many hikers carry beer and wine? Dillon shook his head. Not many. And would they take the time to use the shower? Although, they might have spent the night. All the residents of Pine Bluff knew where the Lazy M cabins were located. One time or another, most had stayed in one. No, it was either a couple of young people who thought they'd party here, or adults known to his family who used the cabin as a rendezvous.

So, who cut the hole in the fence and shot at him and why? And how did they know he'd be on the trail yesterday? Coincidence? It must be. Though anyone who knew him would know he often rode the property. Dillon sighed and finished his beer. *I'm probably worrying about nothing more than boys out hunting and by mistake almost shooting me.* He rose and placed the clean sheets and towels in the dryer. It was all speculation. He'd make sure the cabin was securely locked and hope that whoever was using it wouldn't be back. He could only hope the same went for the shooter.

Dillon remade the bed and took one last check of the doors. As he rode through the quiet landscape toward the barn, thoughts of Diana filled his mind. She and Jenn should be back in Chapel Hill by now. Once Diana was in her own environment, would she realize a cowboy and country life really weren't for her? She seemed to enjoy herself and took to ranch life readily. Diana wasn't the type of person to pretend she felt something she didn't.

In the barn, as he bedded down Flame, he couldn't help but grin. *I'll bet Diana never imagined herself making love in a mound of hay.* He loved watching her let loose and stop acting as she was supposed to, but more like she wanted to. He missed her already. Perhaps after dinner he'd give her a call.

****

Diana was unpacking when her cell rang. A queasy sensation formed in her stomach when she read the caller was Trent. She hadn't known what the cell service would be like at the ranch, so she'd told him she'd talk to him when she got back. She steeled herself, took a calming breath, and answered. "Hello."

"Diana, hello. I wasn't sure what time you'd get home. Did you have fun?"

Diana swallowed hard before she spoke. "Yes, Jenn's family were very nice and the scenery beautiful. How about you? How's the skiing?"

"Fantastic. The weather has been perfect."

"Are your parents enjoying themselves?"

He hesitated. "Oh, that's right. You'd already left when they had to cancel. Something with dad's work. Mom thought since the villa was already rented, I should still come."

"You're there by yourself?"

"That's right. If I would have known earlier, I would have insisted you come to keep me company."

Diana's hand tightened on the phone. Guilt washed over her. "I can't imagine you haven't met some people to hang around with."

"Actually, I did. It's not the same as having you here, but I'm enjoying myself."

"I'm glad to hear that." Diana frowned. It sounded like someone laughing in the background. "Trent, is someone there?"

"It's the people I met. I'm about to join them for lunch."

"Lunch? Oh, I forgot about the time change. Listen, I won't keep you. When will you be home?"

"My flight gets in Friday afternoon. I thought we could go to dinner."

"Sure, that would be nice."

"Diana, are you all right? You sound a little strange."

No, I'm not all right, she wanted to scream. *I've spent the weekend having incredible sex with another man, who I'm afraid I've fallen in love with.*

"Diana?"

Her heart pounded so hard she was sure Trent could hear it. She willed herself to speak normally. "Sorry, I'm here. I'm just tired."

Trent laughed. "I can imagine Jenn kept you pretty

busy. Hun, I'll let you get some rest. I'll see you in a few days. I love you."

Diana opened her mouth to reply, but he'd already hung up. She sank down on her bed. If Trent could tell something was wrong just by talking to her on the phone, how would she ever hide her feelings until she had a chance to explain? If she kept thinking about this, she'd drive herself mad. Needing a distraction, she resumed her unpacking. When she lifted her new western clothes from the suitcase, tears filled her eyes. She hugged the shirt she'd worn to the Stag's Head and smelled Dillon's spicy cologne. So much for a distraction.

****

Trent placed his phone on the counter and joined Belinda in the hot tub. They'd spent the last few days discovering more creative ways to excite each other. He was pleased to find a woman who didn't mind a little rough sex. So far, he'd been gentle with Diana, but he'd soon teach her to give him what he wanted. At first, he was sure she'd be shocked, but she would be his wife and expected to do as he said. If she fought him too much, there were more women like Belinda out there.

Chapter Twenty

Monday morning over breakfast, Chet and Ada informed Dillon they had decided to leave early on their trip. Their ship left from near Cape Canaveral, so they were flying out Wednesday to Orlando to sightsee before the cruise.

"We thought since you were here, there wasn't any reason not to go," Ada said.

"And they're predicting bad weather," Chet added. "I wouldn't want to get snowed in."

"I'm concerned about leaving you here alone," his grandmother said. "I was hoping Sam could stay for a while."

"I'll be fine. I'm half convinced the gunshot came from teenage boys who wandered onto the property."

Chet frowned. "You might be right. I've caught boys up here with rifles."

"No matter who it was, Chet," Ada said, "you need to post more No Hunting signs." She rose and refilled their coffee cups. "Dillon, are you sure you won't be lonesome here by yourself? We could call one of the boys who help us during the season and see if he can come out."

"Gran, you don't need to call anyone. There's plenty around here to keep me busy. Just focus on your trip."

Ada's eyes shone with excitement. "I always wanted to visit Florida's entertainment parks."

"Now that everyone is gone," Chet said to Dillon, "I'd like you to sign those papers Sunny Carstairs faxed over."

Dillon nodded.

"While you boys are busy, I'll run into town for a few things," Ada said. "I'll be back after lunch. There are plenty of leftovers for you to eat."

****

A couple hours later, Ada, her packages stowed in the car, hurried into the Sunnyside Café. Seated at a table were three women Ada knew well.

"Ada, hello, please join us," Janis Dalton said.

Always ready for a good gossip, Ada did so and ordered a cup of coffee and a club sandwich.

"How was your Thanksgiving?" Sue Nielsen asked.

"Just fine. Had some of the kids and grandkids in. How about y'all?"

They caught up on family news, then Bonnie Duffy asked, "What brings you to town?"

"I needed to do some last-minute shopping. Chet and I are flying to Orlando on Wednesday for a few days, then we're leaving on a cruise."

"That sounds wonderful," Sue replied.

"Kevin mentioned Dillon might be staying on for a while," Bonnie said.

Ada smiled. "Not only is he staying on, he's thinking about taking over the ranch for us."

Bonnie's brows rose. "Really? And give up the rodeo circuit?"

"I sure hope so," Ada replied. "Not only would he

be a huge help to Chet and me, he's made it this far without getting seriously hurt. I don't want him to push his luck."

Janis frowned. "Will his wife be joining him?"

Ada's mouth formed a thin line. "Thankfully, no. He finally saw Tonya for what she was, and they're getting a divorce. I try and stay out of my children and grandchildren's business, but I couldn't keep quiet about her."

Sue smiled. "That bad?"

Ada sniffed. "As far as I'm concerned, she was a lazy little gold digger, who cheated on him."

"My goodness, I can't imagine anyone cheating on Dillon," Bonnie said.

"So, while you're gone, Dillon will be at the ranch by himself?" Janis asked.

"That's right," Ada replied. "And after what happened, I'm worried about him."

"What happened?" Sue asked.

Ada leaned forward and told them about the mystery shooter. "Chet and Dillon think it must have been boys with a rifle who didn't see Dillon," she concluded.

"Oh, my God, that's awful," Janis replied.

"Did Dillon contact the sheriff?" Bonnie asked.

Ada shook her head. "Dillon rode up there to see if he could find any tracks, and there weren't any. He thought by then it would be a waste of time telling Sheriff Dunn."

"I'll make sure Kevin knows about this and that Dillon will be alone. He can ride over a couple of times and keep him company," Bonnie said.

Ada nodded. "Thank you. I appreciate it." They

talked for a little while longer, then Ada rose. "I'd better be getting back. If I don't see you girls, have a wonderful Christmas."

"Same to you," they said as one.

By Wednesday morning, the ranch house was in turmoil. Ada made list after list of last-minute reminders, and Chet insisted he and Dillon go over ranch purchases one last time. When he finally dropped them off at the airport, Dillon was exhausted. He decided to stop at the Stag's Head for dinner and a beer before going home.

The middle of the week normally wasn't busy, so he slid into a booth near the bar. The waitress, a pretty dark-haired girl who introduced herself as Mandy, reminded Dillon of Diana. He ordered a burger and a beer and leaned back. He took one sip from his beer and his phone rang. He let out an aggravated sigh when he read the caller was Tonya.

"Tonya, what is it?" he abruptly asked.

"Well, hello to you too," she snapped.

Dillon gritted his teeth. "I'm about to eat dinner. What do you want?"

Her voice took on a whining tone. "You know you don't have to be so mean. I wanted to let you know I heard from my lawyer. He said the divorce papers are ready for me to sign."

"Well, that should make you happy."

She was quiet before she said, "You may think that, but it's not true. Dillon, I'm not sure I'm going to sign. I can't help but wonder if we gave our marriage enough of a chance."

Was she serious? Dillon's temper rose. "It's kind of hard to give a marriage a chance when the bride's fucking someone else."

"I told you I was sorry." Her voice broke. "Dillon, I'd like to try again."

"Tonya, I don't know what brought this on, but forget it. Go find yourself another poor sucker who will fall for your lies."

"You're a real bastard. You know that?" Her whine had turned to a snarl. "You're not so innocent. Are you going to tell me you don't have a girlfriend?"

"My life is no longer any of your business. So, sign the damn papers."

"What if I decide I don't want the divorce? I'm still your wife, and you have to support me."

Dillon clenched his teeth so hard he thought his jaw might crack. "Tonya, staying married to me will do you no good. You won't get a dime out of me."

"We'll see about that."

She disconnected, and it took everything Dillon had not to throw his phone across the room. Instead, he placed it on the table and ordered another beer. Why hadn't he seen how vindictive and manipulating Tonya could be? *Because you fell for a pretty face and a sexy body, and she played you like a fiddle.* What would he do if Tonya didn't sign the divorce papers? A drawn-out battle was the last thing he wanted. A sudden thought made his stomach clench. If Tonya found out about him buying the ranch, and what it was worth, she'd fight for every cent she could get.

After speaking with his grandfather's lawyer and going over his finances, he and his grandparents came to a purchasing agreement. Somehow he had to convince Tonya it would be in her best interest to move on with her life.

He sipped his beer and turned his thoughts to something more pleasant—Diana. With her, there wasn't any hidden agenda. You saw the real person. Sure, with her upbringing she could come across a little serious and reserved. But when she let her defenses down, she rocked him to his core. He'd called her every night since she left. He planned on trying his damnedest to talk her into coming back up after she spoke to Trent.

He finished his burger and was leaving when he spotted Kevin and Bonnie in another booth. He thought about stopping, but judging by their facial expressions, they were in the middle of an argument. Dillon shrugged and headed out the door.

Chapter Twenty-One

Diana, back from Christmas shopping, placed her packages on the table, and flopped down on her couch. She slipped off her shoes and sorted through her mail. There were three more wedding confirmations. She let out a long sigh. It would take an entire day to notify every one of the cancelation. The thought of that daunting task had her up and heading for the kitchen.

She poured herself a glass of wine and turned the radio to a jazz station. Not yet having the nerve to tell her mother the wedding was off, she'd avoided her calls. Thank goodness she hadn't heard from Trent's mother either. She sipped her wine. Soon Trent would be home. *I'm running out of time.* She wished Jenn were here, but she'd left that day on hotel business in Key West.

Thinking of Jenn brought Dillon's handsome face swimming before her eyes. She could write Trent a note, pack a bag, and drive to the ranch. Dillon called her every night, and after each conversation, she missed him more. If anyone would have told her that her well-planned life would flip upside-down, she wouldn't have believed them. But here she was, engaged to one man while lusting after another.

She glanced at the clock—six-thirty. Time to fix some supper. Instead, she poured more wine. She set her glass on the counter and opened the department store bags, removing a deep-blue western shirt she'd bought for Dillon. She couldn't count the number of times she'd been in the mall and hadn't noticed that store, but today the display window had immediately caught her eye. Not only did she buy Dillon the shirt, she found him a vest and herself more clothes. Diana grinned to herself as she removed the lid from a shoe box and lifted out a pair of western boots, rich dark brown leather with a small heel, dressier than the ones she'd bought with Jenn. She sat and slipped them on, switched the radio station to country, and was practicing the steps Jenn had taught her when her cell rang.

"Hello," she said a little breathlessly.

"Diana, it's me," Dillon said. "Did I catch you in the middle of something?"

She turned the music down and laughed. "No. I was practicing dance steps." Just hearing his voice made her feel good. "How are you?"

"I had a pretty hectic day, but finally got my grandparents to the airport. Did you say you were dancing?"

"Ah, yeah, just fooling around. I'll bet it's quiet there with everyone gone."

"Actually, for the moment, I'm enjoying it. I'm not used to so much activity."

Diana chuckled. "I'll bet not. I loved your family, but honestly at times I was a little overwhelmed."

"Tell me about it. So, what about coming up this weekend? We'll be all alone."

Diana glanced down at her new boots and gnawed on her lower lip. *You know you want to, so say yes.*

"Diana? Are you there?"

"I'm here. Let me think about it. Once I break off with Trent, I have to return gifts, notify everybody, and cancel the arrangements."

"You don't have to do all of that immediately. Besides, you can do some of it from here."

He made it sound so easy. Her entire life had been so structured, and she had always known how to conduct herself. Breaking an engagement to run off to the mountains with a rodeo cowboy was not acceptable behavior. She let out a sigh. "Perhaps I can come on Saturday or Sunday."

"When does Trent get home?"

"Friday."

"Are you going to tell him then?"

"Yes, we're supposed to go to dinner."

"Diana, do you want me to come to you? I can get a hotel room."

The thought of Dillon and Trent in the same vicinity was more than she could deal with. "No." She realized how harsh she sounded and softened her voice. "Dillon, I appreciate your offer, but I'll be fine."

"Okay, well, I'm here if you need me."

"Great, thanks."

"Diana, I miss you."

The husky sound of his voice made her knees tremble. "I miss you too."

She hung up, sat down, and removed her boots. There wasn't a reason why she couldn't pack a bag and leave Saturday morning. Considering how angry Trent would be, leaving town might be the smart thing to do. Before she could change her mind, she headed for the closet where her suitcase was kept.

****

Thursday morning dawned sunny with a rise in temperature. Dillon decided to turn the horses out into the corral while he cleaned out their stalls. He climbed the ladder to the loft to throw down bails of straw, but when his foot hit the top rung, it snapped. Dillon, caught off balance, grabbed for the rail but missed. He landed hard on his back, twisting his foot. The wind knocked out of him, he lay stunned, gasping for breath.

As his breathing became more normal, he moved gingerly. He gritted his teeth as pain shot through his lower back. He stared up at the ladder and cursed. The rung was fine two days ago and he knew damn well somebody tampered with it. First the gunshot, now this. If someone thought he'd be intimidated, they didn't know him. Piss him off, and he dug in deeper.

He managed to sit up, then roll onto his knees. When he stood, his left ankle threatened to give way. He hobbled to an old wooden chair and sat down. His back ached and his ankle throbbed, but he dared not remove his boot, for he might not get it back on. He wasn't sure he could walk to his cabin. Perhaps he could make it to the truck parked next to the barn.

The horses were another problem. He had to get them back in their stalls. He'd have to call for help, but who? If Kevin was home, he was the closest. Dillon patted his jacket pocket. "Son-of-a-bitch," he cursed aloud. He must have left his cell on the kitchen counter.

More colorful cursing filled the barn as again he tried placing weight on his foot. He held onto the chair deciding what to do next when a shadow fell across the open doorway.

Dillon, feeling like a cornered animal, glanced

around for a weapon, but saw nothing. He was next to the wall where the harness and tack hung. As the sound of footsteps grew closer, Dillon shuffled behind the chair. It wouldn't help much, but he could swing it at his intruder's head.

Chapter Twenty-Two

When Kevin Duffy stepped through the door, Dillon tightened his grip on the chair and tensed, then relaxed. What was wrong with him? Kevin was a good friend, but he hadn't been acting quite like himself lately, and it would be smart to be cautious.

"Hey, Dillon, Bonnie told me you were all alone over here, so I thought I'd see if you'd like to take the horses for a ride up the mountain?"

Dillon studied Kevin's face. Was this a friendly suggestion, or a way to get him away from the ranch. Before he could reply, Kevin frowned.

"Are you okay?"

Dillon let out a long breath. Kevin had no reason to harm him. "I had a little accident." Dillon pointed to the ladder. "Top rung gave way and I fell. It knocked the wind out of me, and my ankle is messed up."

Kevin picked up the broken rung. "This looks as if it's been cut." Apprehension filled his eyes. "How the hell did this happen?"

Dillon didn't reply. Kevin's features tightened as he stared from the broken piece of wood in his hand to the loft. "Who would do this?"

"I have no idea, but I intend on finding out." He hesitated for a minute before saying, "Did you know the far east fence on the ranch was cut?"

"What?"

"I found it the other day. It's an opening large enough to get a horse through."

"Are you talking about the fence that borders the open land?"

Dillon nodded. "Your property line is nearby as well, isn't it?"

"Our campground extends that far, but I haven't been over there since it turned cold. Did you notice if my fence was cut as well?"

"No. I couldn't see that far."

Kevin shook his head. "I can't imagine why someone would do that. If you wanted to get onto either of our properties, you could climb over the fence. Why cut it?"

Best not to tell Kevin about the other mysterious happenings on the Lazy M. Dillon had a hard time believing Kevin was behind any of it, but his instinct warned him to be careful. He shrugged. "We'll probably never know. I planned on fixing it, but now with this damn ankle, that will have to wait. For now, I need to get the horses back into their stalls."

Kevin laid the wooden rung on a work table. "I can deal with the horses. You sit and rest your ankle. Then I'll take you to get it x-rayed."

"I'd appreciate that. For now, I can somewhat help here in the barn," Dillon said.

As Kevin tossed down the bales of straw, Dillon slowly spread it in the stalls. Even though he wanted to trust his friend, Dillon kept alert for any sudden moves. By the time Kevin led in the last horse, the pain in Dillon's ankle was excruciating. He wiped sweat from his brow and leaned against the wall.

"Buddy, you look like hell," Kevin said. "You'd better let me take you to the emergency room."

Dillon sighed with irritation. The last thing he wanted to do was sit for hours waiting to see a doctor. But he'd be foolish not to accept Kevin's offer. "Okay, let's go."

Hours later, Dillon sat in his cabin, an ice pack laying on his swollen ankle. The x-ray showed it was bruised and sprained, but not broken. Thankfully, his lower back didn't show any severe problem. The doctor told him to stay off his foot for a couple of days, an order Dillon had no intention of obeying. Not only were there chores that needed doing, he'd go crazy just sitting around. Besides, someone had now shot at him and sabotaged the ladder. Whoever it was had to have done it yesterday while he took his grandparents to the airport. So who knew of these plans?

It could be any number of people. His grandparents were so excited about their trip, hard telling who all they'd told. But the ranch was the key. Martin Patrick's face swam before his eyes and he scowled. He could picture him messing with the rung, but shoot at him? Dillon shook his head. He wouldn't have the balls. He paused in thought.

What about the mystery buyer? Was it too far-fetched to believe a stranger hid on Lazy M property waiting for him to ride by? If he was the target, and it wasn't just careless kids with a rifle, the suspect list was down to those who were close to him and his family. Dillon frowned. That logic circled back around to either Martin or Kevin. And his money was on Martin. But what did he think he'd gain by hurting him? Could he actually believe if Dillon was out of the way, his grandparents would sell the ranch? There was only one way to find out, and that was to confront him. Dillon glowered at his foot and cursed. He'd have to wait until tomorrow to face Martin.

When Dillon awoke Friday morning, the temperature had dropped, and they were calling for snow. He managed to hobble into the shower, then to the kitchen. He brewed a pot of coffee and was about to eat a bowl of cereal when a knock came to the door.

Dillon was surprised to see Kevin standing on the porch. "Good morning, what brings you out so early?"

"Good morning. I didn't trust you not to try and take care of the horses, so I came to tell you I've already done it."

Dillon motioned Kevin to come in. "I appreciate that, but you didn't have to do it."

"Were you about to go to the barn?"

Dillon gave him a sheepish grin. "You caught me. Come on and have a cup of coffee." Limping, Dillon led the way to the kitchen. "Have you had breakfast?" He pointed to the box of cereal. "That's all I've got, but you're welcome to join me."

"Sure, I could eat. You sit down. I'll get it. How's the ankle doing?"

"It hurts like a son-of-a-bitch, but I'll live. I only hope I can get my boot on."

"Why, you going somewhere?"

Dillon nodded. "I've been mulling over who may have cut that rung, and Martin Patrick came to mind. I've decided to pay him a visit."

Kevin frowned. "You think this might all be about selling the ranch?"

"Why else would someone take a shot at me and

cause me to fall? Whoever it is knows I'm alone here and is taking advantage of the situation."

Kevin stared into his coffee cup, then up at Dillon. For a second, Dillon thought he saw indecision in his eyes. Dillon waited. Did Kevin know something? Seconds passed in silence, then Dillon asked, "Do you have any other idea who it might be?"

Kevin shook his head. "I'm having a hard time believing anyone would want to cause you harm in order to get the ranch. But something's not right. Would you like me to go with you to confront Martin?"

"Thanks, but I'm going to his office in town. I'll be safe enough. I want to see the expression on his face when I accuse him of trying to kill me."

Kevin laughed. "He'll probably piss his pants. I'll come back later to help with the horses and hear what he said."

As Dillon drove down the mountain to town, he couldn't shake the sensation Kevin knew more than he was saying. But if so, why keep it to himself? The sporting goods store Kevin owned was small, but it was a hangout for a lot of the local men. He might have overheard something and didn't want to say anything until he knew if he was right.

As Dillon rounded a steep curve and tapped his brakes, he frowned. He pressed down harder, and nothing happened. The truck sped faster, and he downshifted into a lower gear. His jaw set and his hands tight on the wheel, he hugged the mountain, avoiding the drop-off on the other side. Grateful it was winter and the road seldom used, praying he didn't meet another car, Dillon swerved around curve after curve, his tires squealing. Sweat trickled down his neck, and his heart pounded in his chest as the truck scraped against the guardrail. When a gravel cut-off near the bottom came into view, he let out the breath he didn't realize he was holding. He jerked the wheel, and the truck slammed into a mound of dirt and snow.

Stunned from the impact and the blow from the air bag, Dillon sat, his hands shaking as he ran them over his face. He sucked in deep breaths, then cursed long and hard. What if he'd hit another car and killed someone? Whoever had messed with his brakes was fucking nuts. It was time for him to talk to Sheriff Dunn. With trembling fingers, he slipped his cell from his pocket and called DT's garage. He'd known the mechanic for years and knew he'd give him a tow.

An hour later, Dillon sat in the cramped Sheriff's office across from Paul Dunn, a tall, heavy man with a reputation of being tough but honest. Paul listened, and when Dillon finished, he leaned back in his chair and crossed his arms over his chest.

"Do you have any idea who this person might be?" Paul asked.

"Martin Patrick comes to mind, but that's only a guess. Other than him, there's the mysterious buyer for the Lazy M."

"Do you want me to talk to Martin?"

"I was on my way to do just that when the brakes went out on my truck. I wanted to inform you of what was happening before I saw him."

Paul cocked his head. "Considering the situation, do you think confronting him is a good idea?"

Dillon's smile was without humor. "You mean because I'd like to beat the crap out of him?"

Paul nodded. "I don't want to have to arrest you for

assault. If you don't want me to go to his office, I suggest you stop off at the diner, get something to eat, and calm down before you see him."

Dillon stood. "I believe I'll do as you suggest. The little weasel isn't worth going to jail for."

Paul also stood. "Call me if anything else happens. Do not investigate on your own." He scowled. "I'll never hear the last of it from Chet if something happens to you."

The garage provided Dillon with a rental truck, so after eating lunch he drove into the lot of Pine Bluff Realty and parked next to Martin's car. As he stepped from the truck, pain from his ankle shot up his leg. He'd been on the damn thing too long. Not wanting Martin to see he was hurting, Dillon gritted his teeth and tried not to limp as he entered the office.

A pretty twenty-something receptionist greeted him with a smile. "Hello, can I help you?"

"I'd like to see Martin Patrick."

"Do you have an appointment?"

"No. Tell him Dillon McCoy is here."

His tone was harsher than he wanted, for her eyes opened wide and she stammered, "Please have a seat, and I'll inform him you're here."

Before Dillon could move, a door opened and Martin came out. "I thought that was your voice," he said, giving Dillon a wide smile. "Please come on back."

Dillon followed him into a well-appointed office. He waited until Martin sat behind his desk. With steel in each word, he placed his hands on the front of the desk and leaned forward. "Someone has been fucking with me, and if I find out it's you, I'm going to have your sorry ass thrown in jail. Don't think for one minute, if I'm killed, my family would sell you the ranch. McCoys stick together. You'd have to get rid of all of us first. And if it's not you, but you know who it is, you'd better tell them the same. I hope I've made myself clear."

Hatred blazed in Martin's eyes as he rose. "Who do you think you are coming in here threatening me? I have no idea what you're talking about, but if someone is fucking with you, then all I can say is, good for them. Now get out of my office."

At the door Dillon turned. "I'm not kidding. Stay the fuck away from me and my ranch."

After Dillon left, Martin sat seething with anger. This had gone far enough. He was done, and fuck the consequences. This would stop now. He picked up his phone.

****

When Dillon arrived back at the ranch and parked next to the barn, the first snowflakes were beginning to fall. He'd quickly bed the horses down for the night and get to the cabin. His foot was hurting like a son-of-a-bitch and his lower back aching. By the time he finished, the wind was howling, and an inch of snow was on the ground. Exhausted from the day, he limped into the cabin. He planned on fixing a sandwich and hitting the sack.

Chapter Twenty-Three

Diana paced nervously through her apartment. For the hundredth time she glanced at the mantel clock—six-thirty. Trent would arrive any minute to take her to dinner. She was about to do the hardest thing she'd ever done. She considered waiting until they'd returned from dinner, but she wasn't sure she could keep up the pretense through a meal.

She stared out the window at the parking lot. A gentle snow fell, dusting the trees, grass, and cars. She'd spent the day rehearsing, but she feared once she faced him, the words wouldn't come. Her palms grew damp, and she wiped them on her wool slacks. She'd decided no matter how she said it, she would hurt a man she cared deeply for. Could she make him understand how sorry she was and that she never meant for this to happen? And if she were to marry him, it would end badly.

Diana straightened pillows on the couch and stacked magazines neatly on the coffee table. *You can do this. No matter what Trent says, you must stay firm. You can't allow him to change your mind.*

Dillon's phone calls had both comforted her and strengthened her resolve. She'd leave for Pine Bluff in the morning. Her suitcase was packed and in the car. Breaking her engagement, then running off to another man was about as contemptible as one could get. She didn't want to hurt anyone, but, damn it, for her entire life she had done what was expected of her. Now she wanted to live her own life. Besides, no matter how hard she tried, she couldn't deny her feelings for Dillon.

If she was lucky, no one would know she was gone. Jenn was in Florida on hotel business, and her other friends were busy with holiday preparations. She let out a long sigh. How had her structured life become so complicated? *Because you finally stepped out of the box and realized you want more.*

When the door intercom buzzed, she jumped. With her nerves as tight as bow strings, she hit the button to open the lobby door.

"Hey, beautiful," Trent said as he entered the apartment. "I've missed you."

Diana forced a smile. "Hi, Trent. Welcome back." She ran an appraising eye over Trent's blond hair, hazel eyes, and athletic build. *He's good-looking enough, but he doesn't send my heart racing like Dillon does.*

"I have a surprise for you." He removed his jacket and slipped a gift-wrapped box from the pocket. "I saw this and thought of you. But first…" He took her into his arms and kissed her.

Diana automatically kissed him back. To her relief, he quickly broke their embrace.

He gave her a quizzical look. "Is everything okay?"

Oh, damn, had she already given herself away? Before she'd enjoyed his kisses, now nothing. Was it her guilt, or knowing what she was about to do?

She swallowed hard and took a deep breath. "Trent, we need to talk."

"Sure." He placed the gift on the table. "This

sounds serious. What's wrong?"

"Let's sit." Diana indicated the couch. "Would you like a glass of wine?"

He nodded.

Diana stepped to the counter that divided the living room from the kitchen. She poured some pinot noir for them both and handed him his glass.

She sat in the chair across from the couch, took a long sip of her wine, and began. "Trent, I want you to know I care deeply for you. You're a good man, and I never meant to hurt you."

Trent interrupted her before she could continue. "Diana, I don't like where this is going. What are you trying to say?"

Diana hesitated, then began in a rush. "Trent, I can't marry you. I'm sorry, but I don't love you enough to spend the rest of our lives together."

For what seemed an eternity, silence filled the room. A myriad of expressions flashed in Trent's eyes—hurt, confusion, then anger.

"What do you mean you don't love me enough? We're four months away from our wedding, and you just realized this?"

Diana bit her lower lip, willing back the tears. "I've had doubts for a while now."

"Oh, really?" Anger dripped from every word. "Well, I'll tell you something, Diana. You can get over your doubts because this wedding will not be canceled. I've put too much into this relationship to have you suddenly change your mind. Not to mention my parents. My mother has gone out of her way to make the wedding perfect, and you won't disappoint her."

Stunned at what she heard, Diana gaped. "Trent,

I'm sorry to disappoint your mother. Mine will be upset as well. But that's no reason to get married."

Trent rose and stood over her. The menacing glare in his eyes and the rigid set to his jaw gave Diana her first tingle of unease. "Is there another man? Is that it? Have you been laying someone else?"

Diana winced, then opened her mouth to tell him the truth, but closed it. His hands were balled into fists, and his eyes blazed. "Trent," she said quietly, "I don't love you enough. That's all. Please, let's end this without any more hurt."

"Hurt, I'll show you hurt." He jerked her from the chair. Squeezing her arms painfully, he shook her. "No one walks out on me." He shook her harder. "Especially a boring little bitch like you." He shook her again. "You're exactly the type of girl my mother expects me to marry, and that's what I'll do."

Shock left her temporarily speechless. Diana expected anger, but not this. "Trent, you're hurting me. Let go."

A cold grin spread across his face. Diana willed herself to remain calm. "Trent, think about what you're doing. Now, let me go and leave."

"Not on your life. I need to teach you how to love, honor, and obey."

To Diana's horror, he shoved her. She lost her balance and tripped over the edge of the coffee table, landing half on and half off the couch. Before she could rise, Trent came down on top of her. She opened her mouth to scream, but he muffled her cries with his hand. "You also need to learn how to please me." He squeezed her breast until she sobbed in pain. "Trust me, you'll learn to like it."

Fear threatened to consume her. How was she to get away? Diana gathered all the courage she possessed and brought her knee up between his spread legs. His intake of breath told her she'd hit her mark. The punch to her cheek left her dazed and crying out in pain. *Diana, move*, a voice in her head screamed. She ignored her throbbing face and raked her nails down his cheek.

He jerked his head away. "You bitch."

Diana managed to shove him off her and stumble to her feet. Trembling from head to toe, her leg throbbing from connecting with the coffee table, she grabbed her purse and ran for the door.

Trent caught her by the hair, and she cried out. "Where do you think you're going?"

If he got her to the couch, he'd rape her. Frantically she looked for a weapon. On a small table next to the door sat a crystal vase Trent's mother had given her. She grabbed it with both hands, swung it over her head, and heard Trent grunt then fall. She opened the door and fled.

Tears streaming down her cheeks, she headed toward her car. Halfway across the parking lot, she slipped on the ice and fell to her knees. Sobbing so hard she could barely see, she managed to get to her feet.

"You fucking bitch," Trent shouted from behind her.

Crying out in fear, she made it to her car, flung the door open, climbed in, and slammed it shut, punching the lock. Her hands shook so badly it took her three tries to insert the key in the ignition.

Like something from a horror movie, Trent's bloody face appeared next to her car.

"I'll kill you," he yelled as he pounded on the

driver's side window.

Diana's stomach heaved, and she swallowed back the bile. She threw the car into reverse, hit the gas, and peeled from the parking lot. Without conscious thought, she headed for I-40 West.

A half-hour later, her tremors subsiding, and her bladder about to burst, Diana stopped at a gas station with a convenience store and hurried inside. She had fled her apartment without her coat, but thankfully she was wearing a sweater. Shivering from the cold, she pushed the door to the Ladies' room open and dashed into a stall.

At the sink, she stared in disbelief at her reflection in the mirror. She had cried most of her make-up off, leaving dark smears under her eyes. Her left cheek was swollen and beginning to bruise, and her hair was a tangled mess. She gripped the edge of the sink. How could she have not seen what Trent was really like? What kind of demon was he hiding? The thought that she'd almost married him made her stomach heave again. She cupped her hands and splashed cold water on her face. She patted it dry with a paper towel and dug in her purse for a comb. She was about finished when her cell chimed letting her know she had a text. Incredulous, she read what Trent had written.

"Diana, I'll be waiting for you when you come home. Tonight was nothing but a misunderstanding. You upset me, and I overreacted. Hurry home, and we'll talk. I love you."

Diana gritted her teeth. Did the arrogant jerk think she'd go anywhere near him? Not hardly. She dropped her phone back into her purse and headed out the door. She bought a bottle of water, filled the car with gas, and headed for the highway.

As the miles passed, her mind kept replaying the scene with Trent. She'd had no inkling of the kind of violence he was capable of. She'd seen him become angry, but never the way he behaved tonight. Eventually she'd have to go home, but for now she knew exactly where she was going. She was heading to Dillon. She wanted nothing more than to fall into his strong arms and have him hold her. She wanted to feel his mouth on hers and hear him tell her everything would be all right.

Thank goodness she'd had the good sense not to confess to Trent about Dillon. She couldn't imagine what he might do to her if he knew the truth. Needing to distract her thoughts from Trent, she turned on her satellite radio. The smooth jazz she normally listened to wasn't calming her, so she punched buttons until she found a country station. She didn't know any of the songs, but they made her smile. One was about a gal taking a Louisville slugger to her boyfriend's new truck. Sounded like a great idea.

The snow fell harder. She loved her little red sports car, and it got great gas mileage, but it wasn't the best for driving in these conditions. Her hands tightened on the steering wheel as the wipers worked to push the thickening snow from the windshield. Should she find a hotel and stop? This stretch of I-40 was pretty desolate. She frowned. When was the last time she'd seen an exit? She glanced at the digital clock. She'd been driving for almost three hours. For a few minutes the snow let up, and a sign came into view—Asheville, 65 miles. There wasn't a lot of traffic, but what little there was moved fairly slowly. With visibility becoming worse by the minute, she could do nothing but follow the slight glow from the tail lights in front of her.

Diana cried out when her car hit an icy patch and slid onto the shoulder. As she fought to get the car under control, the back tires sank into a snow-filled ditch. She hit the gas and tried to go forward, but the tires just spun. Tears of frustration burned the back of her eyes. *I don't even know where I am. This is a living nightmare.* "Damn, damn, damn."

For a few minutes, she sat, drumming her fists on the steering wheel. The wind howled, buffeting her car while the snow continued to fall. *Okay, Diana, calm down and get a grip. Sitting here having a fit won't help get you out of this ditch. You're a big girl. You can handle this. Turn your flashers on and phone for help.* As she was about to make the call, her cell rang.

Chapter Twenty-Four

At the sound of Dillon's voice, Diana broke. "Oh, Dillon, thank God it's you."

"Diana, what's wrong?"

Tears flowed down her cheeks and her words came out in short gasps.

"Slow down. I can't understand half of what you're saying."

Diana took a deep breath and began again, concluding with, "I'm somewhere on I-40 stuck in a ditch."

"Are you hurt?"

"No. I was about to phone for help when you called."

"Stay there. I'm on my way."

"Dillon, I'm not sure where I am. I'll call for a tow truck and let you know when I get back on the highway."

"I don't want you sitting there by yourself. Did you try to drive out of the ditch?"

Diana sighed with exasperation. "Yes. The tires spun and sank deeper."

"What was the last road sign you saw?"

"It said Asheville was sixty-five miles away."

"That gives me an idea of where you are. I think I should come."

Again, she was about to tell him no when flashing lights slowed behind her. "Dillon, someone's stopping."

"Diana, do not get out of the car."

"It's all right. It's the police. I'll call you back."

"If I don't hear from you soon, I'm coming to find you."

Diana dropped her cell back in her purse, rolled down her window, and waited for the trooper. She shivered from the blast of cold air and blinked away the flakes of snow that blew through the open window.

"Miss, are you okay?" the female state trooper asked.

"Yes, but I'm stuck," Diana replied.

"Have you called for assistance?"

"Not yet."

"Hang on, let me see what I can do." She started toward her car, when flashing lights of a truck could be seen stopping behind the cruiser. The Trooper waved her hand and hurried to the tow truck.

Could she be this lucky? She'd expected to be there for hours waiting on someone to show up. The Trooper headed back her way.

"He's going to pull you out. I'm Trooper Morgan. Would you like to wait in my car?"

Grateful, Diana nodded. She grabbed her purse and stepped from the car. Immediately, her shoes sank into the cold wet snow, soaking her feet and pants.

"Where's your coat and boots?" Trooper Morgan asked.

Diana shivered. "It's a long story."

She arched one brow, then led the way to her cruiser. Diana sighed with relief as the warmth of the interior surrounded her.

"Where are you headed?" Trooper Morgan asked.

"Pine Bluff. I have a friend who lives near there. I'm not sure where we are. Do you know how far that is?"

"In normal weather, around an hour or so. But I have to tell you, I heard on the radio the highway up there is as bad as this. You might want to think about stopping for the night. A few miles ahead there's an exit. Perhaps you can find a motel."

"You're probably right. I'll get off and call my friend."

"I'm sorry, I couldn't help but notice the bruise on your cheek. Did you injure yourself in your car? Or, did someone do that to you?"

Diana, not knowing what to say, hesitated.

"Miss, if someone hurt you, you should report it."

Diana swallowed back her tears. This woman was being so kind, she couldn't help but tell her the entire story. "You see, that's why I don't have a coat. I was so scared, I ran." Her last words came out on a sob.

"What is your name?" Trooper Morgan asked, in a gentle voice. "I can contact Chapel Hill and report the attack."

"Oh, please, no. I'm all right." Diana took a deep breath, trying to smooth the panic from her voice. The thought of the police getting involved was more than she could deal with. "My friend is coming to meet me. I won't be going back to Chapel Hill for a while."

"If you're sure." Trooper Morgan replied.

"Yes, but thank you for your help and concern."

"That's my job." She smiled. "Your car is ready to go. Follow me, and I'll guide you to the off-ramp."

Again, Diana thanked her profusely and hurried to

her car. She exchanged insurance information with the tow truck driver, then waited for the police cruiser to lead the way. Diana eased in behind her and leaned forward, peering through the blowing snow. Within a few miles, lights pierced the wall of white. Trooper Morgan switched on her blinker, and Diana spotted the exit. A flashing neon sign for an all-night breakfast restaurant came into view. She fishtailed into the parking lot, barely missing another car.

She turned off the ignition and crossed her arms over the steering wheel, resting her forehead on them. Tension from all she'd been through had her on the verge of screaming. *You've made it this far, don't fall apart now.* A knock on the driver's window made her jump.

Diana turned to see a man's face. "Are you all right?" he shouted.

Diana nodded.

"Roll down your window." He motioned with his hand.

Diana shook her head.

"It's okay." He held up a badge. "I'm a cop."

Diana cracked her window.

"I saw you slide into the lot and wanted to make sure you weren't hurt," he said. "I'm off duty, but I'm Trooper Macy with the North Carolina state police. If you'd like, I can help you into the restaurant. Are you from around here?"

"No. I was on my way to Pine Bluff."

"Trust me, you don't want to travel any further in this mess."

Diana was cold, hungry, and tired of the snow. She nodded and stepped from her car.

"Where's your coat?"

Diana sighed. "I left in a hurry and don't have one."

He gave her a curious glance but took her arm.

Warmth and the smell of coffee and frying bacon hit her as they stepped through the door.

"Hey, Chuck, what you doing out on a night like this?" one of the waitresses asked.

"I was on my way home when the storm hit. I found this young lady in her car in the parking lot. I believe she's in need of something hot to drink."

"Honey, come sit down. What in the world are you doing out without a coat?"

Diana gave the plump, grandmotherly woman a grateful smile and slid into a booth. "I'll be fine, thank you. I'd like a cup of coffee, please."

"Sure thing. How about something to eat?"

Diana's stomach growled. She realized she hadn't eaten since breakfast. "Yes, I believe I will."

"I'll get your coffee while you decide. I'm Lucy."

Diana placed her order, then took in her surroundings. She'd seen this chain of breakfast restaurants with their big yellow signs but had never been in one. She'd never even eaten a waffle. She drew her phone from her purse and called Dillon.

"Diana, where the hell are you? I was about to walk out the door."

"Don't. They say the roads are awful up your way. I'm okay." She told him about Trooper Morgan, the tow truck, and the detective. "I'm going to find a motel."

"I can't believe you drove in this storm."

"I had no choice. I needed to get away. When I

tried to break it off with Trent, it went very badly. I ran out and started to drive and got caught in the snow."

Silence filled her phone before Dillon spoke. "What did he do to you?"

Diana sniffed. "I'd rather not say right now."

"What exit are you at?"

"Hang on. I have to ask."

Lucy came by to refill her coffee. "Can you tell me what exit this is?"

"Stay there," Dillon said, after Diana related the information to him. "I'm on my way."

"Dillon, no." Before she could continue, he'd disconnected the call.

"Here you go," Lucy said, setting a plate in front of her.

"Thank you. It smells wonderful."

"Honey, what brings you out in this storm?"

Diana hesitated. "I'm on my way to visit a friend in Pine Bluff."

"This is none of my business, but that bruise on your face looks pretty bad. Would you like some ice?"

"No, thank you. It doesn't hurt as much as it did."

"I'm glad you got away from him. Honey, I've been there, don't go back."

Seeing the compassion in Lucy's eyes, Diana blinked back tears. "I won't," she managed, her voice barely above a whisper.

Lucy glanced out the window. "Is that your little red car?"

Her mouth full of cheesy scrambled eggs, Diana nodded.

Lucy cocked her head. "You're not going to try and drive to Pine Bluff tonight, are you? You won't make it over the mountain past Asheville. My advice is to find a place to stay right here."

Diana swallowed and patted her mouth with a napkin. "My friend is coming to get me. Are there motels nearby?"

"Sure, but it's almost Christmas, one of the busiest times for this area. It might be hard finding a vacancy."

Diana thanked her, picked up her cell, and began making calls.

****

Dillon stripped out of his sweatpants and threw on clothes. He clenched his teeth at the pain as he forced his swollen foot into his boot. He grabbed his coat and the keys to the ranch pickup. It had four-wheel drive, and he'd packed sandbags in the bed for extra traction. The county tried to keep the road leading off the mountain plowed, but in weather like this the main roads were cleared first.

The snowfall had tapered off, and he cautiously kept the truck in the middle of the twisting road. Cursing the entire way, he managed to reach the bottom.

The state route through Pine Bluff was snow-covered and icy. Dillon crept along until the entrance ramp for I-40 East came into view. The plows had been by, but the highway was still a mess, and traffic crawled slowly along. The windshield wipers worked rapidly to keep up with the blowing snow.

Dillon tightened his hands on the wheel. Whatever happened between Diana and Trent must have been pretty damn bad for her to drive three hours in this mess. If the son-of-a-bitch hurt her, he'd beat the shit out of him. With Tonya being a royal pain in the ass, and not knowing who'd been trying to mess with him, he'd love an excuse to pound on someone.

He was tempted to get Diana, say the hell with it all, and take off where no one could find them. He'd tried his damnedest to give her some space, but he hadn't been able to keep from calling her. She'd been gone less than a week, but it seemed much longer.

The thought of him and Diana being snowed in on the mountain made him smile. As he pictured her lying naked by the fire, the car in front of him spun sideways.

Dillon swore and jerked the wheel heading for the shoulder. He bounced off a snow bank, slid back onto the pavement, hit the gas, said every curse word he knew, and made it past the cars piling up behind him. He punched 911 into his phone and reported the accident.

One thing was certain. If he made it to Diana, they sure as hell weren't driving back tonight. A half-hour later, he pulled into the restaurant parking lot.

When he came through the door, a friendly, gray-haired woman smiled. "I have a feeling you're here for that young lady over there." She pointed to where Diana sat in a booth.

Dillon smiled and nodded. "Thanks."

When he slid in across from her, Diana burst into tears.

"Hey, darlin', it's okay. I'm here." He reached for her hand, then saw her face. For a second, the rage that consumed him left him speechless . "Did he do that to you?" His voice sounded more like a growl.

Diana sniffed, then nodded. "I'm sorry. It's been a horrible night. And I'm so glad to see you."

"He's a walking dead man."

"No, Dillon, don't. It's not that bad, and I probably hurt him worse."

His mouth formed a thin line. He indicated her plate. "Have you finished?"

"Yes. How about you? Are you hungry?"

At that moment, Lucy arrived with the coffee pot. "I thought you could use a cup."

Dillon nodded. "Thanks."

"Will you be wanting something to eat?"

Dillon shook his head. "Just the coffee and the check."

"Diana, we're not going to make it to the ranch tonight," he continued. "I-40 is a mess. We need to find a motel around here."

"I've been calling, and the only opening I found between here and Asheville is an Easy Sleep Inn ten miles away."

"Did you make a reservation?"

"They said they only had one room left, so I thought I should."

"Darlin', have you ever slept at an Easy Sleep?"

"No, but that doesn't mean it won't be perfectly fine." She gathered her things and rose. "I'd like to thank Lucy for being so kind to me."

"We should also let her know we'll be leaving your car here. There's no need for both of us to drive in this."

Diana frowned. "Will my car be all right?"

Dillon motioned through the window at the snow-covered landscape. "Who's going to bother it?"

Diana nodded and headed for the counter.

"Where's your coat?" Dillon asked.

"I don't have one."

"Why not?"

"Because I didn't have time to grab it." Diana let out a long breath. "I'll explain everything once we're settled in a room."

Chapter Twenty-Five

Dillon frowned and followed her into the parking lot. "Which car is yours?"

"Over there." Diana pointed to what could still be seen of her car.

He glanced from her to the car and scowled. "You drove three hours in a blizzard in that toy?"

Diana narrowed her eyes. "It got me here, didn't it?"

Dillon opened his mouth to reply, then noticed her teeth were chattering. "Come on." He took her arm and helped her into the truck. He turned on the ignition and set the heater on high. "You'll be warm in a minute. Which way is the motel?"

Diana, phone in hand, asked it for directions. "We'll be driving away from the highway. I hope we can get through."

Twenty minutes later, the road somewhat plowed, Dillon stopped in front of the Easy Sleep, a two-story building with outside entrances to the rooms.

"Whose name is the room under?" he asked.

"Mine." Diana started to get out, but Dillon stopped her.

"I'll go. You stay here where it's warm."

****

Diana lay back against the headrest and sighed.

She'd never been as happy to see someone as when Dillon came through the restaurant door. In his tan cowboy hat, leather jacket, and faded jeans, he was her knight in shining armor. When he slid into the booth across from her, she tried not to cry but couldn't control her tears. She was safe, and soon he'd be holding her in his arms.

Diana, be careful, a little voice in her head said. *You're caught up in the moment. Don't jump in until you understand what you're feeling.*

But Diana knew it was too late. She was falling in love with Dillon McCoy, and if he broke her heart, so be it. She planned on stuffing the old Diana Thompson in a closet and riding this cowboy until the rodeo was over.

When Dillon opened the truck door, Diana jumped. "That was quick."

He handed her the key. "We're on the second floor." He pointed. "Go up those steps. There's a convenience store next door. I'm going to get some water and beer. Would you like wine or something?"

"Sure. Red wine if they have it."

Diana carefully made her way across the parking lot and up the stairs. She soon found the room and slipped the key in the lock. Darkness greeted her and she fumbled for a switch. She clicked on the lights and stood transfixed. The furniture and lamps might have been there since the fifties. The carpet was threadbare and the curtains thin as paper. She peeked into the small bathroom and stifled a laugh. The fifties motif continued here. Diana laughed out loud, picturing the luxurious marble bathrooms her mother was used to when they traveled. *Diana, you're not in the Ritz anymore.* She lifted the bedspread to find the sheets crisp and white and smelling of bleach. The room may have been in desperate need of an update, but everything was polished and clean.

There was a knock at the door, then Dillon's voice. "Diana, it's me."

She hurried to let him in. He stomped the snow from his boots and handed her the bag. "I hope you like Giant Chicken cabernet."

Diana frowned. "What?"

"The wine. The shelves were pretty empty. So, I didn't have much to choose from."

Diana set the bag on a tiny dresser and pulled out the bottle. A huge red rooster covered the label. "I'm, um, sure it will be fine."

Dillon took off his coat and hat and glanced around. "So, what do you think?"

"It's okay."

He cocked his head. "Kind of like a time warp."

She grinned. "Are they all like this?"

"Not usually this bad, but I haven't been in that many." He picked up a beer and twisted off the cap.

"Did you remember a corkscrew?"

"My pocketknife has one. But I did forget glasses. I'll see what's in the bathroom." He returned with a plastic cup. "Afraid this is all there is."

"It will do." Diana took the cup of wine and sat on the end of the bed, leaving the only chair for him.

Dillon sat, removed his boots, and grimaced. He took a long sip of his beer and crossed his swollen foot over his knee. "Besides the fact the bastard hit you, tell me what happened with Trent."

Chapter Twenty-Six

Diana indicated his foot. "What did you do?"

"I fell."

"What happened?"

"I'll explain later. I want to hear about you and Trent."

She paused for a minute, opened her mouth to say something, instead sipped her wine. "You know, this isn't bad at all."

"I'm glad you like it. Now, what about Trent?"

She sighed and set the cup on the bedside table. She'd debated how much she should tell him and had decided to tell him everything. When she finished, Dillon sat as rigid as stone, his eyes shards of ice, his jaw clenched. Seconds passed before he spoke. "The fucker also tried to rape you?"

She nodded.

"How badly are you hurt?"

"Not too bad. But I actually think I hurt him more when I hit him with the vase."

"We can only hope. You were hurt and he made you run. You could have been seriously injured or killed driving in a snowstorm. Did you call the police?"

"No. I got away, and he'll never touch me again."

"You're damn right he won't. Because I plan on making it clear to him that if he ever comes near you, he'll be dealing with me."

"Fighting with him won't accomplish anything. He's rich, and you'll be the one to end up in jail."

Dillon opened another beer for himself and refilled her glass. "How do you think you'll keep him away?"

"By not being around him."

"The man threatened you. He told you he wouldn't accept you calling off the wedding. What makes you think he'll give up so easily?"

Diana recalled the text Trent sent her and hesitated. In a soft voice she said, "I don't know. He may not."

"This is what I suggest we do," Dillon continued. "We'll go to the ranch and stay there until the roads are passable, then I'll drive you to your apartment where you can get your things."

"I have wedding preparations to cancel. Not to mention explaining this to my parents."

"You can do that by phone, can't you?"

Diana nodded. "Most of the cancelations are the florist, caterers, and the ballroom at the country club." Diana frowned. "Although Trent's mother arranged it all."

Dillon shrugged. "So let her take care of it."

"I suppose. There are still the invitations. We'll have to notify people."

He refilled her glass.

Diana glanced from her glass to him. "Are you trying to get me drunk?"

"Yes."

Diana laughed. "I think it's working. I feel totally relaxed."

"Good." He threw away his empty beer can and placed her glass on the nightstand. He sat next to her and took her into his arms and kissed her.

Dillon folded back the blanket and laid her down on the sheets. When his mouth covered hers, Diana gloried in his embrace. His lips were warm, while his tongue coaxed and teased. Diana feathered her fingers through the silky hair at the base of his neck. Oh, how she wanted this man. He made her feel safe, daring, and free from the rigid restraints she was used to. Dillon deepened the kiss, and Diana softly moaned with pleasure. When his hand ran down her side and over her hip to cup her between her legs, fiery need coursed through her.

He rolled her onto her back and slid his hand under her sweater. Diana's body reacted to his every touch as her desire soared. When he stroked her breast through her lacy bra, Diana winced in pain.

Dillon broke their kiss and stared down at her face. "What's wrong?"

She shook her head. She didn't want him to see how much his slight touch hurt. She blinked back tears. "I'm all right."

"No, you're not. Let me see."

"Dillon." Before she could stop him, he tugged her sweater over her head and unhooked her bra.

"Son-of-a-bitch." His eyes blazed in anger as he stared at her bruised skin. "He did this to you?"

She nodded."

"Where else did he hurt you?"

Tears filled her eyes. "He shoved me, and I fell over the coffee table. He pinned me beneath him and squeezed both my upper arms." Her voice broke on a sob. "Dillon, after he hit me, he twisted my breasts."

Dillon sat up and cursed as she showed him the

purpling marks. "I'm going to beat the ever-living fuck out of him."

"Dillon, please, no. He'd probably have you arrested or something. He's not worth it. The bruises will go away." She lifted her arms to him. "I want you to make me forget all about him."

He brushed a tear from her cheek. "Darlin', I'd be happy to." He slipped off her wool slacks and bikini panties. She lay naked, her hair fanned out on the pillow. "Diana, you're beautiful."

A blush stained her cheeks. "Why don't you join me."

He stood and grinned. "I believe I'll do just that."

He started to unsnap his flannel shirt, and Diana rose to her knees. "Let me." When he stood bare-chested, Diana unhooked his belt, and it joined his shirt on the floor. Dillon's gaze never left her eyes. She reached for the zipper to his jeans. She didn't know if what she did next could be blamed on the wine or the events of the night.

Diana eased his zipper down and pushed his jeans and undershorts over his hips. Without breaking eye contact, she slid her hand along his hard erection. His blue eyes darkened, and his breath caught.

In a raspy voice he said, "Diana, if you keep that up, this will be over before we begin."

She moistened her lips with her tongue and lowered her head.

"Christ, Diana."

Delighting in her power over him, she took him deep into her mouth.

"Diana, you're killing me," Dillon hissed.

"Am I?" She licked the moisture from the tip of his

shaft.

Dillon fisted his hands in her hair. "If you don't stop, I won't be able to control myself."

She took him into her mouth again and held him there until he shouted with his release.

When she lifted her head, heat blazed in his eyes.

"Proud of yourself?" he asked, as he stepped out of his jeans.

She gave him a slight grin. "I've never done that before."

"Darlin', you did just fine. Now it's my turn. Lay back."

Her pulse quickened with anticipation as she did as he asked. He spread her legs and ran his hands up her inner thighs. When he stopped at her soft mound, he circled her hard bud with his thumb.

"Dillon."

He replaced his thumb with his mouth. "Oh, sweet heaven," Diana cried. He used his tongue and teeth, until she thought she'd go mad. She tugged at his hair and begged him not to stop. Every inch of her body hummed with a pulsating need. She cried his name over and over, as the orgasm slammed through her.

She opened her eyes to see Dillon grinning at her. "Darlin', I think you liked that."

Her brain still not quite functioning, Diana couldn't speak. She closed her eyes. Did she screech like a banshee? She reopened her eyes to see the smug expression on Dillon's face. She swallowed before she spoke. "I suppose it was pleasant enough."

Dillon roared with laughter. "Darlin', the way you were hollering, I'm surprised the police aren't at the door."

Diana started to sit up, and Dillon pressed her back. "We're far from done."

"Dillon, we can't possibly."

He eased his body over hers, until he lay fully on top. "Oh, yes, we can." He pressed the tip of his erection against her opening. "Now let me in."

Diana spread her legs and wrapped her arms around his neck. Their lips met.

He slid his tongue into her mouth and his shaft into her welcoming heat. Diana moaned and lifted her hips so he could press deeper. When he moved inside her, she matched him thrust for thrust. As he increased the pace, Diana ran her nails down his back.

Dillon broke the kiss and raised up on his arms, held her hands, and placed them on either side of her head. His voice was low when he demanded. "Open your eyes so I can watch you come."

He slowed his pace. She squirmed beneath him. "Dillon."

"You've got the tightest, sweetest little…"

"Dillon," she cried as she convulsed around him.

****

Dillon gritted his teeth to keep from coming too soon, but the feel of her and the passion in her eyes made him lose all self-control. He let go of her hands and placed his under her bottom. He lifted her slightly as he drove himself deep inside her. They cried as one and sailed together into ecstasy.

Chapter Twenty-Seven

Gray morning light shone through a gap in the curtains. Diana, disoriented, slowly opened her eyes. It took her a few minutes to recall where she was. Naked, her back against Dillon, his arm around her waist. She smiled to herself. Here she was waking up in a cheap motel with a man she hardly knew. If her mother could see her now. Diana couldn't hold back the giggle that escaped.

"What's so funny?" he murmured into her ear.

"I was picturing the expression on my mother's face if she could see me."

He ran his hand over her hip, across her stomach, and cupped her breast. "You don't think she'd approve?"

Diana let out an unladylike snort. "Not at all."

Dillon nuzzled her neck while stroking her breast. "That's too bad, because I certainly approve."

The touch of his hand and the sexiness of his voice had Diana pressing her backside against his arousal. When his hand drifted lower to stroke her wetness, she opened for him.

In a low, husky voice, Dillon said, "Roll onto your stomach."

Diana, her climax aching for release, did as he asked.

He placed one of the pillows beneath her stomach and positioned himself behind her.

"Dillon, what are you doing?"

As the words left her lips, he slid inside her.

When he filled her completely, Diana exhaled a moan of pure pleasure. She dug her fingers into the mattress as he moved with long easy strokes.

On the edge of her climax, Diana arched her back. As her release came, her body tightened around his shaft.

"Christ, Diana," he growled with his own release. "Darlin', you are going to kill me." His arms still around her, he rolled off her.

She gave him a slight smile. "Actually, I think it's the other way around."

He grinned and patted her bottom. "We need to get up and find food. I have to get back to the ranch and the horses."

Diana sat up and brushed the hair from her face. "I'm taking a shower before I go anywhere." She glanced at the heap of clothes on the floor. "Dillon, I have clothes."

"Ah, yeah. I believe you were wearing them last night."

She waved her hand. "No, not those. I have a suitcase in my car. I planned on leaving for Pine Bluff this morning, so I already had a bag packed." She hesitated. "Would you mind getting it for me?"

"You were coming to see me?"

"Yes, well, I thought after breaking off with Trent, leaving for a while would be a good idea."

"Is that the only reason?"

Diana glanced away then back at him. "No. I

missed you."

Dillon gathered her in his arms and kissed her. "I missed you too. I'll take a quick shower, then get your bag. I can also check the roads."

"There's a coffee maker," Diana pointed. "While you shower, I'll make us some." She rose and, searching for something to put on, grabbed his shirt. She rolled up the sleeves and hurried into the bathroom for water. When she glanced in the mirror, Diana's breath caught. The bruise on her face was turning purple. No matter what Trent had done to her, she wouldn't allow him to take her newfound happiness away. There was a sparkle in her eyes that she hadn't seen in a long time. *I don't know where this relationship is going, but if it all falls apart, at least I'll have some amazing memories.*

While she waited on the coffee, she turned the television on. The weather map showed western North Carolina under a snow warning.

"This area isn't used to this kind of storm," the weatherman said. "This blizzard was a fluke and isn't over yet."

Dillon came out of the bathroom, a towel wrapped around his waist. "What is he saying?"

Diana handed him a cup of coffee. "We're in for more snow."

"Damn, Diana, we've got to get to the ranch."

"I'll shower and put on my clothes from last night." Diana placed her extra makeup back in her purse and paused. "What about my car?"

"Hopefully, the roads are somewhat clear, and you can drive it as far as Pine Bluff. I don't think you'll get it up the mountain, but we can leave it in town." He smiled as he took in her appearance. "I like you in my shirt, but I think I'll need it back."

A half-hour later, seeing her car buried in snow, Diana frowned in dismay. "Dillon, what do we do now?"

"Dig it out." He headed to his truck for a shovel. "Why don't you wait in the restaurant."

In no time, Dillon had the snow cleared and joined her inside. "All set. Are you hungry?"

Diana nodded. "Kind of. How about you?"

"Sure. Let's get a quick bite."

After taking their order, the waitress glowered at Dillon.

"Great, people are going to think I gave you that bruise, which looks awful by the way."

"I look too happy for you to have done this."

Dillon snorted but didn't reply.

As they were finishing their waffles, Diana's cell chimed. When she read the text, her eyes narrowed.

"What's wrong?"

"It's from Trent. He stayed in my apartment and wants to know where I am."

"Tell him you're fine and to get out of there."

Diana did as he suggested, and Trent replied immediately.

"What did he say?"

"He said if I don't let him know where I am, he's going to call my parents and say I'm missing. Dillon, that will freak my mother out."

"Give me that," he took the cell from her trembling hands.

"What are you doing?"

"Putting an end to this. He hit call-back. "Trent,

my name is Dillon, and Diana is with me. She's fine, and if you call her parents, she's going to tell the police you punched her and attempted to rape her. So, get the hell out of her apartment and leave her alone. Oh, by the way, if you ever lay a hand on her again, I'm going to beat the fuck out of you." Dillon disconnected and handed her the phone. "Are you ready to go?"

Diana sat, gaping. "Do you realize you threatened him?"

Dillon shrugged. "Bullies like that are only strong when the other person is smaller or weaker than they are. I'm sure he's mad as hell, but he'll get over it."

Diana's cell lit up with another text from Trent.

—*Who the hell are you with!*—

She dropped her phone into her purse and stood.

"I want you to go in front of me," Dillon said as she slid into her car. "Take the Pine Bluff exit, then I'll show you where to park." He frowned. "Are you sure you can drive this car in these conditions?"

"I got this far, didn't I? Besides, I learned to drive in Philadelphia winters."

He studied the little red sports car. "You drove this car in Philly?"

"Um, no. I had a different car. My parents bought me this one for graduation."

"Yeah, well, try and keep it on the road. I'll be right behind you."

Diana rolled her eyes and turned the key in the ignition. I-40 was somewhat plowed, but slushy and slick. Snowflakes drifted past her windshield, As the cars around her kept a slow but steady pace, Diana gripped the steering wheel so tightly her fingers started to cramp. Behind her, Dillon's truck filled her rearview mirror. Before leaving the parking lot, she'd switched on her hands-free cell service. When her cell chimed, she expected to hear Dillon.

"Hello," Diana said.

Trent's angry voice filled the car. "You bitch. Where are you?"

Fear clenched her stomach, and her mouth went dry. Her first instinct was to disconnect the call, but Trent's next words rendered her speechless.

"If you don't think I can track you down, you're mistaken. I found the cowboy shirt you bought your lover, but I don't think he'll be wearing it."

Diana's body trembled. She swallowed a few times before she said, "Trent, get out of my apartment, and leave me alone."

"I'm not a stupid man, Diana," he continued, ignoring what she'd said. "It doesn't take much to put together a cowboy shirt and the fact you went to a ranch with that loudmouth friend of yours. It's obvious you met someone and spent the weekend fucking the bastard. How long do you think it will take me to find out where this ranch is?"

The thought of Trent coming after her and confronting Dillon horrified Diana. "Trent, stay away from me, or I'll contact the police and sign a complaint against you."

Laughter filled the car. "Yeah, try and prove anything. You can tell that bastard lover of yours that nobody takes what's mine."

Diana, unable to listen any longer, ended the call. At the thought of almost marrying such a cruel man, her body shook uncontrollably. When the brake lights of the car in front of her suddenly flashed, Diana slammed her foot on the brake and went into a spin. The sound of screeching tires and metal hitting metal surrounded her as she turned in the direction of the spin. Her head slammed against the side window as she came to a jarring halt in a bank of snow, facing the wrong direction.

Dillon, thankful their exit was ahead, frowned when Diana didn't signal that she was changing lanes. He was about to flash his lights at her, then watched as she lost control of the car. He jerked the steering wheel to the right and drove the truck up and over a mound of snow, stopping inches from her front bumper.

He jumped out of the truck and his ankle gave way. Cursing, he landed on his knees. He used the truck to pull himself onto his feet, leaned against it until the pain subsided, and limped toward Diana. Her blood-streaked face lay against the window. He flung the passenger door open and climbed in.

"Diana, can you hear me?" When she lay still and didn't reply, he grabbed her phone to call 9-1-1 for an ambulance, but sirens could already be heard in the distance. He placed his fingers on her neck feeling for a pulse, and she opened her eyes.

"Dillon?"

"Yeah, darlin', it's me. How bad are you hurt?"

She blinked a few times and looked confused. "What happened?"

"There's been an accident, and you hit your head.

She frowned. "I remember Trent calling me, then—" She paused. "—my car." She frantically glanced around. "Is it wrecked?"

Dillon gritted his teeth. She'd about given him a heart attack, and she was worrying about her damn car.

"I don't know. I'm more concerned about you."

She touched the side of her head. "I'm bleeding."

"Yes, you hit the window. Diana, how old are you?"

She frowned. "Twenty-six, why?"

"Where do you live?"

"Chapel Hill. Dillon, why are you asking me these questions?"

"I need to make sure you're thinking straight."

"There are napkins in the glove box. Will you hand them to me?"

Dillon did as she asked, and Diana held them against her cut. "I think the bleeding is slowing down."

A sheriff's deputy walked up next to Dillon. "Is anyone hurt?"

"My friend hit her head."

The deputy bent down and addressed Diana. "Miss, do you need medical attention?"

"I don't think so."

"Sir, I live near Pine Bluff. That's my truck," Dillon pointed. "I can get her to the clinic fairly quickly. We'll have to leave the car until I find out the extent of the damage."

"Miss, is that all right with you?"

Diana nodded, then winced.

After the deputy left, Dillon helped Diana from the car. She was a little unsteady on her feet and clung to him. "Dillon, please get my purse and bag from the trunk."

"Let me get you to the truck, then I'll come back for the rest."

Tears filled Diana's eyes. "I hope my car is okay."

"For God's sake, Diana, it's only a car that can be

fixed. I'll make arrangements to have it towed to a mechanic I know in Pine Bluff."

A few minutes later, Diana buckled in the passenger seat and her belongings stowed, Dillon drove down the shoulder past the wrecked cars to the off ramp.

"Dillon, I really think I'm fine. Let's deal with my car and go to the ranch."

"Are you sure?"

Diana nodded. "If the bump hasn't gone down by the time we get there, I'll put some ice on it."

"Okay. DT's garage is right ahead. Wait in the car while I talk to him."

They parked, and Dillon headed for the garage. Diana spotted a snow-covered truck parked in the lot which looked a lot like Dillon's. Recalling his hurt ankle, she frowned. Had he been in an accident? He came toward her, obviously favoring his left foot.

"Isn't that your truck?" she pointed as he slid in next to her.

He started the ignition. "Yep."

"Why is it here?"

"The brakes gave out." He drove from the lot.

"What. Where?"

"As I was coming off the mountain."

"Is that how you hurt your foot?"

"No. that happened when I fell from the ladder in the barn."

Diana gritted her teeth. "Dillon, you're making me crazy. Would you please start from the beginning and tell me what's happened?"

"It will be tricky driving up the mountain road. I'll tell you everything when we get to the ranch."

Chapter Twenty-Eight

A half-hour later, after a nerve-racking ride up the mountain, Diana sighed with relief when they stopped in front of Dillon's cabin. "You're not staying in the main house?"

"I like it here better."

Diana grinned. "So do I."

"I'll get you settled, then I have to tend to the horses."

"What about your foot? Let me try and help."

Dillon shook his head. "I'll be all right. Besides, you probably should rest."

"I have a slight headache, that's all."

"Kevin Duffy's been helping me. I'll bet he's already got it done."

"Okay, if you're sure. I would like to clean up and change my clothes."

Dillon nodded and set down her bag. "There's aspirin and clean towels in the bathroom, and my room is the last one on the right."

"Perhaps while you're gone, I can find something for us to eat."

"Good idea. There's stuff in the freezer. If Kevin hasn't been here, I should be an hour or so." He hesitated. "You said something about Trent calling you. What did he say?"

Diana shrugged. "It was nothing."

"I can't imagine it was nothing. What was it?"

She let out a long sigh. "He said some ugly things and threatened to come after me. I told him I'd tell the police what he did to me, and he laughed and said prove it. He had me so upset I wasn't paying attention. That's why I wrecked the car."

Dillon cursed long and hard. "If he calls you again, don't answer. We'll talk more about this when I get back." He kissed her and left.

Diana picked up her bag and headed for the bedroom. In the doorway, she smiled with delight at the spacious room. A maroon comforter lay across a king size maple sleigh bed with a matching dresser, chest of drawers, and nightstands. Thick gray and maroon carpet covered the floor, and sliding glass doors filled one wall. Diana hurried to the sliding doors and was surprised to see a wide deck with a covered hot tub. The snowy landscape, dotted with thickets of tall pines, surrounded the cabin.

She found an empty dresser drawer and hangers in the closet and quickly unpacked. In the adjoining bath, she took a long, hot shower and washed the blood from her hair. She tenderly examined the bruise forming near her temple and sighed. Between her previous bruise and this new one, she looked as if she'd been in a boxing match. She did her best to reapply her makeup, and slipped into jeans and a sweater.

In the kitchen, she poured herself a glass of water and inspected the cupboards and refrigerator. She found a container in the freezer marked spaghetti and smiled in relief. When she'd told Dillon she'd fix something for dinner, she hadn't mentioned how limited her skills were.

By the time Dillon returned, the spaghetti was simmering on the stove, and Diana had managed to light the wood in the fireplace.

"Smells great in here," Dillon said as he took off his coat and boots.

"Thanks to whoever gave you the container of spaghetti."

"That would be Gran. She made sure I wouldn't starve."

"You were gone for a while. I take it that means Kevin didn't help you?"

Dillon shook his head. "He probably couldn't get over here in the snow." He sniffed. "Do I smell coffee?"

"I thought you'd be cold and could use some."

"Could I ever." He grinned. "And you lit the fire. I knew there was a country girl inside you."

Diana rolled her eyes. "Sure, as long as the food only needs to be heated and the fire is already set up."

Dillon kissed her lightly. "It's a start." He took a seat at the table while Diana filled their plates. "Did you hear any more from Trent?"

"No, thank God." She sat across from him. "So, it's your turn. Tell me how you fell from the ladder and why the brakes went out on your truck."

****

Dillon took a few bites of his food while wondering how much he should tell her. Deciding he'd might as well tell it all, he began. When he'd finished, Diana set down her fork and gaped.

"My God, you could have been killed. And you think Martin Patrick is behind it all?"

"I can't be sure, but who else?"

"And you're convinced Kevin can be trusted?"

He let out a long breath. Deep down inside, was he sure? Thinking his friend would try to harm him was too horrible to contemplate. But, still, there was a part of him questioning Kevin's actions. "If not Martin or Kevin, who else is there?"

"What about the person who wants to buy the ranch?"

"That's a possibility. I wish there was a way to find out who it is."

"Do you know any other realtors besides Martin?"

Dillon knitted his brows. "No, but I'll bet Gran does. I'll try and get in touch with her before they leave on their cruise." He picked up his plate and headed for the sink. "I'll help clean up, then let's have a brandy and neck by the fire."

Diana grinned. "I'd love to."

Curled next to Dillon on the couch, Diana sighed in contentment.

His arm around her, his feet propped on the coffee table, Dillon sipped his brandy. "Is your headache gone?" he asked.

She nodded. "I'm fine."

"I was thinking, other than that you're one sexy lady who grew up in Philly and wants to teach, I don't know much about you."

"Funny you should say that. I was thinking the same thing about you. We kind of um…"

"Skipped the getting to know you part and went right to having mind blowing sex," he concluded with a chuckle.

"Ah, yes, I'd say that's about it."

220

"Okay, let's start over. Tell me all about Diana Thompson."

"Well, I collect cranberry glass, so I enjoy rummaging around in antique shops. I like listening to jazz, reading romance novels and murder mysteries. And I love good cheese, chocolate, and coffee ice cream. Fall is my favorite season with leaves crunching beneath my feet and the smell of wood smoke. I remember seeing kids jumping in mounds of leaves after their dad had raked them into the street. I wanted to do that so badly."

"Why didn't you?"

Diana snorted. "My mother would have had a fit if I came home with my clothes covered in dirt and leaves."

Visions of himself and all his cousins rolling down the leaf-covered hills filled Dillon's mind. He would have never thought something so minor would be of such importance to someone else.

"My secret passion is decorating for Christmas," Diana continued. "We didn't have much in the way of decorations in my house. My mother didn't want to take the time or deal with the mess. We always had an artificial tree, and a nativity scene on the mantel, and a floral arrangement on the dining room table. When I have my own house, I'm going to decorate every room."

Dillon kissed the top of her head. "Gran would like hearing that. She'd be right along with you."

"Really, that's great. I'll bet her house looks incredible during the holidays. Okay, it's your turn. Other than riding, what interests you?"

Dillon chuckled. "Mine are a little different. I like

hiking and camping in the mountains, and fishing while the sun rises, listening to country music, and pickup trucks. I read old Louis L'Amour westerns, and my favorite foods are chili dogs, thick steaks, and Gran's apple pie."

Diana grinned up at him. "I like apple pie."

"There you go. We're a perfect match."

Diana laughed. "They say opposites attract." She cocked her head. "The only rodeos I've seen are on TV. Have you ever been hurt?"

Stew's body slamming into the side of the chute flashed in Dillon's mind, and he swallowed hard. "I've been banged up a little, but a good friend of mine was hurt pretty bad."

"I'm so sorry. What happened?"

Dillon exhaled a long sigh. "I got kicked by a calf and couldn't do my next ride. Stew went in my place, and the horse bucked him off. He injured his back and can't ride anymore. The last I talked to him, he was heading home to Oklahoma and his family's ranch."

Diana placed her hand on his cheek. "I can tell by your voice you blame yourself, but it's not your fault."

"Yeah, well, it should have been me on the horse, not Stew."

"Does Stew blame you?"

"No. He said we all know the dangers in riding. But that doesn't change the fact Stew got hurt, not me. I'm beginning to think my grandparents' retirement came at the perfect time. Being home and running the ranch feels right." He chuckled slightly. "Except for the financial aspect. Bookkeeping is not something I do well."

"I love math," Diana said with a grin. "And I'm an

excellent bookkeeper."

"Is that right? Well, you might have to teach me, but first…" He pressed her down on the couch. "I think for the time being, we've gotten to know one another well enough. Let's jump back to what we really have in common."

"What's that?"

He kissed her. "Sex."

In the morning, Dillon awoke with Diana curled next to him. He spent a few minutes watching her sleep. Was their relationship moving too quickly? Probably, but even though their backgrounds were about as different as one could get, he had no desire to slow things down. Now that he had the responsibility of running the ranch, if their relationship was to go forward, she'd have to live in his world. Could she leave the city for life in the country? Deep in his heart, he hoped the answer was yes. He brushed her hair from her cheek and lightly kissed her. He'd go do his chores, then, if he was lucky, she'd still be in bed when he got back.

He dressed, grabbed a cup of coffee, and headed out the door. Snow had fallen through the night, and the landscape had the serene beauty of a Christmas card. He sank knee-deep as he made his way across the yard, thankful the truck had four-wheel drive. An hour or so later, he'd finished with his chores in the barn. About to climb back into the truck, a dark shape, half buried in snow on the other side of the corral, caught his eye. A dead animal? Curious, he headed toward the form. As he got closer, shock clenched at his chest.

Dillon hurried as quickly as he could through the deep snow. "Christ all mighty," he cried as he fell to his knees next to the body of Kevin Duffy. Kevin lay on his side, blood soaking the front of his parka.

Dillon felt for a pulse, but knew it was too late. Unspeakable rage pumped through him. "I'll find you, whoever you are, and God help you when I do," he yelled into the quiet morning. His first instinct was to get his friend's body out of the snow, but he knew better than to move him. On trembling legs, he made his way to his truck to call Sheriff Dunn.

As he waited for the sheriff, guilt and remorse fought for first place in his mind. How could he have ever doubted Kevin's friendship? Had the shooter mistaken Kevin for him? Was he shot this morning? He wasn't sure how much more snow had fallen during the night. What if he'd been there last night and Dillon hadn't seen him? If so, could he have saved him? "Fuck." Dillon punched his gloved hand against the side of the truck, then winced in pain.

This was all his fault. If he hadn't let Kevin help him out, he'd still be alive. He glanced over at his friend's body and whispered, "Buddy, I promise I'll find the bastard who did this to you." His eye caught the front of a snowmobile parked next to a tree. Kevin must have driven it instead of his truck. Then another thought struck him—Bonnie. Had she reported Kevin missing? He sighed in relief when he heard vehicles coming up the road.

After Dillon explained to the Sheriff how he'd found Kevin, and the paramedics removed his body, Dillon expressed his concern about telling Bonnie.

"I called the ranch house, but she didn't answer," Sheriff Dunn said. "I'll drive over there when I leave here."

"If this happened last night, wouldn't she have reported if he hadn't come home?"

"You would think. But perhaps she's out of town. Did Kevin mention to you that she might be leaving?"

"No, he didn't say anything about Bonnie. Paul, I'm afraid whoever did this thought it was me."

Paul nodded. "I was thinking the same thing. We'll search the area for any tracks the shooter made, but in this damn snow, it will be practically impossible." He cocked his head. "Did you talk to Martin Patrick yesterday?"

Dillon nodded.

"And?"

"I told him the ranch wasn't for sale and to leave me alone."

"That's all?"

"Pretty much."

"Did you threaten him?"

"Not really."

Paul snorted. "I'll bet. Well, I plan on having a talk with him myself."

"Hopefully you can get him to tell you who this mysterious buyer is. Because other than Martin, who else could the shooter be?"

Paul glanced to where his men were searching the snow for evidence, then back to Dillon. "I suppose you wouldn't consider leaving for a time while we try and find this person?"

"I can't. Who would take care of the horses?"

"Doesn't Chet have Hank O'Shay come in and help?"

"Only when the cabins are open to guests.

"So, call him and see if he can come."

Dillon shook his head. "I wouldn't be able to relax worrying about the ranch. What if this nut decides to set the barn on fire or one of the cabins?"

Paul sighed. "Did you ever think the ranch has nothing to do with any of this? Is there anyone else who would want you dead?"

Tonya's face swam before Dillon's eyes, but he shoved it away. He didn't think she could find her way to the ranch, let alone kill him. But she could hire it done. No. She was pissed at him, but want him dead? That would get her nothing.

Paul patted Dillon's shoulder. "Go home and let us deal with this. I'm going to see if I can find Bonnie."

Dillon left the sheriff's men combing the area around the barn and corral and headed to his cabin. When he entered, Diana was in the kitchen wearing a robe, her hair in a towel.

"Good morning," she said. "I put coffee on and was about to get dressed."

Dillon hung his hat and coat by the door and sat in a stool by the counter.

"What's wrong?" Diana asked as she placed coffee before him. "Did something else happen?"

Dillon ran his hands over his face and let out a long sigh. "I found Kevin shot dead next to the corral."

Diana stopped with her cup halfway to her mouth. "What? How?"

He told her the little he knew. "I don't know if he was lying there last night and I didn't see him. I was focused on the horses and getting back here. I should have realized something was wrong when I didn't hear from him. Even if he couldn't come, he would have called. The thought of him dying out there in the snow when maybe I could have helped him sickens me."

With tears in her eyes, Diana rounded the counter and held him. "You can't think like that. Even if he was there, it was probably already too late." She leaned her head on his shoulder. "I'm scared someone's going to kill you next."

He kissed her lightly. "I'll be careful."

"Could it honestly be someone who wants the ranch this badly?"

Dillon held her close and stroked her hair. "I can't come up with any other motive for all this. But, trust me, we'll catch the bastard. I feel I should go to the Duffy ranch and see how Bonnie is doing."

"I met Bonnie in a café when I went shopping with your cousins after Thanksgiving. I'd like to go with you."

"Sure, I'd appreciate that. Bonnie's family has been here on the mountain about as long as mine. She was an only child, and she grew up with us."

Diana kissed his cheek. "I'll be ready as quick as I can."

Halfway up the mountain the road forked, to the right the Lazy M and to the left, the Duffy property. Dillon drove into the yard in front of Kevin and Bonnie's log house. Before stepping from his truck, he spotted the Sheriff's car parked next to a new BMW. "That must be Bonnie's car, I can't see Kevin driving a sports car. I'm glad Paul is here, and it wasn't up to me to tell her about Kevin."

Diana placed her hand on his arm. "I'm sure she'll be glad you've come."

Chapter Twenty-Nine

They crossed the porch, and before Dillon could knock on the door, it swung open and Bonnie threw herself in Dillon's arms.

With tears streaming down her face, she cried, "Oh, God, Dillon, who would have done this?"

Dillon held her tight, and tears filled his own eyes. "Bonnie, I'm so sorry." He gently disengaged her arms from around him and led her into the house.

Paul was seated on the couch and he rose. "Now that you're here, I'll go. Bonnie's called some friends, and they're on their way. Thankfully, the sun is out, and the snow is beginning to thaw. The plows should be out and the roads somewhat clear."

Dillon nodded and helped Bonnie into a chair. "Paul, this is Diana Thompson. We'll stay until someone gets here."

Paul shook Diana's hand, told Bonnie again how sorry he was, and left.

Diana crossed to where Bonnie sat. "Bonnie, I'm so sorry for your loss."

Bonnie clung to Dillon's hand and whispered, "Thanks."

Surprise filled Bonnie's eyes, as she glanced from Diana to Dillon. Then dismissing Diana, Bonnie stared up at Dillon. "I didn't know Kevin was missing. I had one of my migraines yesterday and took my medication. It knocks me out, and it wasn't until Sheriff Dunn came to tell me what had happened that I realized he hadn't been here all night.

"Was he here when you took your pills?" Dillon asked.

"No, he left to deal with our horses, then he said he was going to see about yours. My headache was so bad yesterday, I hardly remember what happened." Her voice broke on a sob. "None of this makes sense to me. Kevin was a good man who wouldn't have hurt anyone."

Dillon knelt in front of Bonnie's chair and took her hands in his. "Bonnie, I'm so sorry. I have a horrible feeling the shooter thought Kevin was me."

Bonnie sniffed back her tears. "Why?"

Dillon explained and horror filled her eyes. "You're telling me you think someone is trying to kill you over the ranch? Martin must be crazy to think Chet would sell the Lazy M. Do you have any idea who this person might be?"

Dillon hesitated. "All I know is they want to remain anonymous. You haven't heard anything, have you?"

She shook her head, then wrapped her arms around Dillon's neck and cried, "Dillon, I lost Kevin. I can't lose you too."

Diana, feeling like an intruder, quietly stepped away. She stood near the door debating whether she should wait outside. She glanced back to see Bonnie's face buried in Dillon's neck. She understood Bonnie was devastated with grief, but the sight of another woman in Dillon's arms made her slip quickly through the door onto the porch.

Diana breathed in the cool clear air and told herself Dillon was only comforting her. The sound of a vehicle coming up the road turned her attention from Dillon and Bonnie. A mail truck stopped and a forty-something woman got out.

"Hello."

"Hello," Diana greeted her.

The woman smiled as she came toward her. "I'm late, but I'm finally here." She handed Diana the mail. "Mother nature sure put us to the test. We're supposed to deliver the mail no matter what."

Diana smiled back. "I don't think that means driving up a mountain in two feet of snow."

The woman laughed and headed for her truck. She'd no sooner left than a car pulled in. This time two women got out, one tall with auburn hair, the other a short blonde.

Curiosity showed on their faces as they stepped onto the porch. "Hello, I'm Janis, and this is Sue. We're friends of Bonnie's."

"I'm Diana." She hesitated. "A friend of Dillon's. He's in with Bonnie."

"This is too awful to be believed," Janis said.

"How's Bonnie?" Sue asked.

"She's pretty distraught," Diana replied. "We've been waiting for someone to come stay with her."

"We're planning on spending the night," Janis said.

Diana nodded. "I'm sure she'll appreciate that."

Sue gestured to the mail in Diana's hand. "Can we take that in for you?"

Forgetting what she held, Diana glanced down. "Oh, sorry, the mail lady just left. Please tell Dillon I'll wait out here for him."

A while later, when Dillon closed the door and turned to Diana, the strain of the day showed in his eyes.

"Sorry, I didn't mean to stay so long," he said. "I didn't know how to comfort Bonnie. Because of me her husband is dead."

The anguish in his voice broke Diana's heart. "Dillon, you don't know that for sure. Perhaps Kevin knew something and was on his way to tell you. Come on." She took his hand and led him toward his truck. "Let's go home. I'll fix something to eat, and we can think this through."

Dillon nodded. "I do want to discuss a concern I have, but I'm not up to eating anything."

He was quiet on the short drive back to the cabin. Diana had an uneasy feeling she wasn't going to like what he wanted to discuss.

"I'll light the fire if you get us some coffee," Dillon said, taking off his coat. "Or if you're hungry, we can wait until after you eat."

Diana, becoming more nervous by the minute, knew she wouldn't be able to eat until he told her what was on his mind. "No, I'll wait. I'll get the coffee."

When she returned from the kitchen with two mugs, Dillon was seated on the couch, a crackling fire blazing.

"Thanks," he said, taking the mug from her.

Diana sat next to him, sipped her coffee, and waited.

Dillon let out a long breath, set his cup on the coffee table, and turned to her. "Diana, I think for the time being, you should go back to Chapel Hill. I'm afraid if you stay, you might get hurt."

Diana determinedly shook her head. "I'm not leaving you here alone. Besides, Trent is there. I don't want to confront him alone."

"Can't you stay with Jenn?"

"She's away on hotel business. I have no idea when she'll be home. She doesn't even know I'm here."

"I'm sure you have other friends."

"Dillon, most of them know Trent. I don't want to put them in the middle of this. My other friends are married and are preparing for the holidays." She blinked away her tears. "But if you insist, I'll leave."

He held her in his arms. "It's not that I want you to go. I couldn't live with myself if something happened to you. I already have one death on my conscience."

Exasperated, Diana sat up and faced him. "Dillon, until you know why Kevin was shot, you have to stop blaming yourself. As for me, I'd like to stay right here and take my chances. I honestly don't think I'm in any danger. No one even knows who I am."

"They know you're with me. That might be all it takes. What if they use you to get to me?"

"Do you honestly believe someone wants this ranch bad enough to do something like that?"

Dillon rose and paced the floor. "So far, they've shot at me, cut the rung on the ladder, messed with the brakes on my truck, and murdered Kevin. Yes, Diana, I think someone is crazy enough to do something like that."

"Perhaps we should both go somewhere."

"I can't leave the horses. I wouldn't put it past this bastard to harm them."

Diana gnawed on her bottom lip. "Dillon, I'm

honestly terrified to go home. And I also don't want to go to my parents. I'm not ready to deal with my mother."

Dillon ran his hands through his hair. "If you stay, you have to promise me you'll do exactly as I say. You cannot leave the cabin without me."

Diana rose and wrapped her arms around him. "I promise." She drew his face to hers and kissed him.

He held her close and kissed her with a fevered intensity.

On the floor in front of the fireplace lay a wide, thick rug. One minute Diana was standing in Dillon's arms, the next she lay on her back next to him.

"I've fantasized about making love to you right here, and now I have you where I want you." He leaned close and ran kisses along her cheek and neck.

A thrill of desire skimmed across her body.

He lifted her sweater over her head. "The bad thing about winter is wearing too many clothes."

"I agree." She unbuttoned his flannel shirt.

Soon they were both naked, the glow from the fire warming them. The love Diana felt for this man almost took her breath away. For the first time in her life, she'd met someone who fulfilled her both sexually and emotionally. The more she was with him, the more her structured restraints slipped away. She smiled to herself. Like lying naked in front of a fire in the middle of the afternoon.

Dillon pulled her on top of him and she lay in contented bliss. He stroked her back while she buried her face in his chest. She loved the fresh outdoor smell of him. "What cologne do you wear?"

Dillon chuckled. "I'm sure you've never heard of

it. I started wearing it in high school and haven't stopped."

Diana ran her fingers through his chest hair. "I like it.

He squeezed her bare bottom. "I like the smell of you too."

Diana gazed into his face and gave him a mischievous grin. She rose and straddled him.

Dillon arched one brow. "And what do you think you're doing?"

"I'm going to ride a cowboy." She lowered herself onto his shaft and eased herself down. She pressed her palms on his chest and began to move her body. Their eyes locked, Dillon cupped her bottom as she slid over him.

The pure lust in his eyes emboldened Diana. She brought her moist heat to the tip of his shaft, then stopped. When he groaned aloud, she smiled to herself as she slowly eased him back inside her. She repeated this, but as her own body reacted to the feel of him, she increased her pace.

Her climax building, Diana arched her back as Dillon thrust upward.

As the ripples of her release eased, Diana lay upon his chest, content and exhausted.

Dillon ran his hand down her back. "Darlin', that being your first ride, you deserve a silver buckle."

Diana laughed. "I'll have to try for the gold next time."

"Practice makes perfect." He glanced at the fireplace. "I need to put more wood on before we freeze."

Diana sat up and reached for her clothes when her

phone began to play a jazz tune. "Dillon, what if it's Trent?"

Dillon slipped into his jeans and handed her his shirt. "Answer it. If he gets mean, give me the phone."

Diana slipped her arms into the shirt and grabbed her phone from the table. "Damn, it's my mother." She took a calming breath and said, "Hello, Mother."

"Diana, where are you and what is going on?"

"What do you mean?"

"What I mean is I just received a disturbing call from Judith Sawyer, informing me you've called off the wedding and have gone off to the mountains with some cowboy who Judith says is vulgar and uncouth."

Diana let out a long sigh. "Mother, I'm sorry you had to hear about this from Judith. I was going to call you, but things became complicated."

"Complicated, Diana? What are you talking about? Is what I've been told true?"

"Somewhat. I did call off the wedding, and I am in the mountains, but Dillon isn't vulgar or uncouth."

"Diana, you aren't making any sense. Where exactly are you? Who is this Dillon, and how did you meet him?"

"I'm in Pine Bluff. Dillon is Jenn's cousin, and I met him when I came here for Thanksgiving. He's a rodeo rider, but now he's managing his grandparents' ranch." Diana held her breath at the silence on the other end of the phone.

"Diana, do you need medical attention? I'm sure your father knows a good psychiatrist from the club."

Diana's mouth formed a thin line. "No, I don't need to see a doctor. I realized I don't love Trent enough to spend my life with him. That's all."

"I'm trying to understand, but, Diana, you're not making it easy. After all your time with Trent and the wedding preparations, how could you suddenly discover this."

"Mother, I've been having doubts for a while. As far as wedding preparations, I'll take care of the necessary cancelations and returning the gifts."

"You do know how devastated Trent is. According to Judith, he was so upset, he wasn't watching where he was going and fell. He has a huge lump on his head and scratches on his face."

Diana gritted her teeth. Should she tell her mother the truth? While she was undecided, her mother continued. "Think about what you're doing. You're hurting a good man for what is probably just a fling. I suggest you go home and talk this out with Trent."

Visions of Trent trying to force himself on her floated before her eyes, and her blood boiled. "Mother, the night I broke it off with Trent, he punched me in the face and tried to rape me. He physically hurt me, and if I hadn't gotten away, hard telling what he would have done. The lump on his head is from me hitting him with a vase, and the scratches on his face are from me. So, no, I have no intentions of talking anything through with that man."

Again, silence filled the phone. Finally, in a low voice her mother said, "Diana, you've never been one to exaggerate, so I have to believe you. If he actually hurt you, I don't want you anywhere near him. Tell me, are you injured badly?"

"No. I'm bruised, but okay. Mother, again, I'm sorry I didn't call you sooner, but I was so upset all I wanted to do was get away from Chapel Hill. Trent called me and threatened me, and it sounds as if he's ransacked my apartment. I can't get back until the snow clears, then Dillon is going to drive me so I can see what damage has been done."

"Diana, I have to admit I'm having a hard time taking all this in. I would have never believed Trent would be capable of violence, nor would I have believed you would run to a man you hardly knew. Why didn't you call us and come home?"

Diana closed her eyes praying this conversation would soon end. "At the time I didn't want to have to explain. All I wanted to do was get as far away from Trent as possible."

"How long are you planning on being there?"

"I don't know. I can't leave until the roads are clear."

"Diana, what am I supposed to tell people when they mention the wedding?"

"Say that all you know is that it's been canceled. I'll take care of sending notes to those invited. And Mother, don't take any more calls from Judith. I'll take care of that as well."

"Diana, I have a splitting headache. Please keep me informed of where you are, and what is happening."

"I will."

After disconnecting the call, Diana rubbed her temples. Her own head was pounding.

"That bad?" Dillon asked.

Diana raised her hands and let them fall, then relayed her conversation. "Trent, the little weasel, has lied and made my mother frantic. I need to get to my apartment and pick up my lists. The sooner I start the cancelations the better."

"I've been thinking about that. I'm going to call Hank O'Shay and see if he can take care of the horses for me. He's been working for my grandparents for years, and he's trustworthy. We'll leave early in the morning so we can drive back the same day."

"Sounds good." She hesitated. "Do you think Hank will be safe?"

"He hunts and is good with a rifle. He won't let anyone harm the horses." He stepped to the fireplace and jabbed the poker at the wood. "This has to stop. We have to find out who is doing this."

"Besides Martin, do you have any other suspects?"

"The mysterious buyer. Other than those two, nope." He placed the poker in the stand and helped her up. "Let's find something to eat, then watch a movie and try to think about something else for a while."

Chapter Thirty

The next morning, the sun had barely risen as they drove off the mountain. They stopped at DT's garage to check on their vehicles. Finding his truck ready, they decided to take it instead of the ranch truck. A little over five hours later, they were at Diana's apartment building.

Diana's hand trembled slightly as she placed her key in the lock. When she stepped into her living room, she let out a tiny scream.

"Son-of-a-bitch," Dillon murmured as they took in the destruction. "We shouldn't touch anything. You need to call the police."

Diana stood frozen, staring at the broken crystal, smashed dishes, and overturned furniture. Like a zombie, she stepped over the destruction and made her way to her bedroom. A sob caught in her throat at the sight of the ripped open Christmas packages, their contents sliced and torn.

Dillon came up behind her and wrapped his arms around her waist. "Did he destroy anything that can't be replaced?"

She glanced to where her jewelry box sat upon her dresser as she had left it. "I suppose he had some compassion left."

Dillon snorted. "I doubt it. He probably figured

you wouldn't press charges if he didn't destroy anything too costly or sentimental."

"My antique glass," she cried and headed back into the living room and the curio cabinet which held her collection of cranberry glass. She sagged against Dillon when she discovered it was untouched. "I don't understand how I could be fooled into believing he was a good, decent man. I feel like such an idiot."

Dillon kissed the top of her head. "That's because you're a trusting person he took advantage of."

"Like Tonya did you. Do we have chump tattooed across our foreheads?"

Dillon gave her a slight smile. "Not anymore."

She picked up the shirt and vest she'd bought Dillon. "I was so excited when I found these for you. I should have packed them in the car with my clothes."

****

The tears running down Diana's face made Dillon's blood boil. If he ever got his hands on Trent, he'd beat him to a pulp. Dillon held what was left of the western shirt. "They were perfect. Thank you."

Anger replaced her tears. "If I was a spiteful person, I'd sell my engagement ring to replace what he destroyed."

Dillon grinned. "I would."

"No, I won't give him the satisfaction of telling everyone I wouldn't give his expensive ring back. Besides, if I were honest, I never really liked it. And I'm not calling the police. I don't want to have anything to do with him."

"I don't blame you. Let's get started cleaning this up so we can head home."

A slight smile touched her lips. "Home. I like the

sound of that."

Gazing into her pretty face, Dillon knew he liked the sound of it as well.

Diana let out a long breath. "Okay, if you wouldn't mind sweeping up the broken glass, I'll start in here."

Dillon nodded. "You get some trash bags and I'll take pictures. I think we need to have proof of what he did."

"Good idea. Then let him call me a liar." On her way through the living room she stopped. "Oh, my God, Dillon, where's my laptop?" Frantically she raced from room to room. "I was going to bring it with me to the ranch, but I didn't have time to grab it. Dillon, all my financial and personal information is on it, not to mention wedding lists."

"Where did you have it last?"

"Let me think." She hurried to a small closet next to the front door. Flinging the door open, she sighed in relief. "I found it. I left it here with my heavy winter coat so I wouldn't forget it."

A couple of hours later, Dillon tossed the last trash bag into the dumpster while Diana placed another suitcase of clothes in the truck.

"Do you have the ring?" Dillon asked.

Diana held out a wrapped package. "We need to stop by the post office. I included a note explaining I took pictures of my apartment, and if he bothers me again, I'll take them to the police. I also told him I kept items which would have his fingerprints on them. Hopefully that will be enough to keep him out of my life."

"I would have put down in detail what he could do with the ring, but you're a nicer person than me."

As they drove away from the condo complex, neither noticed the black sports car parked at the far end of the lot.

****

On the long ride back, Diana decided to use the time to check her email and get started on undoing wedding preparations. She turned on her laptop and scrolled through her collected email. One from Trent's best friend's wife caught her attention. "Private" was written in the subject line. Dianna clicked it open.

"Diana, I found this while searching Ted's email for a lost message from his mother. I debated sending this to you, but decided if it were me, I'd want to know. I'm sorry."

"Bastard," Diana shouted at the image of Trent, his arm around some woman, the Rocky Mountains in the background.

"What is it?" Dillon asked.

For a minute, Diana was so angry she couldn't speak. She took a calming breath and read him the email.

"Christ, 'bastard' is right. All the time you tore yourself up over hurting him, and he was in Aspen fucking some ski bunny."

Diana winced at the mental image Dillon's words conjured, but he was right. She'd practically made herself sick with guilt over her feelings for Dillon and for breaking the engagement. She balled her hands into fists. If Trent was here right now, she'd strangle him. She gritted her teeth. "Err." How dare the hypocrite treat her the way he did when all the time he'd been cheating on her.

"By your expression, I'd say Trent's lucky he's not

within reach."

Diana's eyes blazed. "I don't think I've ever been this angry. Yes, what we did was wrong, but I broke the engagement. He had no intention of doing so. He would have married me and probably cheated on me."

Dillon squeezed her hand. "He's out of your life. Let it go. As for me, hopefully Tonya will soon be out of mine."

"You've spoken with her?"

Dillon scowled. "Unfortunately." He shook his head. "I don't understand how someone can change their personality like Tonya did. She'd make a good con artist."

"I suppose the same could be said of Trent. You know, Jenn never liked him. She told me something about him was off. Boy, was she right."

Dillon exited off I-40 onto the Pine Bluff ramp. "How about we stop at the IGA and pick up a couple of steaks, go home, and grill them, then soak in the hot tub. I'll even try and get you some fancy cheese and chocolate."

Diana smiled. "That sounds like a perfect way to end a lousy day."

Later, beneath a star-studded sky, wine glass in hand, Diana sighed as the hot, bubbly water surrounded her. She desperately wanted to push the events of the last few days from her mind, but visions of the destruction in her apartment kept creeping back. The one truth which made her stomach turn to knots was that if she hadn't met Dillon, chances are, even with her misgivings, she would have gone through with her marriage to Trent. Just the idea made her skin crawl. How long would it have taken before Trent's true nature would have reared its ugly head? She never really thought that much about fate, but now she truly believed she was meant to come to Pine Bluff and meet Dillon.

Was she in love with him? Or, was she in love with the newness of him and a lifestyle she found more and more alluring? The simplicity of the ranch and small town life, as opposed to prestigious gatherings, social standings, and proper decorum, which weren't all that important to her anyway. She'd always done what was expected, but now realized that deep inside another part of her was screaming for release. Could she ever go back to her old life? Could she give up a professorship to teach at a rural school?

Diana stared up into the night sky just as a shooting star blazed past. Without hesitation, she made her wish, for Dillon to love her as much as she loved him. For she did love him. And more than anything, she wanted to stay right here and make a life with him, which couldn't happen until they discovered who was behind the threat to Dillon. Diana closed her eyes and sank deeper in the soothing water. She wasn't one to run from a problem, but right now, she wished they could lock the doors and hide away here in the cabin until this was all over.

"You look content," Dillon said, stepping into the hot tub.

Diana opened her eyes to see his naked form sink beneath the surface. God, just the sight of him stirred her desire. She smiled. "This is wonderful. I love being in a hot tub in the snow."

"So do I." He gave her the grin that curled her toes. "Especially when I'm with a beautiful naked woman."

I wonder how many that's been, she thought, then

quickly pushed it away. "I have a confession to make."

"What's that?"

"I've never been in a hot tub without a bathing suit."

His grin widened. "Darlin', are you telling me you've never made love in one either?"

She took a long sip of her wine. "No."

"Well, I think we can do something about that." He took her empty wine glass and placed it on the side of the tub, then reached for her. "Come here."

Diana slowly glided through the water into his arms. The sexual promise in his eyes already had her body at fever pitch. She lay across his lap as his mouth closed over hers. His kiss was tender as his hands slid up her back. He cupped her breast, then ran his thumbs gently across her pink nipples.

Diana arched her back as his mouth closed over one of the swollen tips. A familiar ache blossomed between her legs as he sucked one nipple, then the other.

His mouth left her breast and began a slow descent. As his lips moved down her body, he lifted her from the water, until she was on her knees straddling his lap. "Can you float?"

Lust muddling her brain, she nodded.

"Lay back in the water."

She did as he asked. "Dillon, what are you doing?"

"This." He spread her legs and cupped her bottom. With the warm water surrounding them, he brought his mouth down on her.

"Oh, sweet heaven," Diana cried, as Dillon made love to her with his tongue, his mouth driving her mindless with sweet ecstasy. When her climax burst through her, spasms of the most glorious sensation Diana had ever experienced left her dazed and breathless.

****

Dillon, his own climax bursting for release, watched Diana as she floated, her hair fanned out in the water, the tips of her breasts peaking above the bubbles, and her sweet hot womanhood open to him. He didn't think he'd ever seen anything so erotic in his life.

The pleasure on her face with her climax built the need in him to watch her come over and over again.

He took her hands and guided her toward him. She rose into his arms and smiled.

"I have to say, that's definitely a first for me."

"Darlin', it's not over yet." He placed her over his lap and lowered her onto his throbbing shaft. The feel of her warm, slick heat surrounded him. Dillon gritted his teeth to keep from coming. He wanted to bring her pleasure one more time.

Diana dug her fingers into his shoulders as she moved up and down with the rhythm of his thrusts.

She arched her back, giving him access to her breasts. He licked her nipple as his hips moved faster.

She tightened around him with her release. "Oh, yeah, darlin'," he rasped as he poured himself into her.

Diana collapsed into his arms, his shaft still inside her. "I've never experienced anything like that in my life," she said breathlessly.

Out of breath himself, Dillon chuckled. "Darlin', I want to make you say that over and over again."

She grinned. "You already have a good start. She turned so she was lying between Dillon's legs, her back against his chest, his arms holding her tight.

Sparkles from a quarter moon danced upon the water. Diana sighed in total contentment. "Dillon, do you believe in fate?"

"Hmm," came his sleepy reply.

"Fate," she continued. "I was thinking earlier about the timing of our meeting. If I hadn't shared with Jenn my doubts about marrying Trent, most likely she wouldn't have invited me to come with her. Who knows, I might have ignored my misgivings and married him anyway." At this thought a shiver went through her and Dillon held her even tighter.

"And if my friend Stew hadn't finally gotten up the courage to tell me about Tonya, she'd still be making a fool of me," Dillon replied. "Who knows, if Stew hadn't had his accident, would I have quit the rodeo and taken over the Lazy M?"

Diana nodded her head. "Yes, this is exactly what I mean. It all fell into place."

"True, but we still have a few problems," Dillon said with a sigh. "Tonya, Kevin's death, and the fact someone wants the ranch bad enough to kill me, or cause me serious bodily harm."

"Yes, well, there is that."

He kissed the top of her head. "Which means if fate is truly on our side, Tonya will go away, Kevin's killer will be caught, and we'll discover who's after me." He lifted her from the water and headed for the bedroom. "For now, I think we should help fate along."

****

Eyes burning with hatred in a face hard as stone watched Dillon close the sliding door and pull the curtain closed. *Enjoy her while you can.* The shadowy figure blended into the night and disappeared.

Chapter Thirty-One

Tonya Harper McCoy drove out of the Asheville regional airport and headed for Pine Bluff. The woman working the rental car counter had said she shouldn't have any trouble finding the B&B she booked in town. Tonya glanced into the rear-view mirror and smirked. *Dillon certainly will be surprised to see me. Especially if he's got some tramp at the ranch with him.* Well, she was still his wife, and she wasn't about to hand him over to another woman. Her mama had always told her, a girl had to do what a girl had to do, so here she was going to reclaim her man.

All it would take was a few blow jobs and some hot sex and Dillon would want her back. When Dillon told her he was staying in North Carolina, she couldn't believe her ears. Dillon McCoy would never give up the rodeo circuit unless it was for something he cared for more than riding, and that would only be the ranch. If she was right, he was staying in order to take over the Lazy M. His grandparents were old, so it would make sense for them to turn it all over to Dillon.

Living in the middle of Hicksville wasn't the life she'd imagined, but as long as she could get away to Dallas or Vegas, she could adjust. She'd had just enough money to cover a one-way ticket, the rental car, and a couple of nights at a B&B, with a little left over for food.

She took the exit to Pine Bluff and soon found the large Victorian home which was now the Crabapple Bed and Breakfast.

Tonya rolled her eyes as she took in the decorative gingerbread trim, the wide porch scattered with rocking chairs, and a plaster bear wearing a Santa suit. She snorted. Quaint was not in her vocabulary. On the flight from Dallas, she'd been planning how she'd redecorate the ranch house as soon as it belonged to her and Dillon. Gone would be all that country cozy furniture. She'd replace it with new modern pieces.

As she entered through the glass-paneled front door, Tonya made sure to give Mrs. Potter, the plump, dimple-cheeked proprietor, her friendliest smile.

"Hello, I'm Tonya…" She didn't want anyone in town to know who she was until she had a chance to confront Dillon. "Harper. I have a reservation."

"Oh, yes, Miss Harper, I've been expecting you. I hope you didn't have any trouble finding us."

"No, not at all."

"Wonderful. I've put you in one of our front rooms so you'll have a nice view. Tomorrow is our winter festival parade, and they do pass by right out front. You'll not want to miss it." Mrs. Potter smiled. "In our community hall, we'll have all kinds of baked goods for sale, and my apple butter has won prizes." She patted the neat bun of snow-white hair clipped on top of her head.

Oh, goody, Tonya thought. Aloud she said, "That sounds great. I can't wait. Tell me, where would be a good place to have dinner?"

Mrs. Potter pursed her lips. "Let me see. There's

the diner. Sylvia makes a wonderful meatloaf. And there's also fast food places off the highway. Oh, and there's Kittie's Kitchen. Her pot roast isn't too bad."

Tonya internally groaned. *I'll have to drive back to Ashville to get something decent to eat.* "What about a nice steak?"

Mrs. Potter frowned. "Well, there's the Stag's Head. But, miss, I have to warn you, a young girl like you shouldn't go to a place like that alone. I understand it can become pretty rowdy."

Tonya's gloom lifted. *Hot damn.* The Stag's Head sounded like her kind of place. "Thank you, Mrs. Potter, for your concern, but I'll be fine."

"I suppose if you go early enough. Here's your room key and the key to the front door. I sleep right off the entry here, so if you need me, please don't hesitate to come and get me. Breakfast is on the table at eight. There's water in your room and a one cup coffee maker."

Tonya hesitated. She needed to find out as much as she could about Dillon and what was happening before confronting him. "I was wondering, Mrs. Potter, if you know the McCoys?"

"Why yes. Ada is in my quilting group. She and Chet left for Florida and a cruise. She was so excited, she could hardly wait to leave. Why do you ask?"

"I had a friend from around here who married someone named McCoy."

Again Mrs. Potter pursed her lips. "Now I don't know who that would be. Dillon is the only McCoy to marry, and that was some woman out west. But he's back, and according to Ada he's getting a divorce. Ada didn't want to talk about it, but she didn't seem too upset over the breakup." She lowered her voice. "I also heard he's got some woman up at the ranch with him." She cleared her throat. "But that's none of my concern. What did you say your friend's name was, dear?"

"Oh, it's Jennifer. Perhaps she's from closer to Asheville." Tonya picked up her bag, thanked Mrs. Potter, and headed up the stairs. She'd change and go get that steak. Now that she knew for sure Dillon was cheating on her, she'd plan her next move.

Tonya parked at the Stag's Head next to a black sports car. *I'd surely like to meet whoever's driving this pretty machine.* She ran her finger along the smooth paint. Crossing the gravel parking lot, she tossed her long curls over her shoulder and stepped through the door.

The band was playing a Waylon Jennings tune, and the dance floor was hopping. She found an empty stool at the bar and glanced around. If she played it right, she'd have a nice steak dinner and it wouldn't cost her a dime.

****

Trent Sawyer spotted the hot blonde as she stepped through the door and thought the night might not be a loss after all. She wore low boots with spiked heels, skintight black jeans riding low on her hips, and a sweater which showed off her great tits.

Earlier, he'd followed Diana and that bastard from Chapel Hill to this podunk town and lost them when they turned up a mountain road. While talking to some guys sitting around the bar, he'd discovered the road led up to the Lazy M Ranch owned by a family named McCoy. Dillon McCoy, a rodeo rider, was home, and according to a local mechanic had some dark-haired babe staying with him, who Trent assumed was Diana.

Not knowing what to do next, he'd ordered another drink, hoping to learn more about Dillon McCoy.

Now, seated down the bar from the blonde, Trent signaled for the bartender to bring her another beer. When she glanced his way and smiled, thanking him for the drink, Trent inwardly groaned. He could picture those full red lips wrapped around his cock. He smiled back.

When the heavy-set guy sitting next to her left, Trent picked up his scotch and water and slid onto the empty barstool.

"Do you mind?" Trent indicated the vacated spot.

"Not at all," she replied with a strong southern drawl. "Thanks for the beer."

"No problem. I'm passing through. Is the food good here?"

She laughed. "Honey, I haven't any idea. I'm passing through as well. Although I did hear they have good steaks."

"Well, since we're two strangers here, why don't we find out together. I'm Trent."

"Tonya. And that sounds good to me."

Trent noticed the ring she wore on her left hand and silently swore. The last thing he needed was some jealous husband causing a scene. But she'd indicated she didn't live here. He needed to find out more before going any further. He purposely glanced at her ring. "Are you meeting your husband?"

A cold gleam entered her blue eyes and her mouth formed a thin line. "My husband has left me for some tramp."

"I'm sorry to hear that. It seems we have

something in common. My fiancée has broken our engagement and is shacked up with some cowboy."

"Really. Do you think she's here?"

Trent nodded.

"Then, honey, I have a feeling she's with my husband."

"Perhaps we should tell the hostess we need a table where we can talk in private."

"That sounds like a fine idea."

A few minutes later, they were seated near the back. Trent made sure he could keep an eye on the door but not easily be seen.

While they waited for the waitress, Trent asked, "Where are you from?"

"Austin, how about you?"

He wasn't about to tell her the truth. "Knoxville."

"Oh, I've always wanted to go to Tennessee and Nashville. I just love Dolly Parton."

Trent couldn't stand country music. He'd been trying to ignore the twangy background noise since he'd sat down. He smiled. "So do I."

She giggled. "People say I resemble her. What do you think?"

He purposely stared at her chest. "Oh, yeah." When their eyes met, she smiled.

"So," Trent continued, "what makes you think your husband is nearby?"

Tonya hesitated. Indecision was written clearly in her eyes. She licked her lips and said, "He's from Pine Bluff. His family owns the Lazy M Ranch. I have every reason to believe he's here, and she's with him."

Bingo, Trent thought. How lucky could he get. "I think you may be right."

Tonya waited for the waitress to leave before saying, "What do you plan on doing about it?"

"I intend on getting her to see reason and leave with me."

Tonya sipped her beer. "Good, because I intend on getting Dillon back no matter what it takes." She leaned in closer. "We could drive up there and confront them together."

Trent shook his head. "I'd like to have more information before I drive into the wilderness. I mean, he could have a gun and shoot without realizing who we are."

Tonya nodded. "He is a good shot. What do you suggest we do first?"

Two delicious-smelling steaks were placed in front of them. "I suggest we eat, then compare what we know." He hesitated. "We could go to my hotel where there isn't a chance of either of them seeing us."

Again, he read indecision in her eyes. "Or your hotel if you'd be more comfortable."

"I'm staying at a B&B. I don't think the owner would approve of me bringing a man back with me. Besides, how do I know you're who you say you are?"

Who is she trying to fool? She wants me as much as I want her. I can play her game. Trent shrugged. "I understand. Perhaps we could meet in the morning for breakfast. Somewhere out on the highway. We probably wouldn't be seen there." Trent grinned to himself at the surprise that came over her face.

****

Tonya sat back and studied Trent. She knew from the minute he sat next to her he wasn't some local yokel. She'd learned to spot a man with money and a bullshitter a long time ago. And if she was right, Trent was both. She had no doubt he was after his fiancée, but meet her for breakfast, yeah, right. Her mama always said, "Make them work for it." Tonya twisted a strand of her hair around her finger. "Oh, I don't think that will be necessary. I can follow you to your hotel." *And text my whereabouts to Mama.*

Chapter Thirty-Two

Flora nudged Diana's arm with her nose. Laughing, Diana reached in her pocket for a carrot. "Here you go." She held out her hand. Flora took the offered food and crunched contentedly. Diana glanced around the barn and marveled at how much she enjoyed being here. Who would have ever guessed a city girl like her would look forward to helping Dillon take care of the horses? She wanted to ride Flora along the trails, smell the fragrance of the woods, and feel the clear air on her face. But Dillon didn't think it would be safe for them to venture too far from the cabin and barn. Diana scowled. This situation was becoming tiresome. She wished the sheriff would find out who was after Dillon so they could get on with their lives.

The barn door squeaked open and Dillon came in. "DT just called, and your car is ready."

"Great. Can we drive down and get it?"

"Sure. We should go as soon as we're through here. DT told me they're calling for more snow." He shook his head. *Gran and Gramps sure picked the right time to go on a cruise. We usually don't have snow or cold like this. The weather is certainly changing.*

"Flora is all set." Diana stroked her nose, and she whinnied softly.

Dillon smiled. "You two are a match made in

heaven."

Diana turned to Dillon and their eyes met. *Are we a match made in heaven as well?* she wanted to ask. Instead, she gestured. "Bingo's stall is the only one left to clean, but I'm a little concerned about him. I don't think he's eating the way he should."

Dillon went to where Bingo stood, his head lolling over the door of his stall. "I'll check him out. You've done enough."

"I enjoy helping."

His hands on Bingo's reins, he turned. "Do you really?"

She nodded.

"It's a far cry from Philadelphia society."

"I never liked Philadelphia society. My mother did."

His eyes roamed over her borrowed barn jacket to her faded jeans and muddy boots and grinned. "Jenn was right. We did make a country girl out of you."

Diana grinned back. "Perhaps, but I'd still like to change before we go into town."

Dillon stopped what he was doing. "I'll walk you to the cabin."

"It's not that far. I can go by myself."

"I don't like you on your own. Someone could be waiting."

Diana let out a long breath. "Okay, how about if I take the ranch truck?"

Dillon hesitated, then nodded. "Wait for me there. I won't be long."

A few minutes later, Diana hurried into the cabin, dropping her coat on the back of the couch as she passed. She'd been hoping for a reason to be on her own in town, and this was it. After they picked up her car, she'd send Dillon home while she shopped. She wanted to replace the clothes she'd bought for Dillon that Trent destroyed. She slipped on a deep red sweater and black jeans, replaced her barn boots with stylish ankle ones, and was brushing her hair when the front door creaked open.

"I'm almost ready," she called. When there wasn't a reply, she frowned. "Dillon?" Still nothing. Did she remember to lock the door when she came in? Uneasy, she stepped from the bedroom and quietly made her way down the hall. Before entering the living room, she paused and peered around the corner of the wall. The door stood ajar. A chill crept up her spine. *I should go back to the bedroom and lock herself in until Dillon comes. But what if he's been injured?* She needed to call for help. Damn it, she silently cursed. Her phone was still in her jacket, which lay across the couch. Did the cabin have a land line? *Diana, think.* Yes, she'd seen one. She groaned. In the kitchen.

Diana, about to head toward the bedroom, froze. Her eyes opened wide as the silhouette of a man filled the open door.

A screamed lodged in her throat, then Dillon spoke. "I'm sorry, the ranch is closed until March. If you call back after the first of the year, we can get you set up in a cabin."

Diana, her knees weak, leaned against the wall.

Dillon hung up his hat and coat and spotted her. "Diana, what's wrong?" He hurried to her side.

"I'm all right. When the door opened, I called, but no one answered. I let my imagination run away and thought you were the murderer."

"I'm sorry for scaring you. As I stepped onto the porch, my cell rang. I get better reception outdoors."

"Dillon, we can't live our lives wondering if a murderer is waiting around every corner."

"I know. I'm as tired of this situation as you are. While we're in town, I'll stop and see if the sheriff's made any progress."

Perfect. That will keep him busy while I shop. "If it's okay with you, I'd like to do some errands. Perhaps you can talk to the sheriff, then we can meet for lunch."

Dillon frowned. "I don't know if it's a good idea for you to be alone in town."

"I'll be around other people. Nothing will happen to me."

"We'll see. I'll take a quick shower, then we'll leave."

Diana, a determined set to her jaw, waited in an overstuffed chair.

When they arrived in Pine Bluff, Diana gaped at the crowd of people. "Is there something going on today?"

Dillon groaned. "Yes. It's the Holiday Festival. There's a parade, and they light the Christmas tree. I totally forgot it was happening."

"I'll never find a parking place near Country General. Do you think DT would let me leave the car here?"

"Probably. The problem is, the sheriff's office is at this end of town, and the store at the other."

Diana sighed in exasperation. "Dillon, do you see all these people? There's no reason for you to go with me. I'm sure I'll be perfectly safe."

He hesitated, then nodded. "I suppose you'll be

safe enough. If for any reason you feel someone is acting suspiciously, get into a crowd and call me. Make sure other people are around you at all times."

"I will. You know, it might be fun to stay and enjoy the festival."

His first reaction was to say no. At any other time, he'd be all for it. Considering their circumstances, being around so many people made him nervous. Seeing the excitement in her eyes, he relented. "Okay, we'll stay for a while. Call me when you're done shopping, and we'll meet for lunch. Although, getting in somewhere will probably be impossible.

"If we can't find a table in a restaurant, there are street vendors." She kissed his cheek and waved. An uneasy feeling crept over Dillon as she hurried away, the same sensation he'd get before he rode a bronco knowing it was a mean one. He'd started after her when he heard his name called. He turned to see Sheriff Dunn coming toward him.

"I was on my way to the office when I saw you standing here," Sheriff Dunn said. "There's time before the parade begins. Can you come with me?"

"I hope this means you have news."

"I'm not sure if it means anything. That's why I'd like to run it by you."

****

Diana wove her way through the pedestrian traffic on the sidewalk, enjoying the happy holiday atmosphere. Wreaths hung from the lamp posts. Garland decorated with holly, glittering bells, and candy canes was strung across the street. Twinkling lights showed through store windows, and a beautiful huge Frazer fur stood in the square. How did she miss seeing all this last night when they drove through town? She sighed. *Because your mind was on how you'd like to throttle Trent.* Every time she thought about how close she came to marrying him, her stomach turned.

As she waited at the crosswalk, she glanced across the street. A small parking lot fronted a row of businesses that included a hair salon, florist, real estate office, and bakery. Two people standing near a silver SUV caught her attention. A stocky man with his back to her was in a heated conversation with a woman Diana recognized as Bonnie Duffy. Something about the man seemed familiar, but she couldn't recall why. As the light changed, Bonnie glanced up and met Diana's eyes. Diana smiled and waved. From the expression on Bonnie's face, Diana didn't think whatever she and the man were discussing was going well.

Diana quickly headed for the men's department of the general store and was relieved to see it wasn't as crowded as the rest of the store. It didn't take her long to find two western shirts and a vest she thought Dillon would like. On her way to the checkout, she spotted a women's cowboy hat she instantly fell in love with. Dark gray trimmed in black, it would suit her perfectly. She grinned as she admired herself in the mirror. Diana pictured the horror on Trent's face if he saw her, and she chuckled.

She grabbed a box of dark chocolate candy and headed for the check out.

"What a cute hat," the girl at the register said. "Would you like me to cut the tags off so you can wear it?"

"Sure, why not."

Out on the street, Dianna headed toward the café she'd gone to with Jenn and the girls at Thanksgiving, but the crowd blocked her way. Realizing the parade had begun, in an attempt to see it, she squeezed between a young woman holding a little girl and a plump woman wearing a Santa hat.

The Pine Bluff high school marching band came first, followed by a float carrying the mayor and city council. Next came juggling elves and skating Christmas packages. Diana, thoroughly enjoying herself, wished Dillon was with her. Over the din, she thought someone called her name. "Diana, hello."

Diana turned.

****

Dillon took a seat in Sheriff Dunn's office.

"Now what I'm about to tell you is only a rumor. As of now, we don't have any proof, but we're digging deeper," the sheriff began. "We've interviewed folks from Martin's real estate company, and we suspect he's been taking payoffs to 'adjust' appraisals."

Dillon sat up straighter. "No shit."

The sheriff nodded. "And he also might be in financial trouble from an investment that went south."

Dillon thought for a minute, then said, "Are you thinking whoever wants to buy the Lazy M is blackmailing Martin to press me to sell?"

The sheriff nodded. "Something like that."

"Are you also thinking Martin murdered Kevin and tried to murder me?"

"That's a little harder to swallow. Martin Patrick is an ass, but I can't picture him murdering in cold blood."

"Neither can I. Then either the mysterious buyer is the murderer, or someone working on their behalf."

Again, the sheriff nodded.

"Have you spoken to Martin? He's such a worm, he'd probably crack under a little pressure."

"I was hoping to have more evidence. I'm afraid if I tip my hand, he'll warn off the killer, and we'll lose our edge. If I don't learn any more soon, I plan on bringing him in for questioning."

"What if you confront him, then have him followed?"

"I'm afraid that might be too risky." He glanced at his watch. "Sorry, I have to ride in the parade. I'll keep you informed if I learn anything new."

Both men rose and headed for the door. "And do not go to see Martin alone," Sheriff Dunn said as they stepped onto the sidewalk.

Dillon nodded, glanced around at the wall-to-wall people, and frowned. "I'm supposed to meet Diana."

"Where?"

"I'm not sure. She went shopping, then we were to meet." Cell in hand, he tried her number. It rang a few times, then went to voice mail. "Damn it. I should have never left her on her own."

Sheriff Dunn placed his hand on Dillon's shoulder. "Don't panic. She probably can't hear her phone in all this noise."

"I don't know. I'm going to head toward the other end of town." As he stepped away, Sheriff Dunn called, "Let me know when you hear from her."

Chapter Thirty-Three

Dillon, moving as quickly as possible, searched the crowd for Diana. The store she was headed to was on the opposite side of the street. A float with dancing snowmen was passing, closely followed by a band from Waynesville. Cursing under his breath, Dillon waited for a break, but none came. Majorettes twirling candy canes strode by, then a smiling Christmas queen in a vintage convertible. Dillon's pace quickened. He had to find the end of the parade in order to cross.

****

Diana glanced over her shoulder to see Bonnie Duffy smiling at her. "Hi, isn't it wonderful?" Diana indicated the giant snowball passing by.

Bonnie nodded and leaned close. "Diana, I hate to ask, but could we talk?"

Surprised at Bonnie's request, Diana nodded.

Bonnie smiled and took Diana's arm. "My car is parked right over here. It will be quieter there."

"Bonnie, I hardly know you. What can I help you with?" Diana asked as they stopped next to the car.

"It's Dillon. Let me take your packages." She opened the passenger door. "Please get in, and I'll explain."

Diana hesitated, caught the worry in Bonnie's eyes, and did as she asked.

After stowing Diana's bags in the back seat, Bonnie slid behind the wheel and started the car. "It's cold. I'll soon have us warm."

Afraid something had happened to Dillon, Diana forced back her fear. "Please, tell me. What's wrong? Is Dillon hurt?"

"No, I'm sorry. It's nothing like that. I'm concerned Dillon is blaming himself for Kevin's death."

Diana let out a sigh of relief. "You're right. He does feel responsible. But as soon as the murderer is found, and the reason behind the killing is clear, Dillon will realize there was nothing he could have done."

Bonnie nodded. "I hope you're right. I wish there was some way I could reassure Dillon I don't blame him."

Diana frantically tried to recall what meals were still in the freezer. "Well, if you'd like, why don't you come to dinner tonight."

"That's awfully kind of you. Where is Dillon now?"

"Actually, he's talking to the sheriff. He wanted to see if there was an update on Kevin's death. Then we're meeting for lunch." She placed her hand on the door handle. "I should go in case he's looking for me."

"Why don't I drive you to the sheriff's? I can take back streets, and it would be quicker than you trying to get through this crowd. Besides, you know men. They're probably still talking."

Diana gazed into Bonnie's friendly face and smiled. "I imagine you're right. Thanks, a ride would be great."

****

Dillon finally made his way across Main Street and headed toward Country General. As he wove through the crowd, he pulled his cell from his pocket. "Damn it to hell," he cursed, seeing the low battery signal. As he was about to call Diana, he spotted Martin turning onto a side street. Moving quickly, Dillon caught up. "Hey, Martin, wait."

Martin stopped, his face a chalky white.

"What's wrong?" Dillon asked.

Martin shook his head and continued walking.

Dillon grabbed his arm. "Martin, what's going on?" He was visibly trembling, and sweat covered his face. "Are you sick? Should I get help?"

Martin shook his head. "Dillon I'm sorry. I had no idea it would lead to this."

Fear twisted Dillon's gut. "What the hell have you done?"

****

"Bonnie, isn't that the way to Main Street?" Diana asked.

"I'm going to go around and loop back."

Unease prickled Diana's neck. Sure, she didn't know Pine Bluff well, but this didn't seem right. Bonnie started up the mountain road. Diana's pulse quickened. "Bonnie, where are you going?"

Bonnie didn't reply and only drove faster. Panic clutched at Diana's chest. "Bonnie, stop this car and let me out."

When she glanced at Diana, hatred blazed in Bonnie's eyes. "I'll let you out when we get to the ranch."

Confused at her hostility, Diana stammered, "Bonnie, what are you doing?"

"You know if you hadn't come along, I could have had Dillon as well as the land."

"I don't understand. What are you talking about? You were married. How could you and Dillon be together?" Reality slammed into Diana and her eyes widened. "Oh, my God, did you kill Kevin?"

****

Dillon had hold of Martin and backed him against a wall. "I'm going to pound the ever-loving shit out of you if you don't start talking. Where's Diana?"

"With Bonnie."

For a second, his taught muscles relaxed. Bonnie had no reason to hurt Diana. Then the anxiety in Martin's eyes made the fear race back. "Why is Diana with Bonnie?"

Martin licked his lips. "Dillon, it's all about the ranch."

Blood pounded in Dillon's temples. "Bonnie is behind buying the Lazy M?".

"Yes, but I also think there's someone else involved. Dillon, you have to believe me, I didn't know she was this crazy."

Dillon clenched and unclenched his fists. If Bonnie hurt Diana, he could never forgive himself. He should have never allowed her to go off on her own. "Where is she taking Diana?"

"Your place."

Dillon knew it would take too long to get to the garage and pick up his truck. "Where's your car?"

"There." Martin pointed.

Dillon dragged him down the street and threw him into the passenger seat. "Give me your keys."

Dillon cursed loudly and fluently as he maneuvered

through traffic. "Martin, call the sheriff and tell him to get to the ranch. Damn. He's in the parade, he'll never hear his phone." He glanced at Martin. "All right, start talking, and you'd better tell it all."

****

Stay calm, Diana told herself as the entrance to the ranch neared. *When she stops the car, I'll get out and start running.* Prepared to release the seatbelt and open the door, Diana froze when Bonnie reached under the seat and produced a gun.

"Don't think about doing anything stupid, because I will shoot you."

Even though her insides felt like jello, Diana did her best to conceal her fear. "You killed your husband, and now you think you can have Dillon?"

Bonnie's expression turned sly. "I never said I killed Kevin. Although, if he wouldn't have asked so many questions, he'd still be alive. I knew when he left that night, he would tell Dillon what he suspected. Although he didn't know much. The gullible ass thought it was me who wanted to buy the ranch. Like I'd use my inheritance when I had another willing to buy it for me."

"And do what?"

"Develop the property. What else?"

"So Dillon was right. You plan on stripping the land to build houses."

"Both properties combined, with the location and view, would be worth a fortune."

Diana's mind raced. "Was it you who shot at Dillon?"

Bonnie smirked. "I couldn't believe my luck when I saw you two, but I didn't try to kill Dillon, just wound him. Trust me, if I wanted Dillon dead, he'd be in the ground. You, on the other hand, I should have killed when I had the chance."

"Do you honestly think by killing me you'll have the land and Dillon?"

"Dillon and I were good together. I've seen the way he looks at me, and I know he still wants me. But you had to ruin everything." Bonnie gave Diana a triumphant smile. "I'll tell you a secret. When the two of you were at my house, and you were outside, he kissed me."

Diana doubted that was true, but the longer she kept Bonnie talking, the better the chance Dillon would find her.

"You don't believe me," she sneered. "Well, let me tell you, the little cabin in the woods I saw you and Dillon come out of, that was our love nest. He used to take me there, and we'd fuck all day."

Dillon told her she was the only woman he'd taken to that cabin, and she believed him. Still, a stab of jealousy shot through Diana. Her feelings must have shown because Bonnie's eyes lit with satisfaction.

Bonnie pulled the car into the ranch parking lot and stopped and turned toward Diana.

"That's right. He and I used to go at each other like rabbits. And I know there's no other woman who can please Dillon McCoy like I can."

The thought of Dillon being with this woman both enraged and sickened her. Whatever happened between them was years ago, but she couldn't stop herself from saying, "He was young then. Teenage boys will fuck anything that will hold still."

"Bitch."

The hard slap Bonnie gave her was so unexpected, Diana cried out.

"It's too bad you won't be around to see what I tell you is the truth."

Her head reeling, Diana forced herself to stay focused. "By now Dillon must know I'm with you. After he discovers you're the one who killed me, you'll be the last woman he'll want."

For a second, Bonnie's expression went blank. Then a sly smile spread across her face. "I'll say we were both kidnapped by a masked gunman. Unfortunately, you were killed, but I got away. Trust me. I'll have no problem convincing everyone it was the same stranger who killed Kevin."

"How?"

"That's not your concern. Now get out."

Her hands slick with sweat, Diana fumbled with the handle. When she stepped from the car in front of Dillon's cabin, her legs threatened to give way.

Bonnie came up behind her and stuck the gun in her back. "Get inside. Dillon should be here soon."

Diana stumbled her way up the steps and onto the porch. She had to do something to warn Dillon. Damn it to hell, her cell and purse were still in Bonnie's car. Could she stall? "I don't have the key."

Bonnie snorted. "No one up here locks their doors." She turned the knob. "See." She shoved Diana. "Get in."

****

"Dillon, you have to believe me. I don't know why Bonnie is doing this," Martin stammered. "She found out I've been…"

"Yeah, yeah, I know all about your real estate

scam," Dillon interjected. "So, what, she was blackmailing you?"

Martin nodded.

"Wait a minute. The only way Bonnie could have known that information is if she was also a realtor."

Again, Martin nodded. "I had no idea she'd gotten a realtor's license." Martin snorted. "Ya, well, trust me I wish she hadn't."

"You low-life son-of-a-bitch. Did you kill Kevin?"

"No. No way. I had nothing to do with that."

"You're saying Bonnie killed her own husband?"

"I'm not sure. Like I said, she's crazy. When I ask her why she wants the ranch so badly, she just smiles. I have a small part in this. There's someone with a lot more power and money helping her."

."The buyer for the Lazy M. Martin, who is it?"

"I have no idea. All transactions went through Bonnie."

"What does she think she'll gain by hurting Diana?"

Martin lifted his hands and let them fall. "My original involvement was to get you to sell the ranch. Then today, send you after her. When you saw me, I'd decided I wasn't going to have anything else to do with her. I was heading home to tell my wife everything and accept the consequences."

"How could Bonnie have planned this when she didn't know I'd be in town today?"

"It wasn't until she saw Diana go into the store. She figured you were here as well, and she could put her insane scheme into play. She told me to keep an eye out for you and get you to come after her."

"Well, you managed to do that. Then what? Does

she think by kidnapping Diana, I'll sell her the Lazy M?"

Martin shook his head. "The woman might have killed her husband. Is this a rational person?"

Dillon steered the truck off the road, stopping at the Lazy M barn.

"What are you doing?"

"I'm going to try and get in touch with the sheriff. I'm not about to drive into her trap." He held up his phone and cursed. No signal. "Do you have your cell?"

Martin nodded and felt in his pocket. "It's not here. It must have fallen out when you pushed me."

"Damn. Hopefully when we get closer to the cabin, I'll get a cell signal."

"Why do I have to go with you?" Martin almost whined. "I'm telling you she's dangerous."

"Because your sorry ass is part of this. You had plenty of opportunity to stand up to her and be a man. You could have come to me and told me the truth." Dillon gritted his teeth. "Do you realize you could have saved Kevin's life?"

Martin lowered his head. In a quiet voice he said, "I honestly didn't think she was capable of murder. I liked Kevin. I'm truly sorry he's dead."

Dillon thought for once he was telling the truth. "Then for Kevin's sake, help me stop her before she hurts Diana."

Chapter Thirty-Four

Her encounter with Trent flashed through Diana's mind as she staggered into the cabin. A weapon, she needed a weapon. She spotted a metal flashlight sitting on the entry table. It worked once, it had to work again. She grabbed the flashlight, turned, and swung behind her. She winced as the heavy light connected with Bonnie's head. Not waiting to see how badly Bonnie was hurt, Diana ran to the bedroom. She closed and locked the door behind her and hurried to the sliding doors leading onto the deck. She slid them open and ran.

Once she made it to the trees, the snow was deeper. Sinking to her knees, Diana struggled to move quickly. Knowing her trail would be easily followed, she pushed on. Not having a clue where she was going, Diana hoped to spot a landmark she'd recognize from their trail rides. Was Dillon coming? Did he know she was missing? Surely by now he was looking for her. But how long would it take for him to realize she was at the ranch?

Breathless, her hands and feet numb, she wiped tears from her cheeks. *Stop it. You have to remain strong to survive.* She gritted her teeth. Why had she changed from her sturdy boots to these fancy leather ones. She could almost hear Jenn now, "Girl, what's the matter with you?"

None of this made any sense. What in the world was she doing lost in the woods in the snow running from a killer?

****

Dillon removed the rifle from the ranch pickup, then cautiously approached the cabin. Bonnie's car was parked in front. "We'll go in through the back. Stay low and stay behind me." They rounded the cabin and Dillon halted. Two sets of footprints led from the deck toward the trees. The thought of Diana lost in the woods twisted his gut in fear. She knew nothing about landmarks or watching for dangers. She was most likely half frozen and scared out of her mind.

"At least the prints are clear. We can track them." Dillon glanced toward the sliding doors. He didn't think anyone was still in the cabin, but he had to check. "Martin, I'm going to see if anyone is inside. Stay here in case one of them shows up." He narrowed his eyes. "And, you'd better be here when I return."

He raced up the stairs onto the deck and into the bedroom, where the door to the hall was locked. Rifle raised, he stepped into the hall and then the living room. His eye fell on the flashlight laying on the floor, a streak of red glistening on the end. Diana's or Bonnie's blood? One of them was hurt. Bad enough to slow them down? Hopefully Bonnie. He searched the rest of the cabin and, convinced no one was there, headed back outside. "One of them might be hurt." He told Martin what he'd found. "Let's go."

****

Diana, her teeth chattering and her cheeks raw from the cold, let out a little sob. How long had she been wandering in the woods? She thought she'd been heading down hill, but she couldn't be sure. She blinked. Had she seen something move? She listened, but neither the sound of a bird or the chatter of a squirrel could be heard. Unease crawled up her spine when a shadow a few feet ahead flickered through the trees. *Okay, it's probably an animal who's as afraid of you as you are of them.* She started forward. A scream lodged in her throat when the image of a woman formed before her. She floated above the ground and motioned for Diana to follow.

Mesmerized, Diana couldn't move. Upon the wind, a lilting voice said, "I will not harm you. I will lead you to safety. You must hurry."

"Who are you?" Diana whispered.

"I am Wilhelmina." She gave Diana a wan smile. "I will not harm you. Dillon McCoy is a good man. Now come."

Diana, as in a dream, followed the spirit until a cabin came into view. She quickened her pace. It must be one of the ranch rentals. That meant she could find the road. Could she hide inside? She was so cold, the idea of warmth sent her onto the porch to try the door. Locked. "Damn, damn, damn." She stomped her frozen feet and rubbed her gloved hands. Should she try the windows? If the door was locked, so they would be as well.

She must go on. Hopefully, the road would take her to the ranch or the barn. If she could make it to the barn, the ranch truck would be there, the keys inside. When she stepped onto the dirt road, confusion overtook her. Which way should she go? She scanned her surroundings, but nothing seemed familiar. Diana paused. Where was Wilhelmina? She was nowhere to be seen. Had she actually been there, or, had her imagination conjured her? *Dummy, you can't just stand here. Move.*

To her right the road seemed to rise, so she turned left. The snow wasn't quite as deep, and she was able to walk faster. A sound behind her sent her running. Wilhelmina didn't make noise.

****

"There's blood." Martin pointed to the ground as they entered a thicket of trees.

Tiny red droplets of red were alongside the last set of footprints. Bonnie's? They must be. Diana would be ahead of her. As quickly as possible, Dillon followed their trail. Soon, it was clear to Dillon the women were headed away from Lazy M property and toward the Duffy campground.

"Where the hell are they going?" Martin asked.

"The Duffy property line is in this direction. If Bonnie has Diana, she could hide her anywhere. If Diana is in the lead, she hasn't a clue where she is. She could unknowingly be playing right into Bonnie's hands." Hoping he could get a signal, Dillon slipped his cell from his jacket. Nothing—too many trees. He needed to get to higher ground.

****

Diana, breathing hard, exhausted from running, tripped over a rock in the road and landed hard on her knees, crying out in pain. *Oh, God, this nightmare has to end.* She slowly got to her feet. *Why can't I find the damn barn?* A scraping sound made her jump. She glanced over her shoulder and saw Bonnie step from the woods.

"You bitch, you'll not outrun me," Bonnie called.

Diana had only taken a few steps when pain shot up her knee and she stumbled. Bonnie slammed into her, and they hit the ground. Bonnie, taller and heavier than Diana, knocked the wind out of her.

"Get up." Bonnie grabbed Diana by the hair and jerked.

Diana, gasping for breath, tried to rise, but her strength was fading. *Come on, come on, you can't let her win.* She drew on every ounce of energy she possessed. *She's going to kill you.*

"What's wrong, city girl, too much of a coward to face me?" She kicked Diana in the side.

Diana winced in pain but didn't cry out. Bonnie might be stronger than she was, but Diana was light and quick. She kicked out hard with one foot and caught Bonnie in the shin. Satisfaction soared through her when Bonnie lost her balance.

Diana got to her feet and scanned the area for a weapon. Spotting a thick branch, she lunged for it, but Bonnie got there first. "Oh, no you don't." She threw the branch into the woods. "I already have one head injury thanks to you."

Diana's eyes opened wide, seeing the bruise forming on Bonnie's forehead and the blood caked in her hair. Until recently, she'd never hurt another human being. Now this made two. She was about to apologize, but Bonnie still had her gun, and it was pointing at her.

"You've managed to accommodate me rather nicely," Bonnie said with a grin. "You're on Duffy land, and I know just how to dispose of you."

"Bonnie, you're not thinking rationally. By now Dillon knows I'm with you. He's probably got the entire sheriff's department out searching for us. If I'm found dead, there's no suspect but you. No one is going to believe some mysterious stranger kidnapped both of us and killed me."

"If you have an unfortunate accident, who will know the difference?"

Diana's brows knitted in puzzlement. "What kind of accident?"

"You'll see." She pointed her gun. "Move."

****

"She stopped here," Dillon said as he stepped onto the cabin porch. He'd trailed both sets of prints, the ones in the rear well behind Diana's. If Bonnie had been hit hard enough by the flashlight, she could have been unconscious for a while. That would give Diana a good head start. But she didn't know the area well, and the snow was deep in spots. With each passing minute, Dillon's fear grew. "We should make better time on the road."

"Dillon, I can't go any farther," Martin panted. "I'm not in shape for this."

Dillon glanced at Martin with disgust. "Then wait here." He handed him his cell phone. "Try and get ahold of the sheriff. Tell him where we are and what's happened."

"Where the hell *are* we?"

This is one of the Duffy cabins." He pointed. "The road forks, leading to their barn or off the mountain." Dillon paused. The barn wasn't far away. He could make better time on horseback. He ran.

As he moved, he wanted to call out for Diana but was afraid he'd alert Bonnie of his presence. He rounded a bend and stopped.

He studied the ground. Bonnie must have caught up with Diana and they scuffled. Dillon stepped to the side of the road and picked up a gray cowboy hat. Somehow, he knew it belonged to Diana. *Darlin', I'm coming.*

Their footprints left the road where Dillon knew a path led to a grassy area and a rock outcropping with a high cliff. Diana's words pounded in his brain when he recalled her saying, "I don't mind heights if I'm far enough away, but walking out there, I'd go into an out and out panic." Dillon cursed and ran faster.

In the Duffy barn, it took him seconds to saddle Kevin's horse, Smoke, and head for the ridge.

****

Diana's insides coiled into knots. Ahead, a snow-covered granite block jutted out over the valley. She imagined the view was amazing, but she had no intention of seeing it.

Bonnie prodded her with the gun. "Why are you stopping?"

"I'm not going out there."

Bonnie jabbed her harder. "Yes, you are."

A burst of anger flared in Diana.

She was freezing, she hurt all over, she was tired, and she was done with all of this. "You know what, I've had enough of you. If you want to kill me, you're going to have to shoot me."

Bonnie's eyes opened wide. "Not quite the city mouse I thought you were." She shoved Diana. "But you're still going over the edge."

At this point, Diana's fear of the drop-off was greater than her fear of Bonnie. "The hell I am." She shoved back hard.

Caught off guard, Bonnie lost her grip on the gun, which fell and slid on the snowy rock, stopping only a foot from the cliff edge.

Chapter Thirty-Five

Kick it off, Diana's mind screamed. But her legs wouldn't obey. As Bonnie reached for the gun, Dillon broke from the trees.

"Diana."

With joy and relief, Diana smiled at the sound of Dillon's voice. There he was, her gallant cowboy riding a gray and white horse, coming for her. When she took a step toward him, Bonnie wrapped her arm around her neck and placed the gun against her head.

"Stop right there, Dillon," Bonnie called.

Dillon pulled back on the reins and halted a few feet away. "Bonnie, it's over. Let her go. There's no need for you to do this."

Raw panic engulfed Diana. *Keep your attention on Dillon, not what's below you,* she repeated to herself as Bonnie's arm tightened, and she stepped closer to the edge.

"I've come too far to lose it all now," Bonnie shouted.

"Why are you doing this?"

"You fool," Bonnie shouted. "You really don't understand, do you? I love you. I've loved you since the first time you kissed me. Even though you hurt me bad, I still had hope. I thought once you sold the ranch, and we were together again, we'd leave and enjoy all the wealth together." She jabbed Diana with the gun. "Then she came along."

Dillon's jaw hardened. "Was it you who shot at me, messed with the rung on the ladder, and tampered with my brakes?"

"It was taken out of my hands. I never wanted you dead. Why did you become so obstinate about selling the Lazy M?"

"Taken out of your hands by whom?"

Bonnie shrugged. "Martin, who else."

Dillon shook his head in disgust. "Not going to work. He's ready to confess to all your blackmail threats. Besides, we both know Martin is a candy ass who wouldn't shoot at anyone."

Bonnie's eyes flared with anger, but she remained silent.

"If you love me so much, let Diana go," Dillon continued. "I'll do whatever you ask."

Bonnie snorted. "You don't mean that."

"Yes, I do."

"You'll sell the Lazy M?"

Dillon hesitated. "Are you also the mysterious buyer?"

"No. I have a partner. Once the Lazy M property is sold and combined with mine, we'll split the proceeds from the development. I'll walk away with millions."

Dillon scoffed. "And you believe that?"

"Why shouldn't I?"

"Think, Bonnie. Why would anyone invest that kind of money into building if they didn't own all the land?" Dillon shook his head. "They'll find a way to take it from you, and you won't get a dime."

"You don't know what you're talking about. I've

known him for years, and he wouldn't cheat me."

"Bonnie, who is this person?"

"Someone who you used to knock around, and who has come home to rub your nose in his success."

Stunned, Dillon stared. "What the hell are you talking about. I never knocked anyone around."

"Perhaps not physically, but mentally." Bonnie shrugged. "You weren't the only one. I, on the other hand, comforted him after that stuck up cousin of yours rejected him."

Confusion creased Dillon's face. "Who? What?"

Bonnie gave a dismissive wave. "It doesn't matter now. We've been planning this for years, and I'm seeing it through. Get off the horse. You and your slut can go over the edge together."

"Was Kevin a part of this?" Dillon asked.

"Are you serious? Kevin knew nothing. Well, until recently. If he'd been where he was supposed to be and not in the woods spying on me, he'd still be alive."

Dillon's expression turned stormy. "Kevin Duffy was a good, decent man. Did you kill him?"

"Mr. Goody Two Shoes is more like it. Unfortunately, he saw my friend and me coming out of Red Oak." She smirked. "We did enjoy helping ourselves to such nice accommodations."

"It's called breaking and entering, and it's against the law."

"Not when the door isn't locked."

Dillon scowled. "You were saying…"

"Kevin became suspicious. I tried to convince him he misunderstood the situation, but he wouldn't let it go. He kept asking questions and snooping around. The day he died, I was afraid he was on his way to confide in you."

"Bonnie, as I said, Martin told me everything, and the sheriff is on his way up here. It's time to give yourself up."

Diana cried out when Bonnie's arm tightened on her neck. "Martin's a thief and a liar. He'll make a perfect fall guy. There's no proof I was involved in Kevin's death or, now, yours."

Diana stood rigid as stone and stared into Dillon's eyes, silently pleading for him to do something.

"If you fire that gun, it will echo through the valley and lead Sheriff Dunn right to you," Dillon said, sliding from his horse.

At the same time, Bonnie twisted her body, so Diana faced the rocks and stream below.

****

Dots swam before Diana's eyes, and her stomach heaved. Her heart pounded in her chest, and her legs turned to jelly as her foot slipped, and the snow and ice gave way beneath her.

"Diana," Dillon shouted as Bonnie screamed.

A floating sensation came over Diana as she seemed to hang in the air. To Diana's disbelief, Wilhelmina hovered in front of her seconds before she landed with a thump in a huge mound of snow on a ledge below the rim.

Diana, her breath coming in shallow gasps, gazed up into the brilliant blue sky and Dillon's fear-stricken face peering over the edge of the cliff.

His voice was low and ragged. "Are you all right?"

For seconds, Diana couldn't speak. She licked dry lips, then whispered, "I think so. Dillon, did you see her?"

"What? See who?"

"Wilhelmina. She saved my life."

"Ah, no. I didn't see anyone. Stay still. I'm coming for you."

"No. You'll kill yourself."

"Diana, look around you. You're not that far down and you're surrounded by snow."

"Not on your life am I taking my eyes from the beautiful blue sky above me."

Minutes later, Dillon slid down next to her and grinned. "See, I told you."

Diana took in a deep breath. "Okay, how do we get back onto the ridge?"

"Get onto your knees. We should be able to crawl up."

"Are you insane?"

"Diana, the snow is thick enough you'll sink into it. Bonnie misjudged and thought you were nearer to the drop-off."

Diana grabbed Dillon's arm. "Where is she?"

"I don't know. She screamed, looked terrified, and ran like a spooked horse. Come on, let's get out of here. I'll be right behind you."

Diana gathered all the courage she could muster, focused on a distant pine tree, and climbed. When she reached the top, she dragged herself over the edge and collapsed. Dillon rushed past her, then a horse whinnied. On wobbly legs, Diana stood, frantically searching for Bonnie.

Dillon, in one motion, swept Diana into his arms and kicked Smoke into a gallop.

Nestled in front of him, Diana held tight and burst into tears.

"Hush, darlin', you're safe. I'll soon have you home."

Diana's teeth chattered, and she shook uncontrollably. "Dillon, I was so scared."

"I know, darlin', I know. I'm sorry. I should have never left you on your own."

Diana lifted her tear-streaked face to him. "I was the stupid one who went with Bonnie."

"She had everyone fooled. She's the last person I would have suspected. Martin, on the other hand, didn't surprise me.

"Why?"

"I'll explain later." Dillon steered Smoke into the trees.

"Where are you going?"

"This is a shortcut to the ranch."

"I wandered around lost in here. If I knew more about the area, I might have found my way to your barn. My hope was to make it there and drive the ranch truck to safety."

He held her tight. "Diana, I can't imagine how frightened you were."

She opened her mouth to tell him about Wilhelmina, but hesitated. Would he believe her? "Umm." She cleared her throat. "I had help finding the road. The problem was, I thought it was on Lazy M property."

"Help, from whom?"

"Wilhelmina."

Chapter Thirty-Six

Dillon glanced at the top of her head, her face buried in the front of his coat, and assumed he'd heard her wrong. "Who?"

She lifted her face. "Wilhelmina."

Incredulous, he stared. He finally found his voice. "This is the second time you've mentioned seeing Wilhelmina."

She nodded. "It's true. She saved me from falling, and she led me to the road. The problem was Bonnie was close behind me, and I tripped and fell."

He cleared his throat. "Diana, Wilhelmina is a folk legend. She doesn't exist."

"You told us at the fire pit you saw her."

"Yeah, well, I like to aggravate Jenn. I most likely saw an animal."

Diana snorted. "Legend or not, I have Wilhelmina to thank for my life."

Dillon had heard stories of people being lost in the mountains and imagining help from unexpected sources, but this was usually after consuming large amounts of alcohol. The cold and her fear must be the explanation for Diana's imagination conjuring Wilhelmina. They'd made it to Dillon's cabin, and there was no sign of Martin or his car. Dillon slid from Smoke's back, Diana in his arms. *Where the hell was*

Sheriff Dunn?

"I'll tie the horse here and try and get in touch with the sheriff," Dillon said. "I would have expected him by now."

"How does Martin fit into this?" Diana asked.

Dillon explained Bonnie's blackmail and Martin's role in her scheme. "The last I saw of him, he was supposed to meet the sheriff and tell him which way we'd gone,"

As they were about to enter the cabin, Diana grabbed Dillon's arm and lowered her voice. "Bonnie's car is still here. Could she be inside?"

"I doubt it, but I'll check all the rooms."

Diana noticed the rifle in the scabbard on the saddle. "Why didn't you use that?"

"Bonnie had you so close to her, I was afraid I couldn't get a clear shot. Besides, you were on the edge of the cliff."

Once in the cabin, Dillon made quick work of the search. Diana sighed with relief when he said it was clear. She stared at the blood-stained flashlight still laying on the floor. Her voice barely above a whisper, she said, "I can't believe I actually hit Bonnie. I could have hurt her badly."

"You had no choice. When the sheriff gets here, you can tell us how you ended up in her car."

Diana nodded. "I'd like to take a shower and change my clothes. Damn." She turned for the door.

"Where are you going?"

"My packages from shopping are in Bonnie's car." She frowned. "I bought the cutest hat and lost it somewhere in the woods."

"I found it and left it in the Duffy barn. I'll get it

when I take Smoke back. Take your shower. I'll get your packages."

For a moment, she stood, weariness overtaking her. "Was it only this morning I was happily shopping and watching a holiday parade?"

He wrapped his arms around her and kissed her. "All we have to do is fill the sheriff in on what we know, and then go to bed."

Diana leaned her head against his chest, absorbing his comforting presence. "There were times today I thought it all must be a bad dream, and I'd wake up."

His voice was raw with emotion. "When I found Kevin's body, I should have insisted you leave. You being hurt or killed because of me is something I could never live with."

Diana held him tighter. She knew without any doubt she loved this man deeply and completely. "Dillon, I chose to stay. I knew the danger, and I wouldn't be anywhere else but by your side." She stepped from his embrace and gazed into his troubled eyes. She wanted to tell him she loved him but was afraid his response would come from fear for her life and not his true feelings. She knew he cared for her, but did he love her? She gently kissed his lips. "I'll go take my shower. Hopefully by then the sheriff will have called."

Diana closed her eyes and let the hot water wash over her. She tried her best to ignore her lingering fear. What if Bonnie wasn't caught, and she came back while they were sleeping? *Don't think about it. You're with Dillon, and you're safe. The police will catch Bonnie, and her partner will be exposed.*

She stepped from the shower and toweled dry.

When she entered the bedroom, she halted, staring at the sliding doors leading onto the deck. Sudden terror took her breath. She grabbed the doorframe for support. *Get a grip, Diana, she's not out there. She wouldn't come anywhere near here.*

Diana dressed and made sure the sliding doors were locked. When she reentered the living room, Dillon was pacing in front of the fireplace.

"What's wrong?"

"A deputy was just here. It seems Martin notified the sheriff's office, telling them we were in trouble, but he hasn't been seen. I should have known better than to trust the little weasel. I wouldn't be surprised if he hasn't left town. The deputy was on his way to find us when he spotted Smoke tied up by the cabin. I told the deputy about Bonnie and what happened to us. He said the sheriff was out at an accident, and he'd tell him when he got back."

Diana headed for the kitchen. "I don't know about you, but I need a drink."

He held up his beer. "I'm already there."

"Bonnie would need transportation, and her car is parked outside," Diana continued when she returned carrying a glass and a bottle of wine. "I shouldn't do this on an empty stomach, but at this point I don't care. As for Bonnie, she couldn't have been too far ahead of us. I can't imagine she'd take a chance and go home, so where else would she go?"

"Either toward town, which would be a long walk, or the ski area, which is closer." Dillon paused in thought. "Wait a minute." Fragments of past conversation with his family clicked together in his mind. "Diana, did any of my cousins say anything about the owner of the ski area?"

"No. They talked about how it's being updated, but nothing more. Why?"

"I'm starting to wonder if the new owner of the ski area is somehow involved. I recall Gramps saying some Yank bought it and was pouring tons of money into it. If they were to own both the Duffy land and the Lazy M, and developed the property, they could make a killing. Bonnie said her partner was from here and now has money. Remember she said he also seeks revenge on me for past insults."

"Wait a minute." Diana's brows narrowed in concentration. "Didn't Bonnie say something about one of your girl cousins?" She didn't wait for his reply. "I think one of them can help."

"How's that?"

"Because I believe one of them might have dated the mystery man." Diana relayed the conversation she and the girls had in regard to past boyfriends. "One of them said she dated a guy who was a little odd. The problem is I can't remember which one said it."

"Jenn?" Dillon asked.

Diana shook her head.

"That leaves Suzanna or Sally."

"Suzanna. It was Suzanna."

"Do you recall his name?"

"No, sorry, you'll have to call her." Diana rose. "While you do that, I'm going to make some sandwiches. Suddenly I'm starving."

"Dustin Chambers," Dillon said a few minutes later, after disconnecting his phone. "As soon as I heard his name, I remembered him."

"Did you harass him like Bonnie said," Diana

asked, as she returned carrying a tray.

"No more than teenage boys normally harass each other," Dillon replied. "If I recall correctly, he was a bit of a smart ass. He lived in town and used to ask a lot of questions about the ranch and remarked how nice it must be to own the Lazy M."

"Now we don't know if it was Bonnie or Dustin who killed Kevin."

"I know." He let out a long breath. "Why the hell hasn't the sheriff called? Bonnie and Dustin could be long gone by now."

Diana gave an involuntary shudder.

Dillon placed his hand on her arm. "You okay?"

"I'm sorry. I won't be at ease until Bonnie is no longer a threat. You're going to think I'm a coward, but could we stay in town until she's caught?"

Dillon placed his beer on the table and sat next to her. "Darlin', after what you went through today, coward is the last word to describe you. I have no problem getting a room in town. In fact, a friend of Gran's runs a nice B&B."

"Great. Can you call her?"

"Sure." He paused. "I have an idea."

"What is it?"

"I can take you to Mrs. Potter's B&B, and I'll go to the ski area and watch for Bonnie."

"Dillon, that could be dangerous."

"I'll call the sheriff again and let them know where I'm going. Besides, there will be lots of people around. It should be safe enough."

Diana glanced at her tray of sandwiches and sighed. "Is there a restaurant?"

"Yeah. It's supposed to be good. Why?"

"Because we have to eat, and I don't want you going alone." She raised her hand to stop him. "If you believe you'll be safe, I'll be safe too."

Dillon knew by that stubborn look on her face she wouldn't change her mind. "Okay, but you do not leave the restaurant."

"Fine. I'll put these sandwiches in the fridge, and I'll be ready to go."

Dillon felt in his pocket for his keys. "Damn it. My truck is still in town."

Diana shook her head. "So is my car."

"I'll take Smoke to the barn, and we can use the ranch truck."

"Let's pack a bag so we can go directly to the B&B from the ski area."

Chapter Thirty-Seven

The glass and cedar lodge overlooked the snow-covered ski runs, brightly lit against a velvet sky. Skiers in chair lifts dangled in the air as they glided to the top of the slopes. The smell of wood smoke drifted on the crisp breeze as Diana and Dillon stepped from the truck.

"The lodge is huge," Diana said.

"I haven't been over here since the remodeling. Dustin must have added guest rooms and expanded the restaurant. Remember, keep your eyes out for Bonnie."

"Will you recognize Dustin?"

"If he hasn't changed too much."

"I honestly don't think Bonnie and Dustin will casually be seated having dinner," Diana said.

"No, probably not, but I'm hungry. We'll eat, then you can have dessert while I take a look around."

The lobby was dominated by a large chandelier shaped like antlers. The floor was gray and white tile and the walls paneled. A reception desk sat to their right with the door to the dining room on the left. The people around them were dressed in thick cashmere sweaters and designer jackets.

Diana gazed at her wool coat, black jeans, and western shirt and frowned. "I don't think we'll blend in."

Dillon shook his head. "This used to be a place for people to spend the day, ski, and have fun. Now, it's Aspen in the south. Come on." He led the way to the dining room.

"Good evening," an immaculately groomed hostess said. "Do you have a reservation?"

"No," Dillon replied.

The hostess frowned. "I'm sorry, it will be at least an hour before we can seat you."

"Great," Dillon said with exasperation.

"I can place you on our list," the hostess stated.

Dillon gave a curt nod. "Sure, fine."

She handed him a disk. "I'll buzz you when your table is ready."

"Let's find the bar," Dillon said. "We can wait there."

The lounge, as it was called, had an open circular fireplace in the center and a view of the slopes. As they approached a table, Diana came to a sudden stop, Dillon bumping into her back.

"What's wrong?" he asked.

Diana was so shocked it took her a minute to find her voice. She turned to him and whispered. "Trent is sitting at a table with a blonde."

Dillon peered over her head to where she indicated. His mouth opened and closed, but nothing came out.

"Do you know who she is?"

He cleared his throat. "It's Tonya."

They stood rooted to the floor, Dillon the first to move. He headed directly toward their table. "Tonya, what the hell are you doing here?"

Diana had to admit that Tonya seemed as shocked to see Dillon as he was to see her.

"Dillon, what a surprise." Tonya stared at Diana and smirked. "This must be your little girlfriend."

Trent, his back to Diana, swung to face her. "If it isn't Diana and her cowboy. Funny place to see you, since you're too afraid of heights to ski."

"Trent, how did you find me?" Diana asked.

"I followed you from your apartment. I originally came to bring you home, but…" He glanced at Tonya. "I got distracted."

Tonya smiled and blew Trent a kiss. "Dillon, I came to stay with you at the ranch, but I found myself a real man."

Incomprehensible was the only word Diana could think of to describe Tonya and Trent as a couple.

"As far as I'm concerned, you two deserve each other," Dillon stated with disgust. "Goodbye, good riddance, and good luck."

Diana's curiosity got the better of her, and she asked, "What are you doing here?"

"We saw Dillon earlier and decided to see where he went," Tonya replied. "When he got into a car with some guy, we followed, but a snowplow slowed us down. By the time we caught up, the car was parked in front of Dillon's cabin and they were gone. We waited for a while, but no one showed. We decided the hell with it and came here." Tonya pursed her lips. "Dillon, I can tell you to your face I'll sign the divorce papers. You can have this skinny little mouse."

Trent snorted. "And Diana is welcome to the hick cowboy."

"Um, Trent, will you be taking Tonya home to meet your mother?" Diana asked, barely able to control her laughter. "I'm sure she'll be thrilled for you."

Trent's eyes narrowed, but he didn't reply.

"Diana, I've had enough of these two." Dillon leaned to where his face was inches from Trent's. "Listen to me, you cowardly son-of-a-bitch, if you ever come near Diana again, I'm going to beat the ever lovin' shit out of you."

Diana placed her hand on Dillon's arm. "Come on. He's not worth it."

"I could have you arrested for threatening me," Trent sneered.

"Yeah, well, I could have you arrested for attempted rape, assault and battery, and for trashing Diana's apartment, so bring it on."

Diana tugged on Dillon's arm. "We're drawing attention. Let's leave."

In the lobby, Dillon ran his hand over his face. "Could this day get any more fucked up?"

Diana had a hard time controlling her laughter. "Oh, Dillon, I'd do anything to be there when Trent introduces Tonya to his mother. Talk about her worst nightmare come true."

"Yes, well, here comes our own nightmare." he said as Bonnie hurried through the front door and headed down a hall. "I'm going after her. Wait here until the sheriff shows up."

Diana shook her head. "I'm not staying here alone."

"You need to be here so you can tell the sheriff where I've gone. If you sit over by the hotel check-in, you can keep an eye on the door and the hallway."

Diana reluctantly agreed. "If you aren't back soon, I'll have everyone in this building searching for you."

He kissed her and headed after Bonnie.

****

The short hall was carpeted, with an elevator at the end marked "Private." There wasn't anyone else around, so Dillon slipped in. There were buttons for two floors. He decided to begin with the first one.

Semi-darkness greeted him as he stepped onto thick carpet. The glow from a computer screen and the outlines of desks told him this floor must be Dustin's offices. He was about to reenter the elevator when the sound of low voices led him around a corner. Ahead, a door stood partially open.

Dillon eased forward and peered into the room. He couldn't see the occupants but heard Bonnie's frantic voice clearly.

"I'm telling you she was saved by a ghost."

"Stop this at once," a man's voice said. Dillon assumed this was Dustin. "You must be having some kind of breakdown. There are no such things as ghosts."

Bonnie's voice grew shrill. "I know what I saw."

"Be that as it may, the point is they both escaped, and, we must assume, have already spoken to the sheriff, which means you've led them directly to me."

"They have no proof either of us was involved in Kevin's death," Bonnie said.

"Don't include me in that statement. I didn't kill your husband."

"What do you mean?" Bonnie stammered. "It sure as hell wasn't me."

"Wasn't it?"

"Dustin, you told me you'd take care of Kevin."

"I told you no such thing. You'd better hope you didn't leave any evidence behind."

Bonnie was quiet, then, her voice trembling,

gasped, "Dustin, don't do this to me. I'm telling you there's no proof either of us is involved. We can get away. We'll sell my land and the ski area and leave."

"You truly are mad," Dustin replied. "I've sunk too much into this place to leave. Besides, I'm not through with Dillon McCoy."

"Martin's hands aren't clean. If the sheriff discovers his crooked real estate deals, it would be easy to blame this all on him," Bonnie continued. "I'll say he needed the kickback money from the sale of the McCoy property."

"I don't see how blaming Martin takes care of the problem of your husband's death," Dustin stated. "It doesn't make any sense. Why would he kill him?"

"We'll say he was blackmailing him."

"The little bitch."

Dillon froze. It took his brain seconds to switch from the conversation in the room to the person behind him—Martin Patrick. Dillon eased from his position near the door and faced him. Barely above a whisper he said, "Where the hell have you been?"

Martin motioned for him to follow. "I went home. I've been trying to explain all this to my wife, who has taken my children and left. I have nothing else to lose, so I came to confront Bonnie."

"I thought you said you didn't know who her partner was."

"I wasn't sure, but I've had my suspicions for a while now."

"Because you didn't wait for the police like I told you to, Diana and I were almost killed," Dillon said through clenched teeth.

"I did call the sheriff. I wanted to get home and try

to save my marriage. but…" His voice trailed off when the office door swung open and Bonnie stood there, gun in hand. "Look who's here—the two men who can solve all our problems." She motioned with the gun. "Join us."

Dillon debated his chances of getting away. From the gleam in Bonnie's eyes, he had no doubt she would shoot. The staircase was close. Could he make it?

She stepped forward. "Dillon, if you try anything, I'll kill Martin."

"Bonnie, I have a wife and kids," Martin exclaimed. "Don't do this."

"Shut up, you sniveling coward. If you'd done as you were told, this would be over."

Dillon, realizing he didn't have a choice, proceeded Bonnie into Dustin's office. Dillon easily recognized the man seated behind the desk, even though his hair was receding, and he'd put on weight.

"Dustin."

He stood. "McCoy. As the saying goes, we meet again."

"Yeah, well, I sure as hell didn't expect the next time we met, you'd be trying to kill me."

Dustin's brows rose. "I have no idea what you're talking about."

"The fuck you don't," Dillon growled. "I overheard your conversation with Bonnie, and your hands are as dirty as hers."

"I hired Mrs. Duffy for a real estate transaction, nothing more."

The gun shook in Bonnie's hand. "You back-stabbing bastard. This was your plan from the beginning. You said we'd be partners, and I'd have half the money. I did everything you asked, and now my husband is dead."

"I have no knowledge of your husband's death. And I signed no contract with you," Dustin replied. "I simply asked you to inquire if the McCoys would be interested in selling their property. Whatever you did, you did without my knowledge or consent."

A prickle of unease crawled up Dillon's neck at the rage in Bonnie's eyes.

"Liar," Bonnie yelled as she fired.

Dustin's body jerked once before he crumpled to the floor.

Dillon hurled himself at Bonnie, knocking her down and pinning her beneath him. "For God's sake, Martin, call the sheriff."

Chapter Thirty-Eight

Hours later, exhausted, Diana and Dillon crawled into bed.

"What do you think will happen to Bonnie?" Diana asked with a yawn.

"I have no idea," Dillon replied. "I still can't picture her as a cold-hearted killer. She claims she didn't kill Kevin, but who knows." He shook his head. "She swears Dustin did, but he's not here to defend himself. I feel sorry for Paul and the sheriff's department having to sort it all out."

"I believe she's guilty," Diana said. "She would have killed us as well."

"Over a piece of land. Her greed was a monster she couldn't control."

"I wonder what will become of Martin. Do you think he'll go to jail for his real estate fraud?"

"Hopefully. But he'll probably only lose his license."

Diana laid her head on Dillon's chest. "Did you know Bonnie was a real estate agent?"

"No. If I had, I might have connected her and Martin as partners."

"I found out the day we went to see her after Kevin's death, but it didn't register."

"What do you mean?"

"I went out onto the porch as the mail truck pulled up. I took the mail and glanced at it. On top was a post card with Bonnie's name for a listing in town. I'm sorry I didn't tell you, but I honestly forgot about it."

Dillon kissed the top of her head. "It doesn't matter now. Besides, you didn't know it would be of any importance."

"What will become of the Duffy property if Bonnie goes to prison?"

"There are no children and Kevin hasn't any siblings, so it will probably go up for sale."

"Will you buy it?"

"I don't have that kind of money. It's going to take everything I have saved plus a loan to buy the Lazy M from my grandparents." He sighed. "I know they could purchase the Duffy land, but that would take their savings, and I wouldn't do that to them."

"I still can't believe none of your grandparents' children is interested in the property."

Dillon shrugged. "They don't want the responsibility."

"Do you want the Duffy property?"

"Sure. Combined with the Lazy M, we could expand the stables, have more cabins, and improve the campgrounds. But it's not going to happen. I have to hope whoever purchases it doesn't build multiple condos." He shook his head. "Wouldn't that be ironic after all we've been through to keep exactly that from happening."

"I can buy it," Diana quietly said. She held her breath, waiting for his reply.

"Why would you do that?" he finally asked.

"Because it's important to you and your family to

303

preserve what's here, and it's important to me as well."

He lifted her chin and gazed into her eyes. "You mean that, don't you?"

She nodded.

He tenderly kissed her lips. "I love you. I've loved you since the first time I held your hand."

Diana's heart soared. "Oh, Dillon, I love you so much. You had my heart the first time you smiled at me."

"I'm sure I'm not at all what you expected, but if you'll have this rodeo cowboy, I'd like to make your last name McCoy."

Epilogue

"A Spring wedding, how perfect," Jenn said, helping Diana adjust her veil. "A new beginning for you both."

Diana stared at her reflection in the full-length mirror. Her dress, not the fashion perfect one she'd been expected to wear with Trent, was simple but elegant. Exquisite tiny seed pearls trimmed the neck and cuffs. From the waist, tiers of lace cascaded down the front.

Jenn kissed her cheek. "You're absolutely gorgeous. I'm so happy you're going to be a part of our family."

Diana blinked back tears. "You're going to make me cry."

"And mess up the makeup Suzanna took hours to put on? You'd better not. Are you ready? I'm a nervous wreck, and I'm only the maid of honor."

Diana hugged her friend. "If it weren't for you, I'd never have met Dillon and been so ecstatically in love. Thank you."

Jenn rolled her eyes. "I didn't have anything to do with the love part, but I hope you still feel that way after giving up city life to live in the mountains and teach at a small-town school."

"Trust me. I'm going to enjoy every minute of it."

"Your parents looked a little shell-shocked after meeting my family. I hope your mother isn't too disappointed."

"My mother will come around. She just needs a little time." Diana smiled. "I'm ready."

After a quiet ceremony in a small church, attended by family and friends, Diana and Dillon slipped away.

****

The mountain sky blazed with color as Dillon kissed Diana and helped her onto Flora.

"You're sure you want to spend your honeymoon in the little cabin in the woods?" he asked.

Diana nodded. "That's the first place we made love."

He swung his leg over Flame. "Darlin', it won't be the last."

www.ingramcontent.com/pod-product-compliance
Lightning Source LLC
Chambersburg PA
CBHW070049030726
47506CB00002B/408